A TEMPTING LOVE NOVEL

BEAUTIFUL BETRAYAL

USA TODAY BESTSELLING AUTHOR

NIKKI ASH

Our love isn't simple, but it's so fucking beautiful.

AUTHOR'S NOTE

STOP! This is the third book in the Temptation series, and while it can technically be read as a stand-alone with its own happily ever after, it is highly recommended you start from the beginning with *Sweetest Sin* and then read *Deadliest Desire*, as the plot continues throughout the series.

PLEASE NOTE: *Like real life, the characters are far from perfect, make morally gray decisions, and deal with subjects that may be sensitive for some readers. If you are looking for a safe romance, this series is not for you. Content warnings, which contain spoilers, can be found on my website: www.authornikkiash.com*

For the women who want to be worshipped like a queen
in the streets and be treated like a freak in the sheets.

PLAYLIST

Bleeding Love-Leona Lewis
Desire-Meg Myers
Complicated-Avril Lavigne
i hate u, i love u (feat. Olivia O'Brian)-gnash
Broken-Hearted Girl-Beyoncé
Rock Bottom (feat. DNCE)-Hailee Steinfeld
In Case-Demi Lovato
Back to You (feat. Bebe Rexha)-Louis Tomlinson
Undrunk-FLETCHER
Used to love You Sober-Kane Brown
Knees-Bebe Rexha
I Can Do It With a Broken Heart-Taylor Swift
Before (Feat. Lil Wayne & Jhene Aiko)-Big Sean
My Happy Ending-Avril Lavigne

Listen to Nikki's playlists on her website.

PROLOGUE

Brielle

As I lie on the medical bed, my wrists and ankles strapped down, I can't help but think about how I got here.

One minute, I was in college, in love with my boyfriend, and the next, I was being raped by a monster. A monster who took what he wasn't offered.

"You thought you could get away with this?" Anthony shouted as he held my hands down and took and took and took. "This body was supposed to be mine!"

I wish I could say this was the first time my control had been taken from me, but I was raised by Andrey Antonov, the king of needing to be in control. He might be my father, but family means nothing to him, and women are nothing more than a commodity to be used to further his agenda.

Growing up, if I didn't do as he wanted, he would make sure there were consequences. Rather than demanding respect, he thrived on people's fear.

My brothers, Dominick and Matteo, would try to save me, but I hated that, in turn, Andrey would hurt them. So, I learned from an early age that if I relinquished all control, we would be safe from our father's wrath.

He wanted me to go to a private school. I went.

He wanted me to stay a virgin to marry his business associate's son. I kept my legs closed.

He insisted I go to a college not too far from where we lived. I went to the college he allowed me to go to.

He picked out the apartment I would live in near campus. I thanked him.

But the moment I was out of his home, something in me snapped. Maybe it was the distance that made me bolder. Or being away from home that allowed me to get comfortable.

But little by little, I started to take back my control.

I changed my major from arts and humanities to accounting.

I purchased a second phone so he couldn't track my whereabouts.

I met a boy and fell in love, and I gave him my virginity.

I started to make plans, ones that didn't include marrying Anthony Rothschild.

But me thinking I was in control was nothing more than an illusion.

And that was proven the night Anthony forced himself on me.

I begged him to stop.

But I wasn't in control.

Then my father found out about my boyfriend, and I begged him not to kill him.

But I wasn't in control.

Andrey found out I was pregnant.

And because Andrey Antonov *always* has to be in control, we've ended up here—at a clinic, where he's paying a doctor to abort my baby.

"Please," I beg, unsure if anyone can even hear me. "Please don't take my baby."

"You did this," Andrey hisses, coming into view.

He towers over me, a look of disgust marring his features. "You're a whore who chose to spread her legs, and now I'm forced to fix the problem you created."

"Please," I say again. "I'm sorry. The baby might be Anthony's—"

Grabbing the towel closest to me, I bring it up to my face and scream into it. Even with the material muffling the sound, I'm sure he can hear my frustration out there.

"Brielle!" Theo bangs on the door. "Are you okay?"

"No!" I yell, sliding my heels onto my feet and then unlocking the door. "I'm not okay. I'm horny and unsatisfied, and I've had enough of you treating me like I'm a broken, fragile little thing!"

I stare at him, wishing I could feel something, anything.

He's not wrong.

I am broken.

But I thought maybe Theo could help fix me. He's sweet and loyal and so damn considerate. He's everything I'm supposed to want, yet I still feel this void inside me.

"I can't do this anymore," I choke out. "I think you're a great guy, but you're not the guy for me."

"Because I won't hit you in bed?" he asks, a mixture of confusion and concern written all over his features.

"No." I shake my head. "Because … because …"

"Brielle …" He steps toward me, but I take a step back. "Are you really going to sabotage everything we have when you can't even tell me what's wrong?"

I stare at him for several seconds, trying to put into words what's going through my head, but nothing comes out.

Because Theodore DeSantis, the owner of DeSantis Investing—a thirty-six-year-old man who owns his own condo, has a great relationship with his parents and siblings, buys me flowers and chocolates, and takes me out on romantic dinners—is perfect.

But I'm not.

"You're a whore …"

"… you're now damaged goods."

I shake myself from my thoughts, refusing to let Andrey get into my head.

He's been dead for six years—and haunting me for just as long.

"It's not you," I tell Theo. "It's me."

I walk past him and scoop my purse off the counter.

"So, this is it?" he asks, walking me to the door.

"Yeah," I choke out. "This is it. I just …" I groan, wishing I could find the damn words. "I'm sorry," is what I settle on because I don't know what else to say.

"Are you sure?" he asks, his patient hazel eyes meeting mine. "Because we've done this a few times …"

What he means is, I've ended our relationship a few times.

Because it's always the same thing.

I get bored.

And then I start fights.

I ask for things in the bedroom I know he's not comfortable giving me.

And when he refuses, I push him away.

"I'm sure," I tell him, leaning in and kissing his cheek. "I'm done."

Some women might think I'm doing this for his attention. But I know Theo, and he's not going to chase after or fight for me. He won't beg me to reconsider because he's a good guy and he just wants me to be happy.

And I really wish I could be happy with him.

But I'm not.

"Goodbye, Theo," I say and then head down the hall.

I'm not even to the elevator before I'm texting my friend Nicole and telling her to get ready because I'm picking her up so we can grab a drink. After what went down with Theo, I need a strong shot … or two.

"I still say we should've gone to the country club."

Nicole eyes the bar in disgust and then grabs a napkin in a feeble attempt to clean the area. Unfortunately, there aren't enough napkins—or bleach—to save this place. But points to her for trying.

"We always go there." I slide onto the barstool, praying STDs can't be contracted by touch. "And it's always the same asshats frequenting the bar."

Their hats might be Gucci fedoras, but that's beside the point.

When my heels attempt to leave the ground, they momentarily resist due to the stickiness on the wood floor. I cringe, and Nicole catches it.

"Nope, I can't do it." She stands. "There has to be a place that's cleaner than here."

"Yeah, and my brothers own them all."

And while they don't care what I do, the last thing I want is for word to get back to them that I'm at a bar, looking for a hookup.

Years ago, neither of them would've judged, but now that they've both found love, they can't seem to understand why everyone else in the world hasn't.

I'm happy for them—I am.

Dominick has Peyton and my three adorable nephews. And Matteo has Daniella and a baby girl on the way. And they're all so damn happy that they want everyone around them to be happy.

But what they don't understand is that I *want* to be happy.

I want what they have.

But I'm broken.

"Brielle, please," Nicole pleads, her green eyes begging me to get her out of this place. "You know I adore you, and I'm your loyal wingwoman, but this place is …"

She shivers rather than finishing her sentence, and I glance around, taking the place in. It's a tiki bar on the water in South Harbor Point. I'm sure, at some point, it was beautiful, but now, it's run-down, and it needs a good cleaning—or to be torched—and even the salty air is tainted by the burned smell of fish.

"Fine," I grumble.

She releases a breath of relief. "Thank you, thank you. First drink is on me."

I roll my eyes.

While the gesture is sweet, we both come from money, so neither of us needs anyone to buy us a drink.

Nicole's father is the mayor of Harbor Point and comes from old money. And my family pretty much runs the city—between all the hotels, restaurants, and clubs they own. Even the main port that handles almost all the import and export in South Florida is owned and run by my brothers.

"You're finding somewhere to go," I tell her, immediately regretting it because I already know where she's going to insist we go.

"Gladly," she says as we exit out of the side door. "Besides, if my father knew I was here, I'd never hear the end of it."

I don't know much about her father, aside from the fact that my brothers hate him. When they found out I had befriended Nicole—after chatting with her a few times when I frequented her coffee shop, Lattes and Words—they warned me to stay away from her. But we clicked, and since I refuse to let anyone ever tell me what to do again, I told them that while I appreciated their warning, I wouldn't be heeding it.

And I'm glad I didn't because Nicole has become a close friend and, as she pointed out, the perfect wingwoman.

Our families might not get along, but since neither of us has anything to do with our families' businesses, we've decided their animosity isn't our problem.

We slide into my cherry-red Porsche Boxster—she's a few years old, and she doesn't have all the latest technology, but she's my baby, my late college graduation gift to myself—and Nicole hooks up her phone to my dash so I can see where we're going as I pull out of the parking lot.

"*North Harbor Point Country Club*," I read across the screen.

Of course …

"Look, unless we want to drive out of this city, the hot spots are limited. The country club is clean, safe, and has good drinks."

"It's also where every corporate bigwig with an even bigger ego frequents."

"I take it, this means you broke up with Theodore … *again.*"

"I don't want to talk about it. What I want is to find someone who won't treat me like a porcelain doll, and the country club is going to be filled with a dozen Theodores."

Nicole laughs. "It's Saturday night, so it shouldn't be too bad. And besides, like my stepmom always says, 'It's as easy to fall in love with a rich man as it is a poor one.'"

I snort out a laugh. "Spoken like a dedicated gold digger."

"Eh, she's not bad. At least she's honest with her intentions. She was a struggling single mom and determined to get herself out of South Harbor Point. One night with my dad, and she had him wrapped around her perfectly manicured finger. She might've been broke, but she was young and beautiful, and … well, we both know my dad has bare minimum standards. Thankfully, she's nice, and her daughter and I get along."

"You have a stepsister?" I quickly glance her way before putting my eyes back on the road. "Why have I never met her?"

Nicole and I have been hanging out for months, but now that I think about it, she doesn't talk much about her home life. I know her dad threw a fit about her opening her coffee shop and bookstore, but she used the money her mom had left her when she died when Nicole was little, so he couldn't do much to stop her. Especially since she had moved out and gotten her own apartment so she'd no longer be dependent on him in any way.

"Vanessa is away at college," Nicole says. "My dad might've been keen on having the hot young wife on his arm, but he isn't a fan of raising another man's child."

My thoughts go to my brother Matteo. When he and my sister-in-law Dani found out she was pregnant and it wasn't his baby—due to her ex-husband forcing himself on her while she was kidnapped—he could've walked away, but instead, he insisted the baby was his, DNA be damned.

So many people snub their noses at our family because of our less than stellar business dealings, but listening to Nicole talk about the way the mayor—who prides himself on being a religious family man—could shun the daughter of his wife only reiterates how hypocritical this world is. Mayor Eric Vanderbilt might have this town fooled, but my family has his number, and once my brothers can prove he's as shady as we think he is, I have no doubt they'll take him down.

When we walk into North Harbor Point Country Club, my gaze immediately goes to the bar, which, as I predicted, is filled with a bunch of pompous assholes. They're rich, and they think they're God's gift to women. And they're so wrapped up in themselves that they wouldn't know how to please a woman if her clit smacked them in the face.

I groan, and Nicole laughs.

"Maybe tonight will be different," she says as we walk toward the bar.

We find a spot with two empty seats, and I order my usual whiskey sour while Nicole orders a cosmo.

"Okay, now spill. What happened with Theo?" she asks.

I take a sip of my drink while I try to figure out how to answer her question. I know she won't judge. Unlike Theo, when I told Nicole about my past, she sympathized, but she didn't pity me, and she's never once changed the way she acts around me.

"I think I'm broken," I admit.

She quirks a brow.

"I mean, I know I am. I'm fucked up. But"—I lean in so no one else can hear—"I haven't orgasmed during sex since I was with Owen."

"Owen, as in your college boyfriend?"

I nod, and her eyes go wide.

"Holy shit, Bri, that was, like … years ago."

"I'm well aware," I say dryly. "Theo was the first guy I've been with since I came home."

When I was in college, I met Owen, and we fell in love. We spent months planning our future together until Anthony caught us and then snuck into my apartment and raped me.

A couple of months later, Andrey found out I was pregnant, so Owen and I ran. We ended up in a shitty motel, where Andrey found us, killed Owen, and then forced me to abort my baby.

I moved to Russia to get away and never once even considered looking at a man. I was busy helping my grandfather run his company and trying to heal from the trauma.

But when my brother Dominick dragged me home after our grandparents passed away, I had a lot of time on my hands. So, I decided to put myself out there.

I went on too many first dates and barely any second ones. So, when I met Theo and he seemed to tick all the boxes of what I was looking for, I grabbed ahold of him.

"Girl," Nicole drawls, "you need to get back on the horse. You might as well be a virgin at this point. The man didn't even give you an orgasm, so he doesn't count."

I snort out a laugh. "I want to, but it's hard …"

Nicole snickers at my unintentional pun, and I roll my eyes.

"A couple of times, I came close …"

"To coming?" she questions.

"No." I laugh. "To sleeping with a man. But it never felt right."

"And it felt right with Theo?"

I think about that for a second and then shake my head. "No, it felt … comfortable and safe."

"Maybe that's the problem," she says. "You need to be taken out of your comfort zone."

"Maybe," I agree. Then, because deep conversations like this stress me out, I add, "At least he wasn't allergic to pussy."

"What?" Nicole barks out a laugh.

"When I first came home, I tried to pick up a man. I brought him back to a room at the country club, but his face was only between my legs for about twenty seconds when he told me he was allergic to pussy."

"Oh my God, stop!" Nicole wheezes because she's laughing so hard.

"I mean, I'm not an expert on the opposite sex, but is that really a thing?"

"Excuse me," a gentleman says, sliding in next to me and leaning against the bar. "Can I buy you a drink?"

I glance down at my whiskey sour—which is still more than half full—and wonder how men manage to function, let alone pick up women.

Then another gentleman, who I didn't notice had sat down next to me at some point—or maybe he was here before me?—says, "She already has a drink, and if you haven't noticed from the Saint Laurent purse and matching heels, she's capable of buying her own drink." He raises a finger to the bartender, and when he approaches, he says, "Whiskey, neat."

The asshat standing between us huffs and walks away, giving me a perfect view of the gentleman who just saved me. I suck at guessing ages, but with his messy brown hair, stubbled jaw, and the slight crinkles around his eyes, he looks to be around my age—late twenties. But the way he carries himself in his Tom Ford suit—with his shoulders tense and his back straight, his eyes alert and darting around the bar—it's as if life has aged him several years.

"I'm Brielle," I find myself saying. "And this is my friend Nicole."

I never make the first move, but this guy has me intrigued. And I am here in hope of meeting a man and having sex with him so I can find out if I am in fact the problem.

"Kane," he says, lifting his drink from the bar top and taking a sip.

My gaze goes to his throat and the way his Adam's apple bobs as he swallows while I wait for him to elaborate. When he doesn't, I glance at Nicole, and she quirks a brow, obviously equally intrigued by him.

"Do you live in Harbor Point?" I ask, making conversation.

The city is small, and since it's split between North Harbor Point, where the upper class reside, and South Harbor Point, where the middle and lower class live, I'm surprised I haven't seen him around before.

"I do now," he says cryptically.

Another sip.

No elaboration.

I'm about to give up—because I don't beg for any man's attention—when he turns toward me and says, "Because I think you're the kind of woman who'll appreciate it, I'm going to get straight to the point. I have a room upstairs. Nothing fancy. Just a place to sleep while I wait for my stuff to arrive. Bed is comfortable, and I promise to make you come at least twice before you sneak out ... three times if you spend the night."

I'm so taken aback by his comment that I snort out a laugh, and the drink I was nursing splashes over my glass and all over my hand.

"Excuse me?" I scoff, unsure if I should be turned on or offended. I'm slightly mortified that I'm leaning toward the former more than the latter.

"Don't play games." His eyes, the same color as the whiskey he's drinking, meet mine. "I heard you tell your friend that asshole you were dating was incapable of making you come ..."

"And don't forget about the guy who was allergic to pussy," Nicole adds with a smile at the same time I hiss, "Are you stalking me?"

"Did you not just hear where I'm staying?" Kane says dryly. "I came to the bar to grab a drink, and it wasn't difficult to hear you telling her about your lacking sex life."

Oh, right. He's staying at the country club.

I glance at him just in time to see his tongue slide across his pouty lips, wetting them. I consider playing hard to get, but this guy is offering to make me come twice—yes, I heard the part about three times, but I'm not spending the night. If he can make me come once, it will be more than what Theo could do during the months that we were together.

"And I can assure you that I'm not allergic to pussy." He stands and extends his hand for me to take. "You coming?"

"I sure as hell hope so."

"Are you sure about this?" Nicole asks.

After Kane propositioned me, she dragged me to the restroom to make sure this was really what I wanted to do.

"Yeah, I need to do this. To know if it's me ... if I'm the problem."

She grins. "Look at you, quoting T. Swift."

She starts to sing the song, and I roll my eyes. The woman is a professional Swiftie.

"Okay, go," she says once she's done. "Go see if you're the problem. But make sure you text me his room number in case I need the police to find you and call me afterward so I know you're alive."

"Will do." I pull my keys out of my purse, but she shakes her head.

"I'm good. I'm going to have another drink and then take an Uber home."

After we freshen up, I give her a hug, and then Kane and I head up to his room.

Once we're inside, he goes about taking off his suit jacket, laying it over the dining room chair. The country club only has a couple dozen rooms, but the one he's staying in is on the nicer side with a full kitchen and living room.

"Have you been here for long?" I ask, noticing that the place is bare of any personal belongings.

"A couple of weeks," he says, stalking toward me.

"Why are you—"

"Enough talking."

He takes my face in his hands and crashes his mouth down on mine. His tongue slides between my parted lips, and he tastes like whiskey and determination.

His hands glide down my ass cheeks, and he hoists me into his arms, carrying me into the room, where he drops me onto the center of the bed.

"Take off your clothes," he demands.

And every hope I had about this man is shattered. He wants to dominate in the bedroom, which is what most women would want. A man who is determined to make her come. And it's what I should want, but it's not what I *need*.

I do as he said because we're already here, so I might as well try. But I already know I won't be coming once, let alone twice, tonight.

Once my clothes are off, he spreads my legs and dives right in with gusto. He has no problem finding my clit, but I've already lost the desire for an orgasm.

He licks and sucks, and I get lost in my head, wondering if this is how it's always going to be. I always blame the men, but the truth is, I'm the one with the issues.

After a few minutes—or maybe longer—I notice the licking has stopped, and when I glance down, I find Kane staring up at me.

Was I lost in my head so long that I was already supposed to fake my orgasm?

Well, shit!

"That was so good," I lie, sitting up. "Your turn?"

"What the fuck did you just say?" He leans back and glares at me.

"I said it was good …"

"What was good? You didn't make a fucking sound, and when I stopped touching you for over a minute, you didn't even notice."

Oops.

"Sorry, but, um, it was good."

I reach for his belt buckle, but he moves out of my grasp and stands.

"What is this? Some kind of game you play? You were bitching about not orgasming, yet you checked out before even giving me a chance."

I stare at him for several seconds. I faked my orgasms with Theo every single time, but he never once noticed.

"I'm not playing any games," I tell him, sliding off the bed and grabbing my clothes from the floor. "It's not my fault the male species is so busy banging their fists against their chest that they don't take the time to listen to what a woman needs."

Before I can get my dress on, he snatches it from my hands and grabs my chin between his fingers, forcing me to look at him.

"Tell me what you need."

I take a step back, trying to figure out how to answer his question. I told Theo so many times what I wanted, but is that the same as what I need?

My thoughts go back to earlier tonight with Theo. Where everything once again started to go wrong. He was in control of our pleasure while I had none.

I tried to tell him what I wanted—*please, harder!*—but he wouldn't listen.

"I need to be in control," I blurt out.

"You need to be in control?" he parrots. "Okay. Then you're in control."

"Just like that?" I scoff, taken aback by his simple response.

"Just like that."

I search his face for a hint of insincerity, but don't find any.

And then we stand here for several seconds—maybe minutes—while he waits for me to do something, say something. I start to freak out because I don't know what to do or say. I might crave the control, but I've never actually had it.

I would ask Theo to do things, and when he refused, I'd either fake an orgasm or throw a fit.

"I don't know what to do," I admit, my nose and eyes burning.

This guy must think I'm nuts.

"I'm sorry I wasted your time."

I start to head for the bathroom so I can get dressed without him seeing me lose my shit, but he stops me once again.

"You said you wanted to be in control. What does that look like?"

"I don't know. I've … I've never actually been in control. I just know I need it."

It's more than a need. I crave it, desire it. So much so that when Theo took charge in the bedroom, I'd instantly retreat, and I couldn't get out of my head, to the point where I couldn't find my release.

He stares at me for several seconds, then nods in understanding and retreats. "Get dressed."

My heart sinks. A part of me was hoping maybe he would be different. But I can't blame him. I'm a broken mess, and this guy doesn't owe me anything. He was looking for an easy fuck, and instead, he got a complicated one.

I grab my clothes and disappear into the bathroom to quickly get redressed. Not caring what my face or hair looks like, I head back out to the bedroom so I can grab my heels and purse and get out of here. Only when I step out of the bathroom, I find Kane lying on the bed in nothing but boxer briefs.

"All right, Princess, you have me. Now, what are you going to do to me?"

"Princess?" I quirk a brow, unimpressed by his cliché nickname for me.

"Yeah, you're like the princess in those storybooks," he explains. "The blonde one who's hidden in the castle with the drawbridge up and no way for anyone to get to her."

If only he knew how accurate his statement was.

Usually, I have a guard, Daniil, who shadows me everywhere I go, thanks to the dangerous life my brothers live. But I've worked out a deal with Daniil, and when I go out, he follows behind in a separate car, and he never reports back to my brothers anything I do—not that I've been doing much since I returned to Harbor Point. My life literally consists of spending time with my family, hanging out with Nicole, and taking classes at the local Pilates studio.

"Now, are you going to take control or what?"

Kane spreads his arms wide, and my attention goes to his muscular biceps and forearms. Further down, his chest is chiseled, his skin tan and clean—not a tattoo in sight. I count six abs and notice a thick bulge in his boxer briefs.

"Hey, Princess, you going to stand there, eye-fucking me, or are you going to do something?" He smirks devilishly.

"If I'm in control, then you shouldn't be asking questions."

"Of course I should," he volleys. "Communication is the key. If you had *communicated* that you needed to be in control, you would've saved us a lot of time that could've been spent with me making you scream my name."

I don't argue because he's not wrong, but in my defense, until he asked what I needed, I hadn't pinpointed what the problem was. And honestly, Theo never would've been okay with me taking control.

"Now, tell me, what do you want from me?"

TWO

Brielle

"I NEED A DRINK FIRST," I TELL HIM, WALKING OVER TO THE nightstand, where I left my whiskey sour, knowing I would need it.

"No, you don't," he says, blocking me from grabbing it.

"Um, yes, I do."

Before I have sex, I always have alcohol to take the edge off, and Theo never once questioned me.

"No, you don't," Kane repeats. "You said you need control, and I'm giving it to you. But you're going to do it sober."

"I was drinking downstairs," I point out.

"You were nursing one. You're fine."

My hands shake as I eye the drink, wanting to push past him and down it. It's what I used to numb myself the first time I had sex after being raped, and I've continued the habit ever since.

"Brielle," Kane says, pinching my chin, "it's just you and me. Now, tell me what you want from me."

"I want you to take my clothes off."

"That I can definitely do."

He swings his legs over the side of the bed and then stalks over to me. Without my heels on, he towers a good six inches over my five-foot-six self.

That is, until he drops to his knees in front of me and lifts the bottom of my dress up. He takes his time, gliding his hands up my legs, until he gets to the waistband of my panties. Rather than pull them down, he runs one of his fingers along the edge, and goose bumps prickle my skin.

"Your skin is soft," he murmurs. "And your body is toned. Do you work out?"

"Pilates," I answer. "And a little strength training."

I started working out as a stress reliever when I moved to Russia to live with my grandparents. But I continued to do it after my grandparents passed away and Dominick insisted that I move home. Since I have no idea what I want to do with my life, it helps fill the ample amount of time I have on my hands, and if I'm honest, I love it.

Kane hooks his fingers around the edge of my panties and slides them down my legs, touching every inch of my flesh with his fingertips, until they reach the floor.

Once he sets them to the side, he stands, his body so close to mine that I can smell his scent—fresh, warm, and with a hint of spice. Most men drown themselves in cologne, but with Kane, it's so subtle that you almost can't smell it unless you're as close as we are.

"Arms up," he says.

For a second, I'm confused, having been so lost in the way he smelled that I forgot what he was doing.

But then I remember he's undressing me. So, I lift my arms above my head, and he pulls the fabric up my body. It's a short-sleeved, floral-printed, shirred-waist dress, so it comes off easily, leaving me in only my bra.

His eyes go straight to my breasts, his tongue sliding across the seam of his lips, and I find myself clenching my thighs in anticipation of what's to come.

When he leans in to unhook the clasp of my bra, I feel his lips press a soft kiss to the top of my cleavage, and it takes everything in me not to wrap my hands around the back of his head and beg him to keep kissing me there.

With my bra off, the cool air caresses my breasts, and my nipples grow hard. Kane must notice because the heat that overtakes his gaze could warm the coldest night.

Maybe he could have just a taste. I mean, I am the one in charge …

"Go ahead," I tell him. "Have a lick. But only one."

He doesn't have to be told twice. He takes my breast into his large hand and wraps his lips around the beaded tip, giving it one lick—literally—before he gives the other one attention.

Between his gentle caress and the heady feeling of me being in charge and him complying, I find myself squirming in my spot, more turned on than I can remember ever being.

I knew when I was with Theo, something was amiss. I felt out of control, constrained. But I didn't fully get it until now. When Kane listens to me, my stomach tightens, and my pussy throbs.

He takes a step back, and I think about what I want him to do next. There are so many things I want, things I crave and desire, but we only have one night, and I'm worried I might scare him off. So, I decide to play it safe.

"I want you to lie on the bed, and I'm going to sit on your face. You're going to eat my pussy … unless you're allergic." I tack on the last part with a grin.

"Princess," he drawls, "I'm going to eat that pussy, and if I am allergic, it will be a damn good way to go out."

Ignoring the nickname he's dubbed me with, I walk over to the bed and wait for him to lie down. Once he's situated on his back, I crawl over to him and swing my leg over, holding on to the head-board. I've never done this before, so I hesitate for a second, but Kane doesn't miss a beat. He grips the sides of my legs and pulls me onto his face.

The moment he parts my lips and his tongue swipes up my center, I let out an embarrassingly loud moan, which only increases when he finds my clit and sucks on it.

My hips rock as he devours my pussy—and I mean, *devours*. He'd better hope he's not allergic to pussy because if he is, based on the way he's eating mine, he'll be dead within minutes.

When his finger runs up my ass and circles my *other* hole, I tighten in response and then reach back and knock his hand away from my ass.

"Did I say you could do that?"

He glances up at me, and I wait for him to argue or tell me I'm being ridiculous, but instead, he says, "I'm sorry. You taste so fucking good that I got carried away. Can I finger your ass?"

The thought of giving this stranger a piece of me I've never *willingly* given anyone has me shaking my head, especially since I pretty much have zero liquor running through my body, thanks to Kane making me do this sober.

"No, you can eat my pussy. You haven't earned the right to touch my ass."

He goes back to eating my pussy, and for the first time in a long time, an orgasm starts to build. I find myself grinding my pussy against his mouth, and it only spurs him on.

With every lick and suck and nibble to my clit, my body tightens like a coil. And when it gets to be too much, I do something I haven't done in what feels like forever—I scream out his name as I come harder than I've come in God knows how long.

He doesn't stop until he's wrung every ounce of pleasure from me. I know I need to get off his face, but my legs feel like Jell-O.

Thankfully, he waits patiently, and once I feel like I won't fall over, I lift off him and drop onto the bed next to him.

"Good?" he asks with a knowing smirk.

"Eh, it was okay."

"Just okay?"

He shifts so I'm lying under him, and the action is so fast that flashbacks of Anthony raping me hit me, and I hold my breath, praying Kane isn't about to do the same. But then he shocks me when his hands come to my sides, and he … tickles me.

"Kane!" I screech because I'm beyond ticklish.

"Admit that I ate your pussy like a pro, or I'll keep tickling you."

"Okay, okay!" I gasp. "You did good."

"Damn right I did," he says, removing his hands from my hips. "So, what now?"

I sit up, and because he's still straddling my legs, our faces are only inches apart. Up close, his whiskey eyes are even brighter with flecks of gold mixed in. His facial features are soft, and he has a boyish vibe to him, but underneath, I can see a hint of hardness trying to break through.

"You promised me two orgasms," I remind him.

"Actually three," he volleys.

"We'll stick with two."

His tongue darts out to wet his lips, and my first thought is that I want to taste him … but more than that, I want to taste me on him.

So, I do just that.

Threading my fingers through his hair, I pull his face toward mine and lick across the seam of his lips. He tastes like the perfect mixture of my arousal and something that is uniquely him.

When my lips part on a sigh, he slides his tongue into my mouth, and I find myself pushing him back so I can crawl into his lap to get closer.

The hardness of his erection pokes against my ass, and I grind into it, causing him to groan and deepen the kiss.

"I need you to fuck me," I murmur against his lips.

"You want me to fuck you? Or do you want to fuck me?"

Jesus, this man. He's unlike any other guy I've been with.

"I want you to fuck me just like this." I wiggle my hips. "With me on top."

But then it hits me that I've yet to see his cock, and this might be my only chance.

"But first …" I slide off his lap, and he pouts, making him look even younger. "I want to suck your dick."

His eyes light up with renewed heat as I pull his boxer briefs down and his cock springs free. It's thick and long with a couple of veins running along the length of his erection. There's a single bead of pre-cum peeking out of the tip, and without thought, I lean down and lick it, wanting to know what every part of him tastes like.

"Fucking hell, woman," he moans, tangling his fingers in my hair at the back of my head.

I pause, waiting to see if he'll force himself on me, but he doesn't, so I lean in again and suck on his mushroom head. A few more drops of pre-cum leak out, and I'm reminded that we'll need a condom. I might be on the pill, but I'm not risking it.

I slide off the bed, and I can feel his eyes watching me as I saunter across the room and over to my purse, where I pull a foiled packet out of my zippered pouch.

When I return, I set it next to me and then go back to sucking his dick. As I take him down my throat, rolling his balls gently in my hand, he moans, saying how good it feels, and my legs clench in anticipation. There's just something so hot about bringing this man to his knees—metaphorically.

"Holy shit!" he groans, tightening his hold on my hair yet making sure not to force me to do anything.

The image of him grabbing me by my hair and fucking my face flashes through my mind, and I'm almost positive that my arousal drips onto the bed. I've never let a guy face-fuck me before—when I was with Owen, we were young and had only started experimenting with our sexuality, and when I mentioned it to Theo, he refused.

But now I'm in control …

"Go ahead," I tell Kane, knowing he wants to. When he stills, I glance up at him. "Fuck my face, Kane. I want you to fuck me so hard that I choke and gag all over your cock."

Oh my God! I can't believe I just said that out loud.

Before I can take it back—not because I regret it, but because he's going to run before I get a chance to fuck him—he gets up, and my heart sinks because this is it. I finally found a guy to go along with my craziness, and I scared him off.

"You want me to fuck your face?" he asks, palming my cheek and looking into my eyes.

"Yes," I breathe.

"So hard that you choke and gag on my cock?"

Him repeating my words back to me only makes me wetter.

"Yes," I repeat.

"Lie on your back."

I don't know why he's asking this of me, but I'm so turned on at the thought of him fucking my face that I scramble onto my back.

He gets off the bed and pulls me to the edge so my head is hanging off the side of the mattress.

"If you want or need me to stop at any time, tap my leg."

He grabs my hand and brings it up to show me where to tap, and I wiggle in my spot. If I need to tap, it's because my mouth will be occupied … with his cock.

"Understand?" he asks, his voice deep and commanding.

"Yes." I nod once. "Now, fuck my mouth."

He glances down at me, and a roguish smirk graces his too-handsome-for-his-own-good face as he grips his shaft and strokes it a few times while I watch with eagerness.

With the hand that's not stroking himself, he reaches out and pinches my nipple, and I squirm in desire. He does it to the other one, and I'm about to tell him to hurry this along when his hand goes to my hair and he steps closer, tugging my head back slightly.

The underside of his cock bobs over my face, and I practically salivate. Thanks to the bed being a bit on the higher side, he easily guides his cock into my open and awaiting mouth. I've never done this before, so I don't know what to expect, other than what I've seen from watching porn.

But Kane does not disappoint. He doesn't stop until he's all the way down my throat, and then he proceeds to face-fuck me. With his hands gripping the sides of my face, he takes no mercy on me, thrusting in and out of my mouth. Just as I was hoping for, I gag and splutter, his long, thick length filling my airway and making it hard to breathe.

For a split second, I wonder if I made a horrible decision and this is how I'm going to die. In my world, you can't be too careful with who you trust, and I literally just put my life in the hands of a stranger. But then he pulls back, giving me a moment to catch my breath, and all thoughts of dying fly out the window as I get lost in the moment.

I slurp and suck as he fucks my mouth, and without thought, my hand goes to my pussy, needing to come again.

The tips of my fingers slide between my folds, and I'm soaked. Like, I have no doubt that I'm leaving a wet spot on the bed.

"Fuck, Princess," Kane groans. "Your mouth is perfect."

He picks up his speed, and I do the same with my fingers. As he fucks my mouth, I massage my clit, and within seconds, I'm coming all over my fingers.

I expect Kane to come down my throat, but instead, he pulls out and sits on the bed, pulling me on top of him so I'm straddling his muscular thighs.

He grabs the condom and slides it over his hard length and then looks at me. "Tell me I can fuck you."

The desperation in his tone, mixed with the fact that he's asking rather than taking—once again making sure I stay in control—has me sinking onto him.

We both moan in unison as he stretches me until he's inside me to the hilt.

"Fuck me," I breathe out.

Gripping the curves of my hips, he fucks me fast and deep from the bottom. My fingers delve into his hair, and his mouth connects with mine.

And as I come for the third time tonight, everything hits me like a tidal wave—the control, the pleasure, the chemistry between Kane and me—and before I know what I'm doing, I'm pushing off him and running to the bathroom, not wanting him to see me lose it.

Tears stream down my face as I reach the bathroom, but before I can slam the door, he's following me inside and lifting me into his strong arms.

"Shh, it's okay," he murmurs. "I've got you."

I nuzzle my face into his neck, inhaling his comforting scent while I continue to cry for the broken woman who wants so badly to feel whole.

Somehow, while holding me, Kane manages to turn the water on. He walks us into the shower and then sets me on the bench. Wordlessly, he washes my hair, massaging my scalp, while I continue to silently cry, my tears mixing with the water and swirling down the drain—which is really quite fitting because it feels like being with Kane tonight cleansed the parts of me that Theo had made me feel were dirty.

Not once did Kane tell me no or argue with me. He didn't look at me like I was strange when I told him to fuck my face. He was turned on and enjoyed everything we did.

As Kane rinses me off, my body shakes.

He was just supposed to be a one-night stand. A way to prove that I was the problem. Instead, he knocked down several of my walls, leaving me feeling more vulnerable than I'd ever felt.

Theo was safe.

Kane is dangerous.

And with that realization, my heart begins to race because Kane is dangerous to my heart.

But what if he took care of it? I think as Kane turns off the water and hands me a towel.

We quickly dry off and then he hands me my clothes and says, "It's been fun, Princess," effectively raising every wall he temporarily brought down.

Because Kane isn't looking for more.

He was only looking for a one-off, and now that he got it, he's dismissing me and my heart.

It's for the best, I tell myself as I get dressed, grab my purse, and head for the door.

Theo was safe.

But Kane is dangerous.

THREE

Kane

Tonight wasn't supposed to happen.

I told myself it wouldn't happen.

But then she slid onto the barstool next to me, and just like the rest of the men in my family, I let a woman fuck with my plan. I'd chastised my father over the years for letting women interfere with his business. I'd warned my brother not to take the route he took—which involved getting close to a woman. Both ended up six feet under, thanks to the stupid choices they'd made regarding women.

I knew better.

She's an Antonov.

I want what they have.

What's owed to my family.

But I wasn't supposed to want *her*.

Yet one look in Brielle's eyes, and I was throwing everything out the window for one night with her.

She's nothing like I expected—in the best way.

She's fiercely independent.

Strong.

Beautiful.

And broken.

One conversation with her, and I wanted to be the one to put her pieces back together.

And that only makes what I'm about to do that much harder.

Because I'm not here to save Brielle Antonov.

And then an idea forms … because who says that just because I'm here to avenge my father's death, I can't also have her?

Her family owes mine.

And I'm here to collect.

And now I'm adding one more item to the list—Brielle Antonov.

She's mine.

FOUR

Brielle

"**H**APPY BABY SHOWER, SIS." LORENZO HANDS DANI A CARD and kisses her temple.

My sister-in-law Dani is due next month with a precious little girl. When I suggested planning a shower, wanting to celebrate her pregnancy, she and Matteo insisted they had everything they needed, but that didn't stop me from renting out Pasquale's—their favorite Italian restaurant—to throw them a luncheon anyway.

Dani is one of the sweetest women I've ever met, and she and my brother deserve to be doted on before the baby comes. They've been through so much this past year, and a little celebrating is good for the soul. Since they didn't need anything for the baby, I told everyone to get them something creative.

Dani opens the card from her brother, and it's for a day at the spa. A card from my mom and her husband—who are out of town on vacation, living their best lives—is for baby-and-me classes.

As my other sister-in-law, Peyton, gushes about how much she loves the classes, I keep a smile on my face even though I feel out of place. Not only is Peyton a mother to my three nephews—Damien, five, and twins, Justin and Adam, nine months old—but she and my brother Dominick are happily in love. And now that Dani and Matteo are together with a baby on the way, they'll have marriage and babies to bond over. Meanwhile, all I have is a dead boyfriend, a womb that once carried a baby that was ripped out of me, and an ex who couldn't satisfy me in the bedroom.

My thoughts go back to last night, but I quickly push them to the side, refusing to think about the one man who not only gave me the control I'd craved, but satisfied me in a way that was life-altering.

I force myself into the present when Peyton and Dominick give Dani and Matteo a voucher for a weekend away with babysitting duty included.

"Trust me, after the baby comes, you're going to need it," Peyton says with a laugh, and my heart cracks because they have what I want and fear I'll never have.

When Peyton turns her attention on me, I shake myself out of my thoughts and pull the envelope out of my purse.

"Here's my gift," I say to Dani and Matteo. "It's not as creative." I side-eye Peyton, who sticks her tongue out at me playfully.

"What is this?" Dani asks once she opens it and is reading it.

"It's your baby's first investment. I took out stock, and once she's born, I'll transfer it into her name. I want her to have something of her own so she never feels like she's dependent on anyone," I choke out and then clear my throat, trying not to let my emotions get the better of me. "And every year, for her birthday and holidays, I'm going to add to it."

"Bri," Dani says in awe, "this is so thoughtful. Thank you."

"Yeah," Peyton agrees. "You just got the twins a stroller."

I laugh. "I actually got them each one as well." I go back to my purse and pull out the other three envelopes I was going to give to Peyton and Dominick later. "One for each of the twins and one for Damien. I know their parents are rich, but ..." I shrug.

I want my niece and nephews to always have some sort of independence, unlike I had, growing up. It wasn't until I moved to Russia and went to work for my *dedushka* that I experienced any type of real independence.

At his gas company, Gazcom, I started as a junior accountant and worked my way up to becoming the CFO, earning myself a damn good paycheck. When he decided to sell the company, he offered it to me, but I knew I wouldn't live in Russia forever and that while I was good with numbers, it wasn't my passion. A year later, he passed away, and six months after that, my *babushka* joined him in heaven.

I was shocked to learn that besides a small sum they'd put aside for my brothers, they'd left everything else to me, including the home I'd lived in with them for over four years.

I considered staying in Russia, but when Dominick came to get me, I agreed to come back to Harbor Point, having missed my family.

When Dani pulls me into a hug and thanks me, my eyes and nose sting with emotion, and I shake my head, needing to move on to something less emotional, like dessert.

"Okay, enough of that," I tell her. "I think it's time for some—"

My words are cut off as the last person I expected to see walks through the front door of Pasquale's. He's dressed in a gray business suit, looking as sharp as he did last night. His brown hair is messy, and he hasn't shaved his face.

My heart thumps in my chest as I remember the way his stubble left bumps along the insides of my thighs when he ate me out.

And then his golden-brown eyes lock with mine, and I suck in a harsh breath.

Did he follow me here?

Before I can find out, the guards are on him.

"Sorry, the restaurant is closed," Ian, one of my brother's guards, says.

I'm about to tell them that Kane is here for me—because why else would he be here?—when he says, "Actually, I'm here for the baby shower."

He holds up a small wrapped package and smirks, and I stumble back in confusion because how the hell does he know about the baby shower? I definitely didn't mention it last night.

"And you are?" Dominick asks, taking the lead, like he always does.

"Kane Morgan." He attempts to step around the guards, but they stop him.

He sighs as if they're nothing more than a nuisance, and then he shocks the hell out of me when he adds, "I believe you all are responsible for killing the majority of my family."

"Fuck," Lorenzo hisses. "I knew I recognized the name." He steps toward Kane. "You're Kane Morgan, owner of Morgan Enterprises."

"The one and only." Kane grins, but it's not the same grin he gave me last night. It's cold and calculated.

"And what the fuck do you think you're doing here?" Matteo asks, joining the conversation. "You thought you'd come in here and what? Take us out in the middle of a restaurant that's under our protection with our guards standing right here?"

Kane laughs, and my heart plummets because this man—the one I thought was different, the one I opened up to last night—is clearly a threat to my family.

"That's not the kind of revenge I'm interested in," Kane says to Matteo. "The best kind of revenge is success." He unbuttons and opens his suit jacket. "Feel free to check me. I'm not armed." He tosses the gift to Matteo, who catches it and drops it onto the table behind him. "For my niece or nephew." He glances at Dani. "Congrats, by the way. It's a shame my brother isn't here to watch his child grow up."

His words cause a shiver to race down my spine because only family knows that their baby isn't biologically Matteo's. She was conceived when Dani's husband kidnapped and raped her, but the moment Matteo found out she was pregnant, he accepted the baby as his own. They told us the truth, not wanting there to be secrets in our family, but nobody else knows.

Except Kane. He knows, which means he's been stalking my family.

"Don't fucking talk to my wife," Matteo sneers. "That baby is ours. End of story."

Kane raises his arms in a silent *I'm not a threat* sort of way, and the guards pat him down. Once they've confirmed he's not carrying any kind of weapon, they nod toward my brothers to let them know he's clean.

"So many deaths over women." Kane shakes his head. "All I want is to save my father's legacy."

"Your father?" Dominick steps toward him. "You mean the man who kept you hidden?"

"You mean the man who kept his cards close to his chest," Kane replies. "Who left me his entire empire."

As I try to connect the dots, Lorenzo says, "The third party who bought Rothschild International," but I have no idea what he's talking about since my brothers don't keep me in the loop regarding their business dealings.

When I returned home, my relationship with my brothers was a bit shaky because I had spent years thinking they knew Anthony had raped me and Andrey had forced me to have an abortion, only to learn that they had been kept in the dark.

I was pissed at Dominick for forcing me to come home, but I also understood that I had been hiding from Harbor Point, not wanting to face my past.

I thought Dominick would ask me to join the family business, especially since Peyton did, but he never broached the subject. And since I let my pride get the better of me, I never brought it up to him, in fear of him turning me away. Which is honestly for the best because I don't have the desire to work for Antonov Enterprises—I think, deep down, I just wanted the option to do so.

"Joseph was grooming me to work alongside him. Only he died before I could officially do so," Kane says, forcing me to snap out of my thoughts ... because what in the *Jerry Springer?* Joseph, Anthony's father, who was *also* Enrique's father, is Kane's father as well?

"He knew Anthony was a loose cannon," Kane continues. "His only hope was the marriage he arranged with your family ..." His eyes go to mine, and bile rises in my throat as I realize, last night, he knew who I was. "And Enrique was too emotional," he adds. "He never would've cut it in the business world."

"You don't seem too torn up about your brother's death," Dominick notes.

"He chose to make it personal," Kane says, his gaze bouncing from me to Dani. "I loved my brother, but I warned him to keep it strictly business. He chose to avenge our father's death his way, and he got what was coming to him. He was a grown man who knew the risks."

Business.

That's all I was to Kane last night.

Business.

That's why he'd sought me out.

Let me take control.

It was part of his revenge.

"And what makes you think we won't kill you the same way we killed the rest of your family?" Matteo says.

"I haven't done anything to you." Kane shrugs, not taking the threat to his life seriously—even though we both know my brother would shoot him point-blank in the head without thought. "And from what I've observed, you both are honorable men."

Honorable … what a fucking joke. My brothers and Lorenzo might be honorable, but Kane is nothing but a deceitful asshole who played with my emotions last night.

"Get to the point," Matteo demands, obviously losing his patience. "What do you want?"

"I want what my father was owed," Kane says easily. "Our families made an agreement years ago, and I'm here to collect. A third of the business and"—his eyes go straight to me—"her."

Oh my God.

My heart starts to race as I wrap my head around Kane's words.

He wants to marry me.

The way Anthony was supposed to marry me.

This can't be happening again.

Thankfully, before my panic attack hits, Dominick says, "My

sister isn't a chess piece to play with. Besides"—he grins—"you really want the woman your *brother* was obsessed with?"

"Anthony wanted her," Kane says, his gaze not leaving mine, "but—let's be honest—he never had her."

He smirks, no doubt remembering that he had me last night, and I sneer his way, which only makes his smirk strengthen.

"Our father's biggest mistake was thinking with his dick, the same way Anthony and Enrique did."

"I never wanted him," I hiss. "The same way I'll never want you. You're barking up the wrong tree."

Kane laughs—and not just a small laugh, but a full-blown belly laugh. "We'll see about that."

He slides his tongue across the seam of his lips, and I glare, hating that I was stupid enough to be with him. Nothing I say will change that he was already buried in my pussy, and he knows it.

"How about this?" Kane says, moving his focus from me to my brothers. "You guys think on it, and while you're doing so, keep in mind that I've already gotten the approval for my Section 8 housing project that will conveniently be built adjacent to your waterfront project, thanks to the newly appointed city official and a certain video that involves him snorting powder off a prostitute's ass."

"What a fucking cliché," Dominick mutters dryly, trying to appear unaffected when I know he's pissed.

The South Harbor Point waterfront expansion is his baby. He's already dished out millions of dollars and spent thousands of hours on it.

"You want to talk about cliché?" Kane scoffs. "When you guys were fighting with my idiot brothers, I bought out twenty acres of waterfront property right out from under your noses. I honestly thought it would be harder than that." He shakes his head and tsks. "But it was like taking candy from a baby. And you know why?" He pauses for dramatic effect. "Because you are no different from my father and brothers. You're so busy thinking with your hearts and dicks that you can't make proper business decisions."

"Jesus fuck," Lorenzo bites out. "You not only resuscitated a dying company, but you got enough funds to purchase all that property—and for what? Revenge?" He whistles softly. "A for fucking effort, man."

I glance around, unsure what's going to happen now that Kane has thrown down the gauntlet when Matteo pulls out his gun and points it directly at Kane's head.

Dani and Peyton gasp while Dominick and Lorenzo step toward Matteo to show a united front. And I stand frozen in my spot as memories of my father killing my boyfriend flash before my eyes.

"Please don't do this," I beg as my father's men grab Owen's arms and twist them behind his back. "Please, Dad, I love him."

My eyes meet my father's, and it's in this moment that I realize my mistake. I was trying to appeal to his emotions, but how do you do that when he doesn't even have a heart?

I should've promised to leave him alone, but it's too late to take my words back because at my father's demand, one of his men pulls out his gun and, before I can stop him, shoots Owen between the eyes.

"Stop it!" I scream, caught somewhere between the past and present. "No more bloodshed," I plead. "Please. I'll … I'll marry him."

"Bri, no," Dominick says.

"Yes," I hiss. "I can't keep doing this. Owen, Anthony, Enrique, Lorenzo and Dani's parents …" *My baby,* I think, but don't voice. "So much fucking blood on everyone's hands. You guys were supposed to be making this place safer. You have three babies," I say to Dominick. "A baby on the way," I tell Matteo. "It's not worth it. *He's* not worth it." I nod toward Kane but keep my eyes on my brothers. "This is never going to stop. The waterfront expansion is your dream, and I'm not going to be the reason you don't get it."

"Fuck the expansion," Dominick barks. "You're more important." He steps toward me. "I'm not letting you marry that asshole."

"Fuck him," Matteo agrees, then glances at Kane. "I'll kill you in your sleep, and then it will all be over."

"Except I left everything to my mom," Kane notes, throwing yet another curveball.

"Your mom is dead," Dominick points out.

"Wrong." Kane chuckles. "You guys were so focused on getting my brother that you didn't dig deep enough." He glances at Lorenzo. "Your dad tried to kill her when he took out my dad, but thankfully, I was close by, visiting from college, and found her in time. No one, not even Enrique, knew that she'd survived. I wasn't about to risk her life, especially since Enrique had lost his shit after our father died, so I faked her death and hid her away to keep her safe."

"Holy shit," Lorenzo breathes. "I remember this now. My dad said when he showed up to kill Joseph, there was a prostitute there, but …"

"She's not a fucking prostitute!" Kane barks. "She was a woman in love with a man who was forced to be with someone else."

"And yet you're going to force our sister to marry you," Matteo points out.

"He did what he did for the success of his business, and I don't fault him for that," Kane says. "The only way to ensure that our families are unified is through marriage and producing an heir. That's why our fathers made that deal, and that's what we're going to do." His eyes bounce between each of us. "My father lived and breathed and died for this city, and I want it back for him."

"Why would you want to be part of a family who doesn't want you?" Peyton asks.

"Because while I'm powerful on my own, the power of the three families is stronger, and I want to honor what my father wanted, even in his death. Matteo and Daniella already secured the alliance between the Antonovs and Russos, so that just leaves us." Kane looks at me. "I don't just want marriage. I also want a baby."

I suck in a harsh breath, trying like hell not to cry.

He wants a baby … with me.

All my hopes of finding a man who will love me are thrown out the window.

Of creating a baby out of love …

Rather than stopping the vicious cycle, like my brothers did, we'll be continuing it.

"Bri, you don't have to do this," Matteo mutters. "We'll figure out another way."

"I can't let you do that," I murmur. "He's covered his bases, and if I don't marry him, you'll not only lose the waterfront expansion, but there'll be bloodshed."

And I can't have more blood on my hands.

"I'll marry you," I tell him.

He nods. "You have a month, during which time I'll publicly court you and then we'll announce our engagement and plan the wedding."

"Bri …" Matteo sighs. "I thought you wanted to marry for love. And what about Theodore?"

"She broke up with him yesterday," Kane says with a smirk that I want to smack off his face.

"How the fuck do you know that?" Matteo barks.

"Stop." I rest my hand on Matteo's arm, not wanting to explain that I slept with Kane last night. "I broke up with Theo last night. I got to experience love once, and I knew Theo wasn't the one for me. Besides, I'm starting to think that maybe we're only destined to fall in love once in our lifetime."

"Bri …" Dani begins, but I shake my head.

"I want to do this for you guys … for our family." I glance at Dominick. "Make sure Kevin double-checks the contract. I'll be pissed if I do this and that asshole still finds a way to fuck you and your waterfront expansion over." Kevin is the attorney my brothers have on retainer.

" 'That asshole' isn't going to fuck anyone over," Kane says. "As soon as the marriage is official and you guys include Morgan Enterprises as an equal investor in the waterfront project, I'll sign the twenty acres over to the project."

"And what if I can't have a baby?" I ask.

"You can," Kane says confidently. "I had your records pulled. You're healthy and able to conceive." He grins. "I look forward to making a baby with you."

"I think I just threw up in my mouth," I mumble.

Kane chuckles and steps back. "I'll let you guys get back to it." He looks at Dominick. "I'll be in touch."

We watch him walk out the door, and once he's gone, I release a harsh breath.

"I think it's time for cake," I say, trying to lighten the mood, only there's no use because the afternoon has been ruined, and thanks to Kane, so has my entire future.

FIVE

Kane

THIS WASN'T THE GODDAMN PLAN.

The plan I'd spent years formulating and executing.

The plan was to fuck over the Antonovs and Russos the way they fucked my father over.

I waited patiently for the right time, and when the parcels became available and I learned what Dominick and Lorenzo were planning, I slid in quietly and scooped up twenty acres, knowing it would hurt their plans just like they hurt my father's business.

Section 8 housing would be a nightmare for their beloved waterfront expansion.

But after doing my research and learning how profitable the expansion would be, I tucked away my emotions and thought like the businessman my father had taught me to be.

He should've been part of that expansion.

And so we will be.

I could've accomplished what I needed to without her.

But after tasting her cunt and being buried deep inside her, I knew I needed to make her mine.

And why shouldn't I?

That was the deal—Daniella marries an Antonov and Brielle marries a Rothschild.

I'm righting the wrong.

Taking what my family is owed.

It's nothing personal.

SIX

Brielle

"**I** SPOKE TO OUR TEAM OF LAWYERS, AND THERE'S NO OTHER way. With Kane owning the twenty acres adjacent to the waterfront property, if he goes through with the Section 8 housing, property values will tank." Dominick scrubs his hands over his face, stress evident in his features. "I think we should call the whole thing off."

"And lose the millions you've already invested?" I point out.

We're sitting in Dominick's downtown office. I was at my morning Pilates when he texted me, asking me to meet him, Matteo, and Lorenzo to go over what his lawyers told him. It's only been two days since Kane threw the bomb at us and walked away, but Dominick didn't waste a minute trying to figure a way out of this mess.

"I'd rather lose millions than get into bed with that asshole." Dominick huffs.

"And what about the other investors?" I mention. "You'll piss them off and burn so many bridges."

"He's a smart businessman," Lorenzo points out, making Dominick and Matteo glare at him. "I'm just speaking as a businessman," Lorenzo says, putting his hands up. "Joseph's company was failing because our fathers were slowly pushing him out. When he died, Kane not only saved it, but it's now a Fortune 500 company with a pristine reputation. I had Eddy look up his connections." He whistles. "Fucking impressive. He's got contracts with several large development companies, including a few that we work with. If we pull the plug on this project, it will cost us billions, not millions."

"Yet he wants to taint it by joining forces on this project." Dominick scoffs.

"He wants revenge," I correct. "And to get what his family was promised. You guys own the largest real estate development companies in South Florida—hell, maybe even the East Coast. He saw a way to hit two birds with one stone and took it."

"Maybe we can convince him that we'll do business with him without involving Brielle," Lorenzo says. "He doesn't have to marry her to get what he wants."

"Good luck with that," I mutter just as there's a knock on the door.

"Mr. Antonov," Dominick's assistant says, "Mr. Morgan is here to see you."

And speak of the devil …

"Let him in," Dominick says, his voice tight.

"Gentlemen … and lady," Kane says, strolling in. "I came to deliver the contracts to Dominick, but it looks like I get to see my soon-to-be fiancée as well."

"I hope you get hit by a bus," I deadpan.

Kane grins.

"We were talking, and we'll agree to your terms," Dominick says. "You can get in on the waterfront expansion, if you'll agree to cut the marriage out of the deal. There's no reason for you to marry Brielle."

"There's every reason to marry her," Kane says. "For one, that was the deal that was made between our fathers."

"Before your father went behind my father's back and fucked the woman he was in love with," Lorenzo points out.

"Is that what Maria said?" Kane tsks. "Let's get one thing straight. My dad didn't do shit behind your dad's back. He got fucked up one night, and Maria seduced him. He didn't even remember being with her until she came to him and told him she was pregnant. He tried to tell Giuseppe and Andrey that, but Giuseppe was too emotional and wouldn't listen. So, he manned up and took the brunt of it.

"But Maria never stopped fucking around. She just made sure she didn't get pregnant again. Meanwhile, my dad had fallen in love with my mom, and she got pregnant with Enrique, but it was too late, so she became the mistress. And because she loved him, she accepted it."

Kane sighs and glances at Lorenzo. "Our dads were best friends, and he hated what it did to their friendship, but since he couldn't fix it without making Maria look bad, he delved into the business, giving it damn near all of him. And he thought once the families were unified and blood was mixed, maybe things would be different. Until he died and you pushed his company out."

"It was business," Dominick says. "Not personal."

"And so is this." Kane shrugs. Then he turns his attention to me. "It's time we're seen in public. I'll pick you up at your place on Saturday night." He pulls his phone out. "What's your number?"

I consider telling him to go fuck himself, but it will only create more animosity, so instead, I give him my number.

"I'll text you," he says before he walks out.

"I hate that fucking guy." Matteo seethes.

"Yeah, well, you'd better learn to like him because he's about to become your brother-in-law," I mutter.

"I appreciate you meeting me."

Theo smiles softly at me and reaches across the table to take my hand in his. "I care about you, Brielle, and I would do anything for you."

I swallow the lump in my throat, wishing I could feel something, anything for this man. On paper, he's perfection personified, but unfortunately, he's not perfect for me. And since I've agreed to marry Kane, I owe it to him to end things for good.

"I appreciate that," I tell him, "but the reason I asked you to meet me is because—"

"Princess," a masculine voice says, cutting me off. "I was hoping to run into you, but I must admit, seeing you with your ex only a few days after I was buried deep inside your tight cunt isn't what I was expecting."

Theo's eyes go wide at Kane's crass words and then morph into something that looks a lot like anger. "Brielle, what's going on?" Theo accuses.

"Kane," I grit out as I stand and shove him away from the table. "What the hell are you doing?"

"Reminding you that you're mine."

"I'm not anyone's!" I whisper-yell, then quickly lower my voice, not wanting to draw attention from the other patrons eating their breakfast at the country club. "And I'm especially not yours."

"You sure about that?" he asks, stepping toward me.

He glides his fingers down my cheek and tucks a wayward strand of hair behind my ear, and a shiver races up my spine. "Because the other night, when I ate your pussy until you screamed my name, it felt like you were mine."

He leans in, his face so close to mine that I hold my breath, waiting for him to kiss me—equally wishing he would and hoping he wouldn't.

"And when your pussy was choking the hell out of my cock," he whispers, his lips grazing the shell of my ear and sending a tremor throughout my body, "it felt *a lot* like you were mine."

He stands back as a dark grin graces his features, knowing he's affecting me. "You came not only on my tongue, but on my cock. How many times did that guy make you come?"

His words are loud enough for Theo to hear, and that pisses me off that much more because the last thing I wanted was to hurt Theo. It's why I asked him to meet me in person when he called this morning, asking if we could talk. I wanted to apologize for everything I'd done and officially end things with him in a calmer manner than me running out in the middle of shitty sex.

"Brielle, is what he just said true?" Theo hisses, showing a side of him I haven't seen before. "Did you have sex with him?"

"Yes," I admit, focusing my attention on Theo and ignoring Kane and his knowing smirk. "I'm sorry. I planned to tell you."

"And this is what you want?" he asks, nodding toward Kane. "A man who would air your dirty laundry out in front of everyone."

I want to tell him that the last person I want is Kane, but for the sake of my brother's project, I nod. "I'm sorry."

Theo shakes his head, then shocks me when he hits me with a look of disgust. "Shouldn't have wasted my time with you," he spits. "I knew you were a cocktease but—"

"Enough," Kane cuts him off. "Take the breakup like a man and walk the hell away."

Theo leaves, and once he's gone, I stomp past Kane, shocked by Theo's harsh words and annoyed that Kane had caused all this. But before I can get away, Kane grabs my wrist and pulls me down the hall of the country club and backs me into the corner.

"Don't touch me!" I shout, yanking my hand out of his hold. "You already got what you'd wanted. Did you really have to be an asshole about it?"

"Stop acting like I'm coming between you and some crazy love," he says, crowding my space. "If anything, I'm saving you from a lifetime of self-induced orgasms."

"Which is what I'll be stuck with by marrying you."

"What are you talking about?" Kane scoffs. "We both know I was able to satisfy you better in one night than that guy did during your entire bullshit relationship."

"And now you're forcing me to marry you!" I yell, poking his chest with the tip of my manicured nail in frustration. "Now, step aside. I'm done with this conversation."

Kane grinds his jaw, but moves to the side so I can leave.

Me: Shopping trip 911

Nicole: Can't. It's rush hour at the coffee shop.

Shit, I forgot what time it was and that, unlike me, she has responsibilities.

Since I don't want to be alone, I text my sister-in-law Dani to see if she's up for some shopping. She works with her brother, Lorenzo, at Russo Property Group, but with her due in a month and being married to my overprotective brother, she's started her maternity leave.

Dani: Sure! Meet you downtown?

Me: Sounds good.

I hand the valet my ticket, and I'm waiting for them to bring my car around when Kane walks up next to me.

"I see you're continuing to stalk me …"

He hands the valet his ticket. "I don't need to stalk my soon-to-be wife. Speaking of which, do you have any plans on Friday night?"

"I'm drying my nails."

He chuckles. "Cute."

"We already have plans on Saturday night. I don't think I could stomach being stuck with you two nights in a row."

"Soon, you'll be *stuck* living with me twenty-four/seven," he notes with a smirk.

I open my mouth to argue when what he said hits me—I'm going to be living with him. I've never lived with a man before. I barely live with my brother Dominick and his wife, Peyton, since their house is so big that they're on one side with their kids and I'm on the other.

One time, I tried to spend the night with Theo. Only I freaked out and left in the middle of the night. And now I'm going to have to live with Kane … in a hotel room?

"If you think I'm going to live at the country club, you've lost your mind."

"I wouldn't dream of it, Princess. I'm only staying there while our future home is being finished. Would you like to go see it?"

The valet drives around with my car and then stands next to my door, waiting for me to get in.

"I can't," I tell him. "I have shopping plans with my sister-in-law."

Kane chuckles. "Of course you do."

"What's that supposed to mean?" I bite out, not liking his tone.

"Nothing." He shakes his head. "I just noticed that you like to shop."

"When you were stalking me?"

"It's a small town." He shrugs. "But that doesn't change the fact that you're bored with your life."

Before I can argue—or at the very least tell him to go fuck himself—he walks away, ending the conversation and leaving me to think about what he just said.

I want to tell him he's wrong, that he doesn't know a thing about me or my life. But the truth is, he isn't wrong.

I am bored with my life.

But something tells me, thanks to Kane, my life is about to get a bit more chaotic.

"What do you think?"

I step out of the fitting room and twirl around in the silky red dress. With the low-cut A-frame design, the dress shows off my cleavage—giving me the illusion of having a bit more than what I've actually got, which isn't much. It's fitted up top but flowy the rest of the way down, stopping several inches above my knees.

"It's beautiful," Dani says, waddling over with her cute belly. She rubs the material between her fingers. "And soft. Do you like it?"

"I do." I turn to look at it in the mirror. "It's sexy and feminine and way too pretty for my date with Kane on Saturday night."

"On that note ..." She sits on the seat and looks up at me. "What were you thinking, agreeing to marry him?"

"I was thinking my brothers had spent their entire lives trying to protect me, and now it's my turn to protect them," I admit. "They're working so hard to legitimize their businesses, and with *the asshole* coming after the family and trying to mess everything up, this is the last thing they need."

"Ugh, don't remind me." Dani visibly shivers at the mention of the asshole.

Since we don't know who the person is, I refer to him or her as *the asshole*. Someone has been coming after our family for the past two years, and we don't know who it is or why. All we know is that they want the Antonovs out of Harbor Point so they can take over. And instead of coming out and making themselves known, they're acting like a little bitch by playing games.

Messing with the shipments at the port my brothers own and run, which handles a huge amount of import and export from companies that have seven-figure contracts with Antonov Enterprises. They've ransacked businesses in South Harbor Point that are under our family's protection. They took Dani from The Underground and brought her to the port, just to prove they could take one of us anytime they wanted. Dani is the only person who has seen the asshole, and she swears it's a woman. If it is, I wish she'd show her face so I could fuck it up. And the most recent occurrence was at Matteo and Dani's wedding. They left a bottle of expensive scotch as a gift with a note that read, *Congratulations. Hope you make it long enough to be a husband and father.*

We can't prove it, but we also think the asshole could've been working with Anthony—before I shot and killed him—because he had men go after Peyton and Damien, and he was broke, so someone was bankrolling him. And he might've even been working with Enrique—Dani's ex, who seduced her to try to steal her family's company after he killed both her parents in a fire to avenge his father's death. Enrique had Matteo and Lorenzo thrown into jail, but they were thankfully able to get the charges dropped.

I freeze in my spot and glance at Dani. "Have you noticed that everyone who has come after us is connected to Kane?"

She tilts her head to the side as she thinks about what I just said.

"Anthony is Kane's half-brother; Enrique is his brother. What if whoever is coming after us is linked to Kane as well? Or … what if the asshole *is* Kane?"

Dani's eyes widen. "At the baby shower, Kane made it seem like playing dirty wasn't the type of revenge he was after."

"Doesn't mean he's not working with someone who's playing dirty."

"You should tell your brothers. If we can confirm that Kane is working with whoever is coming after us before you get married, maybe they can find a way to catch whoever it is and take out Kane at the same time."

"Or …" I start, an idea forming. Dani gives me a disapproving look. "Just hear me out. I can seduce Kane and try to get any information he might know about whoever it is."

I glance back at myself in the mirror. "I'm going to need a new pair of heels to go with this dress. Should I go with black or red?"

"Well, since you're insisting on playing with fire, I'm going to go with red."

"I agree." I smirk at my sister-in-law through the mirror. "And as long as Kane is the one who gets burned, it'll be worth it."

SEVEN

Kane

"**W**HAT DO YOU WANT?"

I eye the guard I always see with Brielle and consider telling him it's none of his fucking business, but instead, I swallow my retort down and say, "I'm here to pick up Brielle for our date." If I'm going to be marrying into this family, I need to play nice.

Fuck. I can't believe I'm marrying into this family.

This wasn't the damn plan.

I was only supposed to fuck them over regarding the waterfront expansion, force them to pull out, and in turn, destroy their business relationships with several investors, along with their reputation.

Shifting from destroying the expansion project to getting in bed with the Antonovs I could justify. It was a smart business decision—one my father would've approved of. Not only will it help Morgan Enterprises make additional useful contacts, but it will pad the company's portfolio and bank account.

But marrying Brielle Antonov is another story. I told my father and brother not to make shit personal, yet here I am, doing the same fucking thing.

"You're lucky the Antonovs have given us orders not to kill you *yet*, but if you so much as lay a single finger on Brielle, I won't hesitate to put a bullet in you."

"What's your name?" I ask him, wondering if he genuinely cares about my future wife or if she's fucked him and he's become infatuated with her. I'm quickly learning that she has a way of bewitching men.

"Daniil," he says, jutting his chin out.

"Well, *Daniil*, I can guarantee I will be laying more than a finger on Brielle, and when I do, she'll be screaming my name."

"You motherfucker—"

As he reaches behind him, presumably for his gun, the door opens, and Brielle steps out.

"Daniil," she chides when he points it at me. "What if I were Damien?"

Daniil puts his gun away. "I'm sorry, Brielle. But he was disrespecting you."

"It's Miss Antonova," I correct, adding the *A* to the end, like the Russians do when referring to women.

I can feel Brielle's glare aimed at me, but I'm too busy taking her in. She's in a silky red dress that puts her perfect tits on display. It's loose on the bottom, but short, showing off her toned, tanned legs that end with a pair of matching red heels that I want digging into my back as I fuck her.

"Kane!" she barks, forcing my eyes to ascend to meet hers.

Her blonde hair is freshly highlighted, her face is full of makeup that makes her blue eyes pop, and she's wearing her signature red lipstick that I always see her wearing. The fact that she's gone out of her way to dress up and look this fucking delectable tells me that despite hating me, she still wants me.

As if she can hear my thoughts, she scoffs. "I only look like I care because I refuse to go out in public looking like a slob. This"—she waves her hand down her body—"isn't for you. It's for me."

"Whatever you say." I shrug. "You ready to go, or do I need to go inside and meet the parents?"

Before she can answer, the door opens again, and Dominick fills the doorway. "Morgan."

"Future brother-in-law." I smirk, and he growls like a fucking animal.

But I've done my research, so I know he's the bark while Matteo is the bite.

"Dominick, don't," Brielle warns.

"Where are you taking my sister tonight?" Dominick asks.

"To dinner …"

And then I have something planned for afterward that I think she'll enjoy, but I'm not about to tell him what it is since it's none of his business. His sister is a grown woman, even if they refuse to treat her like one.

"Daniil will be joining you," Dominick states. "And before you argue, since you claim you're not the one fucking with our business, that means there's someone out to get my family. I don't give a fuck if they kill you, but Brielle needs to always be protected."

I remember him asking if I was messing with them when I showed up at the baby shower.

"And you don't have a clue who it is?" I ask. "Possibly the mayor?"

"What do you know about the mayor?" Dominick accuses.

"Only that my brother was in contact with him."

"Which one?" Dominick quirks a brow.

"Enrique is the only brother I have."

"You mean *had*," Brielle retorts, "since the piece of shit is dead."

"Regardless," I say, "Anthony never knew we existed. My father made sure to keep our families separated, knowing Anthony was a ticking time bomb."

"So, Enrique was working with the mayor?" Dominick confirms.

"He didn't keep me abreast of his plans since he knew I was against them, but I saw him talking to the mayor a couple of times."

"The mayor doesn't have the balls to execute the shit this person has done. Kidnapping Daniella, fucking with our shipments," Dominick notes. "They stole a pharmaceutical shipment and switched it out with drugs to frame Ilan Cohen."

I whistle and shake my head. "Ilan is not a man you want to burn bridges with."

"You know him?" Dominick asks.

"My company is an investor in Cohen Health."

He nods in understanding.

"Anything else they've done?" I ask.

"Why do you care?" Dominick crosses his arms over his chest.

"Seeing as my plan hinges on Brielle not dying …"

"Can't mess with the human incubator," Brielle grumbles under her breath. "Can we go now? I'd like to get this over with."

I'd like to continue this conversation with Dominick—I haven't gotten the company to where it's at without doing my due diligence—but if we don't leave now, we'll be late for our dinner reservation.

"She needs to be home by midnight," Dominick says, making me bark out a laugh.

"You do realize she's twenty-seven, right?"

"Dominick, it's fine," she says with a sigh. "We're just going to dinner, and then he's dropping me off."

"How much?" Dominick asks.

"What?" I scoff in confusion because there's no way he's—

"How much to end this bullshit?"

"I don't need your money." I chuckle humorlessly. "If you've done your research, you know I'm worth millions, my company billions. I've spent the past six years reviving my father's legacy. This"—I nod toward Brielle—"is about righting wrongs. The waterfront expansion, the marriage, the *heir*." I glance at my future wife, who's scowling my way. "The day Giuseppe shot my father and damn near killed my mother and you cut my family out, I vowed to get what was owed to my family. My father had gone along with your father's bullshit for years because the business was his entire world, only to be fucked over in the end. Nothing but death will stop me from getting what's owed to my father, and even then"—I grin like a Cheshire cat, knowing it'll piss Dominick off—"I won't stop."

"There's no point in going rounds," Brielle says. "Let's get this dinner over with. I have an early morning Pilates class."

I catch a whiff of vanilla as she saunters past me. It's the same scent she wore the other night, and immediately, my cock swells as flashbacks of our night together hit me. The way she took control. The taste of her cunt …

I don't give a shit what the Antonovs offer—that woman is mine.

"I'm surprised you didn't take me to the country club," Brielle says as the hostess guides us to our table with Daniil following.

I assumed he wasn't joining us, until I noticed we were being followed and Brielle noted that he went everywhere she went.

"It's the most public place in Harbor Point."

"I'm sick of eating their food," I admit.

We're at a popular seafood restaurant called The Brown Pelican. It's downtown, on the water, and since it's a nice night, we're sitting outside. The restaurant is packed, and as we were walking through, I could feel several eyes on us. Brielle might not have anything to do with her family's business from what I've seen, but she's still the infamous, unattainable Antonov princess. Aside from that dickhead Theodore DeSantis, she has no history of dating anyone in Harbor Point. And since they only just broke up, us going out is going to get people talking, which is what I want. My association with the Antonovs and Russos will open doors.

At least, that's what I tell myself as I pull out Brielle's chair. Wanting her has nothing to do with the fact that I have been with countless women who bored the fuck out of me. But one night with her, and I've been fiending for her pussy like a goddamn drug addict. It's about taking from the Antonovs. That's it. Nothing more, nothing less.

The hostess hands us menus and then excuses herself, and I watch as Brielle focuses on the menu, trying to ignore my presence while Daniil stands in the corner, glaring daggers my way.

When the waiter comes over, she orders a whiskey sour, but I step in, refusing to let her numb herself. Especially with what I have planned for after dinner.

"No alcohol," I tell her, earning a death glare.

"Excuse me?" She scoffs.

"No alcohol," I repeat, refusing to speak her business in front of an audience. "We'll take sparkling water and the grilled oysters with furikake butter."

The waiter nods and rushes away.

"Let's get one thing straight," Brielle hisses. "You do not own me, and I will not let you—"

"Actually, technically, I do own you." I cock my head to the side. "Well, I will once we sign the marriage certificate." I shrug. "But one has nothing to do with the other." I lean in and meet her eyes. "You use alcohol to numb yourself, and you're not going to do that anymore. Life is hard, and it's time to start dealing with it."

"You know nothing about my life," she grinds out.

"I know you require a drink just to fuck a man …"

"Since I won't be having sex with you tonight—or anytime soon for that matter—it's a moot point," she sasses.

Her words are spoken just as the waiter returns with our drinks, but if he heard, he does a good job of pretending he didn't. But that doesn't stop Brielle from blushing in embarrassment.

"It's okay." I shoot her a wink. "Your pussy is worth waiting for."

She gasps, her eyes darting between the waiter and me, and I laugh. The woman is so prim and proper in public. Thank God she's nothing like that in the bedroom.

Then maybe you wouldn't be so intent on forcing her to marry you …

I order the steak and lobster, and Brielle orders a salad and scallops. When the waiter walks away, she glances at the water, and

I can't help but look at her. I've been thinking about her all week, and I'd be lying if I said I hadn't considered calling off the marriage a dozen times. But then I'd see her—at her brother's office, working out at the gym, eating lunch with her friend at the country club—and it'd renew my need to make her mine.

"Brielle?"

We both glance up and find a beautiful older woman standing there with a gentleman by her side.

"Mom, I didn't know you were home." Brielle stands and gives her mom a hug.

"We got in this afternoon. Decided to come home sooner since Matteo thinks Dani might go into labor earlier than her due date," her mom explains. "The house hasn't been stocked, so I dragged Walter out." She laughs, her blue eyes lighting up with mirth, and her husband chuckles. "Are you going to introduce us?" she asks, glancing at me curiously, which tells me that Brielle hasn't told her mom about our arrangement.

"I'm Kane," I say, standing and shaking her hand. "Kane Morgan."

I shake Walter's hand, and he nods.

"Walter Freedman, and this is my wife, Larissa."

"W.F. Asset Management," I note. "I have an appointment with your firm on Monday."

"Ah, yes," he says. "I thought I recognized the name. What has you relocating to Harbor Point?"

"A business opportunity I couldn't pass up," I tell him, glancing at Brielle with a small, knowing grin. "My financial adviser decided to retire, and since I plan to place roots in Harbor Point, I figured it was time to find a new adviser."

Brielle glares my way, and her mom must notice because her brows furrow in confusion and probably a little bit of concern. But before Larissa can comment, the waiter comes over with our oysters.

"Brielle," her mom says, "let's do brunch soon." She gives her daughter a kiss on each cheek, then glances at me. "Kane, it was nice to meet you."

"You as well," I tell her.

Once they excuse themselves, I look at Brielle with a raised brow.

"What?" she hisses, plucking an oyster off the platter. "I wasn't about to tell my mother over the phone that I was being forced to get married." Her eyes dart around the area, like she's making sure nobody can hear her. "And I was hoping you'd die before she returned and there'd be nothing to tell her."

I chuckle as she pries the oyster shell open and forks the meat like she didn't just wish me dead. She dips the meat into the butter and then brings it up to her plump lips, parting them and slowly sliding it into her mouth. My gaze is stuck on her red lips and the way she gracefully chews and swallows.

"What?" she repeats when she notices me staring.

"You're a contradiction." I take a sip of my water, wishing it were something stronger. Being around Brielle is fucking with my head.

"Most men would call that bipolar. You sure you want to marry me?" She quirks a perfectly shaped brow. "I could easily kill you in your sleep, and everything you've done would be for nothing. It wouldn't be the first time I killed a man." She shrugs nonchalantly, and for whatever crazy reason, her threats are as much of a turn-on as her sucking my dick.

"I think I'll take my chances," I say, opening an oyster. "I've tasted your pussy and stuffed it with my cock, and it's worth risking my life over."

EIGHT

Brielle

THIS MAN. THIS COCKY, ARROGANT FUCKING MAN IS GOING to drive me to insanity.

I hate him.

I hate everything about him.

But then he reminds me of our night together, and like a conditioned dog at the sound of a bell, I salivate at the thought of him bringing me to another orgasm.

"I hope you enjoyed my pussy," I tell him, "because it's never happening again."

He wants to force me to marry him—fine. But that doesn't mean I have to participate in any sort of wifely duties, including having sex with him.

"It'll be hard to create a baby without having sex," he says with a laugh, thinking he's got me backed into a corner.

"It's called in vitro fertilization."

He drops his smug grin and leans in, his eyes filled with heat, and I hold my breath, waiting for the threat to come. I've been around enough assholes like him to know that they don't take kindly to being told no.

But once again, Kane proves to be different when he says, "So, you've thought about this, huh? Having my baby? If that's what you want to do, that's fine. I happened to like your mouth wrapped around my cock. And there's always your ass."

He waggles his brows, and I swallow thickly as thoughts of Anthony taking me from behind hit me.

"The amount of times I've thought about fucking that tight little—"

"Enough!" I bark, then lower my voice when I realize I'm drawing attention over to us. "That night was a mistake, and it will never happen again. Any of it. Not in my pussy or my mouth and definitely not in my ass," I choke out.

Kane sits back, his eyes assessing me, trying to figure out why I just lashed out. I'm so used to Theo and his golden retriever vibes that I'm not prepared for Kane and the way he notices everything.

Thankfully, the waiter arrives with our food and waits for Kane to cut into his filet.

"Perfect." He pops a bite into his mouth.

Then his eyes meet mine, and I hold my breath, praying he's not going to call me out.

Instead, he smiles and says, "Eat up, Princess. We have plans after dinner."

I almost wish he had brought up the anal talk because the knowing look on his face tells me he's up to something, and whatever he has planned can't be good.

A sex club.

He brought me to a freaking sex club.

"Mr. Morgan," a gentleman says, greeting us at the door. "I'm Evan Mariano, the manager of Satisfaction. Thank you for accepting my invite. We're looking forward to showing you what our club has to offer."

Kane shakes Evan's hand. "This is my girlfriend, Brielle Antonova."

The mention of my surname has Evan widening his eyes, obviously having heard of my family. Exclusive memberships to places like this are based on word of mouth, and since Kane is new to town and clearly has connections, it would make sense Evan would reach out.

"And this is her guard, Daniil," Kane notes.

"Welcome to Satisfaction"—Evan grins—"where fantasy and reality become one."

He nods toward a petite woman, who saunters over. She's dressed in a tight black pencil skirt and an equally tight black top, the buttons undone, showing off her cleavage that's spilling out of her black lace bra. Her stiletto heels are also black—the perfect mix of professional and sexy.

"Unfortunately, only guests can be brought inside." Evan eyes Daniil. "But you're welcome to wait out here."

Daniil glances at me, and I nod that it's okay. We have a deal that I do what I want, and in return, I pay him a large sum off the table, which helps support his family in Russia.

"We'll just need a bit of information from you," Evan continues, "and then Mira will show you around. If you need anything, please don't hesitate to ask."

As Mira guides us into the office, I take note of how different the club looks from what I'd expect. With high ceilings, tasteful art donning the walls, and marble floors spanning across the area, both luxurious and tasteful. There are lavish couches and love seats in the main area with two gorgeous spiraling staircases leading up to the second floor, which makes it look more like a mansion than a sex club.

A few gentlemen and women are sitting on the couches, talking and laughing and drinking, and for a moment, I wonder if this is some kind of joke that Kane is playing on me because nothing about this place screams sex.

"This is the sitting room," Mira explains. "They're waiting for their table to be ready. We have two restaurants on-site—Lucia's and Flynn's, both run by Michelin-starred chefs."

Rather than walking up the stairs, we veer right, and after she scans her card, we enter an office, which is just as upscale as the sitting room.

"We already have Mr. Morgan's info, but we'll need to put your license into our system and gather a bit of information from both of you regarding your limits," Mira says.

"I'm not planning to join," I tell her, wondering how the hell we went from eating dinner to checking out a damn sex club.

"Anyone who enters Satisfaction must have their IDs on file and sign an NDA," Mira says. "It's to protect the guests. Mr. Morgan and you have been given a limited elite pass for the night. Because you haven't provided your STI test results, you may not interact with any other members, other than to observe. However, you can try out any of the rooms you wish"—she grins—"with each other."

Elite pass?

STI tests?

Observe?

"I'm sorry. Can you give Mr. Morgan and me a moment to discuss this?" I ask Mira, who simply nods and stands.

"Of course. If you decide to move forward, please provide your license and fill out this info." She hands us each an iPad. "And then I'll give you a private tour of the facilities. If you change your mind, I'll be waiting outside to escort you out."

Once she's gone, I turn to look at Kane.

"What the hell is this?" I hiss.

Of course, he grins. "A sex club."

"And why in the world would you think it would be appropriate to bring me *here* on a first date? Or any date for that matter." I stand, more than ready to leave, when Kane grabs my hand and pulls me onto his lap.

Instinctually, I try to push myself off him, but when his strong hands slide around my waist and down to my ass, I'm reminded of the last time we were in this position—with both of us naked and me riding him—and I freeze.

"Princess," he drawls, and I glare, which only makes him chuckle. "I know you've got a stick shoved up your ass in public—"

"Fuck you!"

"I'm definitely not opposed." He grins devilishly.

"It's not happening," I reiterate. "Now, tell me why the hell we're here. If you want to fuck other women, feel free. As far as I'm concerned, this sham of a marriage is in name only."

"If I wanted to fuck other women, I sure as hell wouldn't have brought you here," Kane growls, tightening his grip on my waist. "Now, instead of making assumptions, take the stick out of your ass for a damn minute. From the little you told me during our night together, you have certain wants and needs, and what better place to explore them than at an exclusive sex club, where nobody is judging?"

I open my mouth to argue, but realize I don't know what to say because he actually makes sense.

"I was invited tonight by the owner in the hope that I'd sign up," he continues. "He obviously thought I was single at the time, but I figured we could check it out together. There are all types of relationships, including ones where the woman is given the control, like what you crave."

"That's rich, coming from you." I scoff. "You might've given me the control that night, but the next day, you took it away."

"I did what I had to do," he says, refusing to show an ounce of remorse for forcing me to marry him. He lifts me off his lap and stands. "Now, do you want to check out this club or not?"

I want to be stubborn and demand he take me home, but I am curious about the place. "I'm not going to have sex with you. You can force me to marry you, but you can't force me to have sex with you."

"And I have no intention of doing so," he says dryly. "The next time we have sex, it will be because you're so desperate for my cock that you'll be begging me to fuck you."

"Over my dead body," I mutter, grabbing the iPad to fill out the info.

There are a million questions, and I barely glance at them, wanting to get it over with so I can check out the place—and sate my curiosity—and then leave.

Once we're done, Kane gets Mira and tells her we'd like her to give us a tour.

"Fantastic," she says, pulling out her phone and tapping on it. "Looks like we have all the necessary information, and neither of you has any limitations, so let's get started, shall we?"

She begins with showing us the private rooms on the second floor, which have king-size beds, elaborate bathrooms with massive bathtubs, showers that can fit multiple people, and plunge pools on the balcony.

"Is this like a hotel?" I ask.

"In a way," she says as we head toward the elevator. "You can rent the room by the hour or for the night. It's for members who are looking for the complete experience. We provide room service, and you can book a couples massage while staying in the suites."

We enter the elevator, and she presses the number three.

"As you ascend, each floor will increase in darkness," she tells us as we step out onto the floor. "As you can see, this floor is light, filled with pinks and whites, and the relations you'll see are on the lighter side."

Some of the rooms have the curtains closed—which, according to Mira, means they're not viewable to the public—while some are open, allowing outsiders to observe. Each room has velvet couches facing the windows, where people can get comfortable to watch, as well as couches in the rooms, for those who want to hear everything that's happening.

We stop at one room, where a couple—appearing to be in their early thirties—is having sex with the curtains open. The man is on top, lovingly kissing down her bare breasts. When he looks up at her, his eyes are filled with so much adoration and heat that my heart clenches in my chest. He brings his lips down to hers, and I can feel the love between them, so much so that I walk away because it feels wrong to watch the intimate encounter—despite the curtain being open.

"You good?" Kane murmurs, the softness in his tone startling me.

It reminds me of the night we spent together—before I knew he was the enemy. Kane evoked feelings within me that I had kept buried deep, only for me to learn that his feelings were fake. He's a manipulative asshole with an agenda.

"I'm fine," I spit, moving on to the next room.

Mira shows us a few more rooms and then walks us over to the elevator.

"As I mentioned before, each floor increases in darkness and intensity," she says, pressing the number four.

We step off the elevator and stop just before the first room.

"You might find group sex, similar to the scenes on the third floor, but more intense. They might use toys or act out various scenes that you wouldn't see in the rooms we were just observing."

We step in front of the window, and I'm immediately taken aback by the scene in front of us. A man and woman are both naked. She's lying on her back, and he's thrusting a dildo in and out of her. We can't hear her from out here, but her head is thrashing from side to side, and I imagine she's screaming in pleasure.

My thighs clench in desire, and I glance at Kane, wondering if he's as turned on as I am, only to find him staring at me instead of at the couple. His eyes, usually golden brown, are dark, filled with raw heat, and I force myself to look away, not wanting to give him any part of me.

We view a few more rooms, and Kane was right—I am intrigued. I always knew my sexual tastes weren't *normal*, but being with Kane and then watching these couples have confirmed it. I crave control, but it's more than that. I don't want to be handled like glass.

My brothers, Theo, even my mom handle me with kid gloves.

They want to protect me, keep me safe, but what they don't understand is that it's too late for that. I've already been broken, my pieces shattered, and I've picked them up and dragged them along with me. I'm a survivor, strong and capable, and I want to be treated as such.

"And this is our darkest floor," Mira says when we step onto the fifth floor.

The first window is open, and there's a couple in the room, standing and facing one another. At first, I wonder why they're on the darkest floor—there are no toys that I can see, and they're both dressed.

I'm about to ask Mira when the woman turns away from the man and he pulls her back to him. Her mouth opens in what I assume is a scream as she tries to get away, but he grabs her—hard—and throws her onto the bed. He towers over her, ripping her shirt and then shorts off her body, and I'm transported back to six years ago.

My clothes being ripped off.

Screaming in protest.

Anthony forcing my legs open.

My eyes are on the woman and man as he flips her onto her stomach, spreads her cheeks, and forces his way into her ass, but my mind is stuck in the past.

The excruciating pain.

Begging him to stop.

Him refusing to do so.

And before I realize what I'm doing, I'm running from the room—from my past. I see the sign for the stairs, and I shove the door open, flying down each flight of stairs, needing to get as far away as possible. But it's pointless because no matter where I go, my past will always follow me. It lives within me, is a part of me, and I can't escape it.

"Brielle, stop!" I hear Kane shout, but I don't listen.

When I reach the final door, I push it open, and I'm met with the cool January air. I suck in a harsh breath, looking both ways, ready to run—to where? I don't know.

But before I can, strong arms wrap around me from behind, caging me in, and because I'm still stuck in my head, I kick and scream, until Kane lets go of me.

I take off in a sprint, running as fast as I can in heels, and I don't stop until I'm down the driveway and near the guard gate.

"Brielle! What the fuck?" Kane shouts, grabbing my shoulders and spinning me around. "What the hell is going on?"

NINE

Kane

I SEE THE LOOK ON BRIELLE'S FACE. SHE MIGHT NOT WANT TO be here, but she's intrigued. On every floor, she watches the couples with a mixture of curiosity and fascination. I'd bet all the money in my bank account, if I slid my hand under her dress and panties, I'd find her soaked.

And I'm trying to figure out how to go about testing my theory when we approach a room where a couple seems to be arguing. Quickly, I realize it's a fantasy rape scene. He throws her on the bed and rips her clothes off. Then he flips her onto her stomach and is about to fuck her ass when Brielle releases a choked gasp and takes off running down the hall.

I follow her down five flights of stairs, out the emergency exit, and halfway to the guard gate when I finally catch up to her and pull her into my arms from behind. "Brielle! What the fuck?" I have no clue what is going on, but her entire body is shaking, and I'm assuming the scene triggered something inside of her. "What the hell is going on?"

I spin her around, and her eyes are red and glassy.

"I want to leave—now," she demands.

"Okay, but first, you need to tell me what happened in there. One minute, you were turned on, and the next …"

The next, we were watching a rape scene.

Could that be it? Could Brielle have been a victim of rape?

My first thought is, *Who the fuck raped her? And do her brothers know about it?*

And my next thought is, *If whoever did it is still alive, I'll slowly fucking kill them.*

"Brielle, did someone—"

"I said, I want to leave."

She backs out of my touch, and I want to demand she let me in and tell me what happened, but I can see the defiance in her eyes. Her walls have been fully erected, and she's not going to let me in tonight.

Of course, Daniil—who has the worst timing ever—approaches, and since I don't want to continue this conversation in front of him, I relent.

"Okay," I tell her, "let's go."

Since she clearly doesn't want to be touched, I head back to the car with her an arm's length away, Daniil following. Brielle might think this conversation is over, but I'm going to find out who made my future wife like this, and once I do, heads are going to fucking roll.

The drive back to Brielle's is quiet, and once we pull through her brother's guard gate, she starts taking off her seat belt, ready to bolt.

But before she can get out, I place my hand on hers to stop her. "What happened back there—"

"Is none of your fucking business," she finishes, shaking my hand off her and getting out of my car.

"Brielle!" I yell once I'm out of the car, trying to get her to stop, but like the stubborn woman she is, she ignores me and goes inside, slamming the door behind her before I can get another word in.

"Good date?" the guard asks with a smirk.

"Tell Dominick I need to speak to him."

If anyone would know what happened to Brielle, it's him.

The guard clenches his jaw, but pulls out his phone.

A few minutes later, Dominick steps outside. "It's late."

"This couldn't wait." I glance at the guard, making it clear I don't want to talk in front of him. Dominick nods toward him, letting him know he's free to go, and I wait until we're alone to ask, "Who hurt your sister?"

I don't bother asking if she was hurt. I already know she was. So, the only question is who fucking hurt her.

Dominick's face turns dark. "Why are you asking that?"

"Because it's clear someone hurt her, and I want to know if they're still alive so I can end their life."

Dominick barks out a humorless laugh. "No, he's not alive. Brielle killed him."

I can't help the smile that spreads across my face. Brielle is such a fucking contradiction. I wasn't supposed to want her, yet I can't stop. She wasn't supposed to be anything more than revenge, yet I find myself wanting more.

"My sister's been through a lot," Dominick says, snapping me out of my thoughts. "You wanted in on the expansion, you got it. You wanted the contacts that came along with it, and you have them. You don't have to take her too."

He's right—I don't need her. But fuck if I don't want her.

And the fact that marrying her aligns with my plan to avenge my father's death only makes it that much sweeter.

"The deal was that the three families are united by marriage and produce heirs," I remind him—and myself. "And that's what's going to happen."

"Dom," a woman says, poking her head out the door. "Is everything—oh. Hello," she says, stepping out and going to Dominick's side. "We haven't formally met yet. I'm Peyton, Dom's wife." She extends her hand, and I don't miss the way Dominick grinds his jaw at the thought of his wife shaking hands with me. "And you're the asshole who's forcing my sister-in-law to marry you."

I chuckle and nod. "That's me."

"She'll never love you," Peyton says matter-of-factly.

"Good thing I'm not looking for love," I tell her.

Which is the truth. Love is a wasted emotion. It causes men like

Dominick and my father to make shitty choices. I base my decisions on logic, data, and facts.

Yet you're forcing Brielle to marry you.

I shove the thought to the side.

I'm doing what my dad would've wanted.

What's best for the future of the company.

And Brielle is nothing more than a pawn in this game of chess.

The Antonovs and Russos made their moves.

And I made mine.

Check-fucking-mate.

TEN

Brielle

"Oɴᴇ ᴍᴏʀᴇ ʙʀᴇᴀᴛʜ ʜᴇʀᴇ. Gᴏᴏᴅ. Lᴇᴛ's ʀᴇᴀᴄʜ ᴜᴘ ᴀɴᴅ ᴏᴠᴇʀ. A nice stretch here. Good. Exhale. Now switch sides." The Pilates instructor lowers her left arm and then swings her right arm up.

"Oh my God, it feels like I'm going to stretch this baby right out of my uterus," Dani murmurs, making me laugh.

Several of the women in the class glare our way, but I just glare back, making them look away. With my family's reputation, all it takes is one look for them to go running in fear for their life.

"Well, at least if you do go into labor, you're full-term," I point out.

She started going to Pilates with me a few months ago when she mentioned her body feeling stiff from the pregnancy. Since she's a newbie, when we go together, we go to the beginner class so it's safe for her.

Unfortunately, this is also the class all the pregnant women in Harbor Point seem to go to. Being surrounded by happy, pregnant women isn't easy, but I always thought that maybe, one day, this would be me. Now, I'm not so sure anymore.

"Yeah, but the doctor said she's on the smaller side, so she'd like for her to bake as long as possible." Dani rubs her belly, and I can't help the envy I feel toward her.

She has it all. The loving husband, a precious little girl on the way. She works for her family's real estate development company alongside her brother who values her thoughts and opinions.

Meanwhile, I have brothers who want to protect me yet don't really know me. A fake boyfriend, who will soon become my fake fiancé and then my fake husband. And thanks to Kane, starting a family is out of the question.

He thinks I'm going to give him an heir once we're married, but little does he know that I'm on the pill, and I have no intention of getting off it. I considered getting the shot or something more permanent, like an IUD, but the pill is what I was prescribed when my gynecologist found cysts forming on my ovaries, and she recommended that I stay on it since it seems to be working.

We finish our session, and then Dani and I head out to grab a coffee at Lattes and Words—the coffee shop and bookstore Nicole owns.

"There she is!" Nicole exclaims when we walk inside. "I was beginning to think you'd dropped off the face of the earth."

"Dramatic much?" I mutter, walking up to the counter.

"Not when we hang out almost every Friday night and I don't hear from you."

"She had a date," Dani chimes in.

"Oh!" Nicole's eyes light up. "Not with Theo, I hope?"

"No." I clear my throat, preparing to drop the bomb. "With Kane Morgan."

Nicole's eyes go as wide as saucers. "The one-night stand?"

Dani whips her head around to look at me in shock.

"Don't repeat that to my brothers," I warn.

I might be close with my sisters-in-law, but their loyalty lies with their husbands.

Dani shakes her head. "You hooked up with Kane? When?"

"The night before your baby shower."

She curses under her breath, and Nicole says, "What am I missing?"

I glance around to make sure no one is eavesdropping. Daniil and Dani's guard, Ian, are standing by the door, and there are a few customers drinking coffee in the corner.

"It turns out that Kane's family has history with mine, and he's blackmailing my brothers into working with him and … forcing me to marry him."

I don't get into him being related to Anthony since that would lead to questions from her that I don't want to answer.

Nicole gasps. "That asshole. Why do all the good-looking ones have to be so horrible? What are you going to do?" she asks.

"Marry him." I sigh. "And since I can't choose between my sisters-in-law, you'll be my maid of honor."

Nicole smiles sadly. "I would be honored to. When's the wedding?"

"I don't know," I admit. "He said within the month. He wants to publicly court me and propose, and then we'll get married. You can't say anything," I say to Nicole. "Especially to your dad."

The last thing I need getting out is that our marriage is a sham, which will make Kane look bad and lead to him possibly screwing my family over in retaliation. Powerful men like my brothers and Kane take their reputation seriously.

"I would never." Nicole shakes her head. "But I hate this for you. I know how important finding love is to you. Do you think there's any chance he could possibly love you?"

I think back to the night we spent together. The way he took control, yet gave me the control I needed. It was only sex, but it felt like so much more.

And then he ruined it by showing up the next day and snatching every ounce of control he had given me away.

"A man like Kane isn't capable of love," I say. "He cares about one thing—business."

Nicole nods in understanding. "He'd get along great with my dad," she mutters.

"Let's hope not," Dani interjects. "Working with the mayor is the number one way to piss off Matteo and Dominick."

Nicole cringes. "I hate the man my father has become."

"Enough talk about men," I grumble, sick of them infiltrating our lives. Everywhere I turn, there's a man trying to fuck with my life. "I need a proffee and a strawberry muffin."

"Oh! Same," Dani agrees with a grin. "I've been trying to keep it to one coffee a day, but I can barely stay awake, thanks to this little one keeping me up all night."

She rubs her hand lovingly across her bump, and my heart squeezes in my chest. I hate that I never got to feel my baby in me—and thanks to Kane, I never will.

As if I've conjured him by thought alone, the door dings, and in walks the devil himself. He's staring down at his phone, looking every bit like the business mogul he is—dressed in a sharp black suit, his hair freshly cut, and his angular, stubbled jaw tense in concentration.

As if he can sense me staring at him, his head shoots up, and his whiskey eyes meet mine. His features soften slightly, replaced by a cocky smirk.

"Oh, you're here." He saunters over to me. "Just saved me a text. I have a business dinner tonight. We're going to Archies," he says, referring to one of the most exclusive restaurants in North Harbor Point, "so dress accordingly. I'll pick you up at six.

My jaw drops, and when I glance at Nicole and Dani, they both look equally flabbergasted by Kane's abrupt tone.

"Oh, so we're making demands now?" I say sweetly, reminding myself that I can't murder this man in the middle of Nicole's coffee shop. "In that case, I demand you go fuck yourself."

Nicole snorts out a laugh, and Dani covers her mouth. Kane doesn't look amused in the slightest. Good. I'm not either.

"I have plans tonight with Nicole." I pat his chest condescendingly. "So, it looks like you're on your own."

Kane: Where the hell are you?

Kane: I told you I was picking you up at 6:00.

Kane: Brielle, stop playing fucking games.

"Can you believe the nerve of that asshole?" I grab the bottle of tequila sitting on the bar and pour myself another shot. I sprinkle some salt on my wrist, lick it, then throw the shot back. It burns, going down, numbing both my belly and my brain. "It's not enough that he's forcing me to marry him, but now he thinks he owns my time?" I grab a lime and bite into it, shaking my head as the bitterness chases away the taste of the tequila. "Fuck that and fuck him!" I slam the shot glass on the bar top.

Nicole looks at me with sympathetic eyes, but she doesn't bother to say anything because there's nothing to say that will make any of this better.

"I hate him," I tell her. "I hate him and …" *Fuck, I want him.*

No matter how much I hate him, I equally want him.

In bed. His body against mine.

I want to taste him. Suck him. Kiss him. Fuck him.

"Fuck! I hate him."

Just as I pour myself another shot and throw it back, my phone rings, and Kane's name pops up, making me regret giving him my number. I consider blocking him, but the drunken part of me has other ideas.

I click Accept. "How was it?"

"I had to cancel," Kane says. "You were supposed—"

"No," I cut him off. "I meant, how was fucking yourself?"

I bark out a laugh at my joke, and Nicole joins in.

"Where are you?" Kane growls over the line.

"In hell."

"Brielle …"

"Is this seat taken?" a guy asks.

"Nope," I tell him. "It's available, just like me."

"Brielle Antonova, I swear to—"

"Gotta go," I singsong. "And if all goes well, unlike you, I won't be fucking myself."

I end the call, drop my phone into my purse, and pour Nicole, the man sitting next to me, and myself a shot.

"A toast," I say, lifting my shot glass. "To not fucking ourselves."

ELEVEN

Kane

THIS WOMAN IS GOING TO BE THE DEATH OF ME.

What the hell was I thinking?

The entire reason I've avoided any type of commitment is because I know how it ends. Women are like witches, casting their spells on the men around them and forcing them to ruin their lives. I love my mom, but I watched what loving her did to my dad, and I told myself I wouldn't make the same mistakes he'd made.

Yet, here I am, forcing Brielle Antonova to marry me simply because her cunt tasted delicious and felt amazing, wrapped around my cock.

Since I'm still on the street Brielle lives on, I turn around and go back to the house, demanding to speak to Dominick. He's controlling enough to keep tabs on his sister.

"She giving you a hard time?" He smirks when I ask him to locate her. "It's not too late to change your mind. The contract has been drawn up for the waterfront expansion."

When I don't respond, he simply chuckles. "Sorry, but if she doesn't want you to know where she is, that's between you two."

"She's drunk at a bar somewhere. I understand your priority is your wife and kids, but who's making Brielle a priority? And before you try to sell me on that waste of a guard, who's wrapped around her finger, I doubt he's doing anything to protect her."

Dominick's jaw clenches, and he pulls out his phone. "She's at The Tavern."

I thank him and turn to leave when Dominick calls my name.

"It's not that I don't make Brielle a priority," he says. "Matteo and I spent years trying to protect her. But we failed her."

I turn back around to look at him and can see the guilt written all over his features.

"This life … it broke her, and I don't think she'll ever be the same."

She's sitting at the bar with her friend Nicole and the guy I heard over the phone. She's got a bottle of tequila in front of her, and she's pouring another shot.

The guy says something to her, and her entire face lights up. She throws her head back in a laugh, exposing her slim throat, and the guy eyes her, no doubt imagining what it would be like to spend the night with her.

And I don't blame him. Brielle is every man's fantasy. Blonde hair and blue eyes. A smile that lights up the fucking dark. She's got luscious tits, a toned waist, an ass that is perfect for fucking, and legs for goddamn days. But that's only on the surface.

Men in our world want a woman like her on their arm. But they couldn't handle her. The first word out of her mouth would have them shutting her down. It's why she gravitated toward Theodore DeSantis. Rather than standing up to her, he gave in.

But that's not what she needs.

She needs boundaries.

She craves control because she feels out of control.

Dominick thinks she's broken, but he's wrong.

She's just a little fucking bent.

She turns to look at her friend, and she must see me in her peripheral vision because her back goes straight and her head whips around, her eyes meeting mine.

"You can go now." I dismiss the guy, who's now looking at me as well when I grab the purse hanging on the back of Brielle's chair.

"What? I—"

"Walk away," I warn the guy.

"Fuck you, bro. I found her first. She's mine."

He reaches for Brielle, but before he can touch her, I shove him off the chair and against the wall, hooking his arm behind his back. He screams out in pain, begging me to let him go.

"Let's get one thing straight," I tell him as I push his face into the drywall. "She isn't yours. She was never yours, and she'll never be yours."

I shove his arm up, and he screams louder. A little more, and I'll dislocate his shoulder.

"Is this what you wanted?" I bark at Brielle, who's staring at me with wide eyes. "You wanted to use this man to get under my skin? To prove that you're in control?"

"Kane, stop, please," she begs.

"You did this," I bark. "You risked his life—and for what?" I smash his face into the wall harder. "To make me jealous? We both know this man couldn't satisfy you."

I shove him toward Daniil, who has walked over to join the party. "Get him out of here. And then take Nicole home. And, Daniil … if you allow this shit to happen again, you'll be looking for another job."

"You can't do that!" Brielle shouts, stalking toward me.

"I can, and I'd bet your brothers would agree if they knew the shit he's been letting you pull." I grab her face in my hand and look into her eyes. "His job is to protect you, and he either does so or he's gone."

She swallows thickly.

"You want control in the bedroom," I murmur so only she can

hear. "You can have it. You wanna fuck me, suck me, do whatever the hell you want to me. But I'm not going to let you run around this goddamn town, acting like a fucking whore because you need attention. You want attention, baby? You have mine."

"Fuck you!" she sneers.

"Not tonight, Princess. You're drunk."

She shoves away from me, and since I've had enough of her shit, I lean down and haul her over my shoulder, ensuring nobody can see her ass as I walk out of the bar with her kicking and screaming.

When we get to my car, I set her in the passenger seat and buckle her in and then take off toward my house. The design team finally finished it, and I moved my stuff in this week—leaving room for my future wife, of course.

Speaking of which …

I glance at Brielle, and she's already passed out, her head lolled slightly forward. The plan was for her to move in once we were married, but after tonight, the timeline is going to be moved up.

The house I purchased is in a new development in North Harbor Point, not too far from her brother Dominick's house. It's a modern two-story home with a pool and Jacuzzi and an in-law suite I hope I can convince my mom to move into once I know for certain her life isn't being threatened. The home is backed up to the Atlantic with a privacy fence and a bridge that takes you right onto the beach.

I pull into one of the six parking bays, and Brielle doesn't move. I don't know how much she drank, but she's passed the fuck out.

I lift her into my arms—this time bridal-style—and carry her up the stairs to our room. I remove her heels and undress her, carefully putting one of my shirts on her. Once she's under the sheets, I grab her phone from her purse, use her face to open it, and set it to where she's sharing her location with me.

I consider going through her texts, but don't do it. Brielle is full of secrets, but when her brother refused to share them with me, I realized that I wanted her to tell me all of them. And she will—once she trusts me enough to do so.

I find an extra charger and plug in her phone. Then I grab a bottled water and a couple of pain relievers for when she wakes up and set them next to her phone on the nightstand.

After brushing my teeth and stripping down to my boxers, I climb into bed. For several minutes, I watch her chest rise and fall, wondering what the hell I'm doing. My focus is supposed to be on the business. She's the one thing I need to stay away from, yet I'm drawn to her like an addict to meth.

And like any addict, instead of pushing her away, I lean in and drag my nose down her neck, inhaling her sweet scent, knowing this isn't going to end well, but still choosing the high she gives me.

TWELVE

Brielle

"THAT'S IT, PRINCESS. BEND OVER AND SHOW ME YOUR ASS."

I do as Kane said and roll over onto all fours, jutting my ass out and wiggling it playfully. His hand cracks down on one cheek, and I moan as the pain radiates through my body.

Fuck, that feels so good.

"Again," I demand.

He smacks my other cheek.

"Oh God," I moan. "Again."

Another smack, and I clench my thighs, worried that my arousal is going to drip down the inside of my thighs and onto the sheets.

I reach between my legs, needing the release, but I can't seem to find it.

It's so close, resting on the precipice, yet no matter what I do, how fast or slow I massage my clit, I can't seem to tip over the edge …

"Please, Kane," I beg in frustration. "I need help. I need to come."

"Fuck, baby. Open your eyes and say the word, and I'll help you come."

Open my eyes?

But they are open …

My eyes fly open, taking in my surroundings, and I quickly realize that I was dreaming.

I glance down, finding myself in nothing but a men's shirt and my hand in my panties.

Oh God.

No, no, no.

I wasn't just dreaming.

I was fantasizing about being with Kane.

Only it wasn't just a fantasy because the wetness between my legs and all over my fingers is real.

"Fuck," Kane groans, his eyes igniting with lust. "Even in your dreams, I'm satisfying you. Tell me, baby"—he smirks—"what was I doing to you?"

"It's not what you were doing to me. It's what I was doing to you."

"Oh, yeah? And what were you doing to me?"

"Murdering you," I deadpan.

Kane chuckles. "Hmm … so, you're telling me, if I reach between your legs, I won't find you soaked?"

He glances down, and I quickly pull my hand out of my panties, instantly regretting it when my fingers shine with my arousal.

"What can I say?" I shrug, trying to play it off. "The thought of killing you turns me on."

"Oh, Bri." He tsks. "You want to hate me, but you can't deny the way you want me." He grabs the hand that was just in my panties and slides my pointer and middle finger into his mouth, making a show of licking and sucking the juice off my digits. "The way you want this …" With my hand still in his, he brings it down to my material-clad pussy and uses my own fingers to push the fabric aside. "Go ahead, baby. Finish what you started."

I grind my molars, not wanting to admit the truth—that I can't finish. I've tried countless times since the night I spent with Kane, but every time, I get lost in my own head. It's like once my body got the taste of true satisfaction, it no longer wanted the imitation. Even in my damn fantasy, I couldn't finish.

"I'm not in the mood," I mutter, pulling my hand away.

"No?" His brows furrow. "Can I?"

He nods toward my pussy, asking permission to touch me, and a lump of emotion forms in my throat. He doesn't know what happened to me, only that I crave control, and he makes it a point to give it to me.

Except when he's forcing you to marry him …

My legs, apparently with a mind of their own, fall apart.

Kane reaches into my panties and, when he finds me soaked, smirks devilishly. "Oh, baby, you're definitely in the mood."

He pulls the material down my legs and drops them off the side of the bed. I have no idea where we are or whose room we're in—because it's definitely not my room or one of the rooms at the country club—but before I can give it any more thought, Kane pushes two fingers deep inside me, making me arch off the bed and moan in want.

"That's it, Princess," he murmurs, shifting so he has easier access to my pussy. "Now, while I finger your tight pussy, tell me what you were fantasizing about."

Oh God.

I shake my head, refusing to admit what we were doing in my dream, and Kane stops fingering me.

"If you want to come, you're going to tell me every detail of your dream."

Fuck, I really want to come.

"Okay," I breathe out. "Keep going."

He quirks a brow.

"We were in bed together."

He goes back to massaging my walls with his fingers, and I moan in pleasure.

Kane's right—I might hate him, but I can't deny how much I want him.

"Keep going," he warns.

"And I was on my hands and knees, and you were behind me."

He shocks me when he pulls his fingers out and flips me onto my hands and knees.

"What are you—"

He reaches between my legs and thrusts his fingers back inside me, hard and deep.

I drop my head onto the pillow, releasing an embarrassingly loud moan, and I hear him chuckle darkly from behind me.

"And what were we doing in this position?" he asks nonchalantly, like he's not finger-fucking me into oblivion.

"You were …"

He adds a third finger, and I curse under my breath at how full I feel.

"I was …" he prompts, finding my clit and stroking it with what I assume is the pad of his thumb.

"You were spanking me."

He stills, and I glare back at him, needing him to keep going.

"You want me to spank this sweet ass?" he asks, rubbing my ass cheek with the hand that's not buried inside me.

When he stops, I move back slightly, silently begging him to keep going.

I'm like an attention-starved cat.

I can't stop craving Kane's touch.

I shouldn't want it.

Hell, I should be repulsed by it, but my body isn't on the same page as my brain.

It wants his touch. His warmth.

For years, when I was in Russia, I yearned for a connection like this. It was why I settled for Theo even though the attraction wasn't there.

But now that my body is getting what it needs from Kane, it can't stop craving more of him.

"Please," I cry in frustration, needing him to make me feel good.

"Tell me to spank you, and I'll give you what you need."

Fuck, this guy.

How the hell does he manage to make me feel like I'm in control while not giving up an ounce of it?

"Princess …" He circles my clit, and the beginning of an orgasm stirs within me.

"Yes!" I hiss. "Spank me and make me fucking come—now!"

His hand connects with my flesh at the same time he pushes his fingers back inside me, and my body lights up like a Christmas tree.

And fuck if what he's doing to me isn't the best damn gift I've been given.

Just like in my dream, he alternates smacking each ass cheek while he fucks me slow and deep with his fingers. His thumb massages circles along my swollen nub, and before I know what's happening, the most amazing orgasm takes over my body. My legs shake, and my heart thumps so hard that my ears ring. My vision goes blurry, and …

"Fuck, baby, you just squirted all over our fucking bed."

Our fucking bed.

Oh my God.

I'm in Kane's bed.

And then it all hits me …

I was at the bar, drunk, and he picked me up and carried me out.

I must've fallen asleep in his car, and he brought me to his house.

The house he'd told me I would be moving into once we were married.

And then I fantasized about him spanking me, and he turned it into a reality.

I flip onto my back, pulling my shirt down to cover my bare pussy, internally groaning when I realize I'm wearing Kane's damn shirt.

"This changes nothing," I tell him, shuffling to the edge to get away from him now that the high from my orgasm is being replaced with regret.

"And why the hell am I in your house?" I hiss, glaring at him. "You should've brought me home last night."

"I did." He shrugs, leaning back on his elbows.

His gaze roams down my body, and even though I know the shirt is covering the important parts, I still feel exposed.

"This is my home … and now, it's yours as well."

"Not until we get married," I argue.

"Actually, there's been a change of plans," he says dryly. "Since you can't be trusted to behave like a respectable adult, I've arranged for your belongings to be packed up and brought here. You'll be moving in with me, effective immediately."

"You can't do that!" I shriek, the thought of having to share a house and a bed with this man making me hysterical.

"It's already done."

I grab my phone on the nightstand and don't find a single text from my brother.

What the hell? I know he's busy with his family, but damn.

"Daniil is delivering it all this morning."

Fuck! I thought I had another few weeks—and I was hoping to prolong it more than that. I've never lived with a man before. And the last man I spent an entire night with—aside from last night, which I don't even remember, thanks to the tequila shots—was Owen.

At the thought of him, my heart sinks as a flashback of the last time we were together hits me hard.

"It's going to be okay, babe." Owen wraps his arms around me from behind and settles his hands on my nonexistent bump. "We'll hide, and eventually, your old man will give up."

I wish he were right, but that's not the type of person my father is. He won't give up until he finds us and drags me back home to marry that psycho Anthony.

Bile fills my mouth at the thought of having to spend my life with the man who raped me. I'd rather die than spend a night with him.

But I need to live because I have a baby growing inside me. I don't know whose sperm it is—Anthony's or Owen's—but it doesn't matter. The baby is part me, and Owen told me he'd love the baby, no matter what.

"I love you," I whisper, shifting closer to him so my back is flush against his front and I'm surrounded by his warmth.

"I love you too." He strokes his thumb up and down my lower belly. "And I love this baby."

It doesn't matter that we're on the run, hiding out in a dingy, gross motel, in hope of escaping my father—one of the most dangerous men I've ever known. When I'm in Owen's arms, I feel safe.

We fall asleep in each other's arms, and I dream of what life could be like if we could escape my father. Raising our little boy or girl together. Family breakfasts, trips to the park. Christmases filled with love and laughter.

I've never experienced anything like that—my father sucking the joy out of everything and everyone—but I've seen it on TV and when I've visited my friends. And it's what I want. A doting husband who will make me and our children his world. A life with love and happiness.

Only when I wake up, reality is nothing like my dream. Owen is being dragged out of the bed. I'm screaming for my father to stop. Begging him to let him go.

"Brielle," Kane says, bringing me back into the present.

I don't even realize I'm crying until Kane reaches out and swipes my tears from under my eyes.

"I don't share," he says, tipping my chin up with his finger. "And the next time I see you flirting with another man, I will end his life. So, think long and hard before you use another man to make me jealous. If he dies, the blood will be on your hands."

The blood will be on your hands …

"Just remember, you did this," my father says as one of his men points the gun at Owen and ends his life. "You chose to run, and now his blood is on your hands. Let's go. We have an appointment at the clinic to get that bastard taken out."

"You can force me to live with you, but I won't be sleeping in this room," I blurt out. "I want my own room. I need my own space away from you."

Kane's jaw tics, but he nods, thankfully choosing not to argue.

"I need to go," I choke out, needing to get away from this man, from this life.

Every time I take one step forward, I'm knocked three back.

I pull up the rideshare app, and Kane must see because he says, "Your car is here. The keys are downstairs. I had Daniil drop it off for you."

Daniil …

My thoughts go back to last night. Kane threatened his job because he'd found out that Daniil allowed me to do as I pleased behind my brothers' backs.

Another life in my hands.

I follow Kane downstairs, taking in what is now the place I'll be living, and while it's beautiful, it's clear that it was professionally decorated, not a personal item in sight.

It's probably because he recently bought the home, but I always pictured my first home to be warmer, filled with pictures of my loved ones.

This isn't your home, I remind myself. *It's just another prison, where you're being forced to live.*

"The kitchen is here," he says. "I need to order groceries, so if there's anything you want, let me know. And I've hired a cook to make meals since I prefer not to cook. She'll make them and deliver them. If you have any foods you enjoy, I can add them to the list for her to make."

The way he's nonchalantly discussing meals—like we're a regular couple, taking the next step and moving in together—only moments after he threatened to kill any man I flirted with, is dizzying.

I should be used to this since I was raised in a world where violence was the norm, but I've always avoided anyone like my brothers—hence me dating Owen and then Theo.

"Can I go now?" I ask, feeling dead inside.

Kane stares at me for several seconds before he nods and swipes my keys off the counter, handing them to me. "Your stuff will be here shortly. I'll put it in the guest room upstairs for you to put away."

Since the only thing I can think to say in response is *thank you* and I have no intention of thanking him for forcing me to move in with him, I nod and walk out the door.

Not wanting to go home—since it's no longer my home, and if we're being honest, it never was—but needing to shower and change, I call Nicole, who tells me she's home and I can come to her place.

"What the hell happened last night?" she hisses when I walk inside her apartment.

It's on the smaller side, above the coffee shop and bookstore she owns, but it's adorable and all hers.

"My future husband is a fucking psycho," I say, heading straight to her kitchen to make myself a much-needed coffee.

"Daniil took me home," she says. "I was so wasted that I threw up twice on the way," she groans. "So, he came in and stayed with me until I fell asleep."

I glance at her, taking in the softness in her eyes, and wish my life could be that simple.

"Daniil works for my brother," I remind her.

"I know," she says, waving me off. "But it was still sweet."

I pour milk and creamer into my coffee and mix it, then take a large sip, sighing as the hot liquid flows through my body.

"How did it go with Kane?" she asks, chewing on the corner of her lip.

"Oh, you know … after he threatened Daniil and the guy at the bar, he brought me back to his house. When I woke up this morning, he gave me a mind-blowing orgasm and then told me my stuff was being packed and I'd be moving in with him immediately since I couldn't be trusted." I roll my eyes. "Then he warned me if I acted like that again, he'd kill the guy."

Nicole snorts out a laugh. "A mind-blowing orgasm, huh?"

I shake my head. "Of course you would focus on that detail. Did you not hear the part about him forcing me to move in with him now?"

"Yeah." She waves me off. "But he lives alone, right? You always complain that your brother's house is like Grand Central Station, so at least now you'll have some quiet."

Oh, Nicole. Always the optimist.

"I need to go to the gym. You coming?"

"I can't. I have to head down to the shop before the morning rush."

I finish my coffee, then grab a quick shower to rinse last night and this morning off my body. Then, after I borrow some of Nicole's gym attire, I head to the gym to get a workout in. I notice there's a boxing class this morning, so I join it, hoping to relieve some of the built-up tension, thanks to Kane's demands.

When I arrive at my brother's place a couple of hours later, sweaty and a bit lighter from my workout, I find everyone in the playroom. Peyton is on the floor, reading the twins a book, while Damien colors at the kids' table.

"Hey," she says when she notices me standing in the doorway. "I was hoping you wouldn't leave without at least saying goodbye."

"It wasn't my choice," I tell her.

"What do you mean, it wasn't your choice?" my brother barks from behind me. "Kane said you requested to have your stuff sent to his place."

"He requested it, not me. You didn't even bother to text me to confirm, so …" I shrug. "Anyway, it's for the best. Now you can use the room when you undoubtedly knock up your wife again." I chuckle, but even to my own ears, I sound petty.

God, when did I become this bitter, angry person?

"You know you're welcome here anytime," Peyton says with a frown. "And we're done with three, so the room isn't being used for anything."

"It's fine." I wave her off. "I'm just going to make sure Daniil grabbed everything."

I turn on my heel and make it a few steps before Dominick catches up.

"It's not too late," he says. "Say the word, and I'll call the expansion off."

"And set you back millions, possibly billions, of dollars while pissing off several bigwig investors? It's fine. You and Matteo did a lot for me, growing up, so this is the least I can do."

And it's the truth. They might think they failed me because of what happened with Anthony and Andrey, but that was only one incident in a sea of hundreds.

When I messed up, Matteo would step in between Andrey and me, not allowing him to hurt me. When I wanted to join the cheerleading team, they helped me hide it from Andrey. When I wanted to go away to school, they went to bat for me.

We might not be close, but they've always had my back in their own way, making sure I was as safe as I could be. Now, it's my turn to protect them.

"If you need anything, we're here," Dominick says as I step into my room.

It's been cleaned out, only the queen bed and furniture left behind. I don't have much stuff because I didn't bring anything with me when I moved back here from Russia, and since I've been home, I've just been kind of coasting.

"It took an army of men to box up your clothes," Dominick says dryly. "And I'm not sure you have enough shoes. I think he lost count after a hundred."

I laugh softly, imagining the look of horror on Kane's face when he sees all the clothes, shoes, and makeup I have.

I should move into his room just so I can take over his closet.

And with that thought, an idea forms.

> Me: Change of plans. Put all my stuff in Kane's master bedroom.
>
> Daniil: You're lucky I kind of like you.
>
> Me: You mean, I'm lucky I pay you well.
>
> Daniil: That too.

THIRTEEN

Kane

WHAT IN THE ACTUAL FUCK?

I glance around my room as Daniil and a couple of other guys pile boxes and boxes of shit into my master bedroom and bathroom.

"She only had a bedroom and bathroom at her brother's place. How the hell does she even have this much stuff?"

Daniil shrugs. "The woman is a shopper, and she had two rooms at her brother's. One for her to sleep in and the other for her wardrobe. Wait until you see all her makeup and shit."

"She needs to find something else to do with her time," I mutter as I walk out of my room so they can finish bringing in her boxes.

"Oh, you're home," Brielle says, sauntering into the house. "Have they finished bringing my stuff in?"

"No, it will probably take them the entire day with all the shit you have. You know you have a problem, right?"

"If you don't like it, I can live elsewhere." She shrugs smugly.

Speaking of which …

"I thought you wanted your own room, but Daniil just spent an hour moving all your stuff from the guest room to the master."

"Changed my mind. Your closet is bigger"—she steps into my space and runs her hands along my biceps—"and your bathroom is nice. Feel free to move to the guest room if you wish."

Ahh, so this is the game she's playing. Torture me in my own home until I've had enough and I regret my decision to force her to marry me. What she doesn't realize is that I lived with my mom for the past several years since my father was killed, and since she had to keep a low profile, she resorted to online shopping, filling the house up with too much random shit.

"I'm good," I tell her. "Since we didn't make it to dinner last night, I've rescheduled for brunch this afternoon, and I'd appreciate you accompanying me."

"Are you asking or demanding?" she asks.

"Depends on what your answer is."

She sighs. "Whatever. I don't have anything else going on anyway. I already got my workout in."

I drag my gaze from her face down her body and notice she's still in her workout attire—a tiny light-blue sports bra that shows off the swell of her tits and matching leggings that wrap around her thighs and ass like cling wrap. The woman is fucking gorgeous, but more than that, she's in shape.

"How often do you work out?"

"Every day."

"Damn, that's commitment."

"I have nothing else to do." She shrugs. "Might as well do something that benefits my health."

That's the second time she's insinuated that she's bored.

"Didn't you go to college?"

Her shoulders tense. "Yeah. So?"

"Did you graduate?"

I should know this, but her education wasn't really a priority when I was doing my research on the Antonov family.

"Yes," she spits. "With a degree in accounting, and I got my MBA online as well while I was in Russia. I also took and passed the CPA exam when I returned to the States. Any other questions?"

"No need to get defensive," I say, shocked by her choice of degree.

"Brielle," Daniil calls out. "Do you want your jeans hanging or folded?"

"Hanging," she replies with a huff. "Jesus, what crazy person folds their jeans?"

She disappears upstairs to no doubt redo everything they've done while I'm left wondering about the conundrum that is my future wife, starting with why a woman with her degree isn't working for her family's business.

Choosing to give her some space, I head to my office to get some work done and then to the private gym I had built in my house to get a workout in. When time has run out and I have to shower and get ready for brunch, I head upstairs.

When I walk into the bedroom, all the boxes are gone, and I think maybe I was wrong and she wasn't trying to play games, until I open the closet door and find her shit has overtaken the entire room. Dresses, skirts, shirts, jeans take up every inch of space aside from the corner, where she's pushed all my clothes together.

Above and below the hanging racks are hundreds of pairs of shoes—from heels to sandals to workout shoes. I count at least three dozen pairs of tennis shoes. Who the fuck needs this many pairs of workout shoes? Most of them don't even look like they've been touched.

I close the door and walk into the bathroom so I can shower, only to stop in my tracks when I find shit all over the counters. Lotions, makeup, hair products. It looks like a fucking Sephora in my bathroom.

I open the cabinet, ready to shove it all underneath, only to find it's full of her shit. The woman isn't just *a shopper*. She's addicted to shopping. Nobody needs this much stuff.

"Excuse me," Brielle hisses, poking her head out of the shower, which I didn't even notice was running, too distracted by my bathroom being overrun with crap. "Have you ever heard of personal space?"

Since my shower is doorless, with only a glass pane separating her from me, I have the perfect view of everything from the waist up. Her hair is covered in product, her face free of all makeup. Her body is wet, water sluicing down her overheated flesh, and her nipples are erect from the cool air.

Every time I've seen her, she's always been put together. Even when she works out, she has some kind of makeup on. But right here, she's stripped down, all natural, and she's never looked sexier.

I take a step forward, my cock guiding my movements, but I'm stopped when she says, "Don't even think about it. I meant it—what happened this morning changes nothing and it won't be happening again."

My future wife clearly likes to play games, and while I'm not usually one to do so, playing with her seems like it could be fun.

"That's fine," I say, stripping out of my clothes.

Since the sight of her naked body has my cock hard, it springs out, bobbing and hitting my torso.

"Kane, what are you doing?" she accuses.

"Showering." I step into the shower behind her.

It's a large area that could easily fit several people, but I still purposely brush my front against her back, earning a hiss from her.

"Since we're sharing a bathroom and I need to get ready for brunch, I don't see any reason why we can't share a shower."

She turns and glares my way, her arms crossing over her chest to hide her pert nipples, only making her perfect tits even more enticing. The water is still dripping down her body, thanks to the ceiling showerheads, and my eyes can't help but follow the drops as they slide down her toned belly and neatly trimmed pussy, disappearing between the apex of her thighs.

They clench in want, and I chuckle at how turned on she is.

"Sure," she murmurs sarcastically. "Feel free to impose on my personal space. It is your home after all."

The woman has made it her mission to hate me, but no matter what she does, what she says, her actions speak for themselves, and they're making it clear just how attracted she is to me.

"It's now *our* home," I correct her. "And I'll be quick."

"This place will never be my home," she mutters.

I go out of my way to ignore her the rest of the time we're in the shower, soaping up my body and washing my hair. I make a show of washing my dick and balls, and the entire time, I can feel her eyes on me even though she pretends like she's not watching me.

I finish before her and slide past her, once again rubbing my body against hers. She sucks in a harsh breath, and I smile to myself.

My future wife might like to play games, but she has no idea just how competitive I am. Challenge accepted.

All the clothes the woman owns, and she's wearing a pair of cutoff jean shorts and a tank top that reads *Save a horse, Ride a cowboy*, paired with brown cowboy boots. I haven't the slightest clue why she owns an outfit like this, but regardless of her name, the country club won't let her in. Which is precisely why she did this.

Another fucking game.

She's standing in the foyer, waiting for my response—I either tell her to change, to which she'll refuse, or leave without her, and she'll get out of this business meeting.

But she's not going to get either from me.

"You look beautiful," I tell her, plastering a smile on my face.

It's not a lie. She could wear a brown paper bag, and she'd look beautiful.

"Is there a particular cowboy I should be worried about?"

I arch a brow playfully, and she furrows hers, confused as to why I'm not reacting the way she expected.

"Just remember what I threatened after the bar incident."

I smirk and grab my keys out of the bowl, then head out to the garage. On the way, I text Malcolm Johnson that there's been a change of plans. He and I go way back. We both attended the University of Miami and were roommates for the last two years of college.

> Me: My future wife is playing games. Country club is out. Let's go to The Terrace.

Malcolm and I co-own The Terrace, so while it does have a dress code, we won't be kicked out for her not adhering to it.

"Umm, where are we going?" Brielle asks when I head south instead of west toward the country club.

"To brunch with a business associate of mine. His name is Malcolm Johnson and his wife—"

"Malcolm Johnson, the NFL player?" She gasps.

"Yep, we went to U of M together, and his wife is a good friend of mine as well."

Brielle peers down at her outfit and cringes, and I almost consider turning around so she can change, but she made her bed, and now she's gonna lie in it.

Twenty minutes later, we arrive at The Terrace, and Malcolm and his wife, Genevieve, are standing by the valet, waiting for us.

Brielle takes one look at how elegant Genevieve looks and glances at me. I quirk a brow, waiting for her to admit she fucked up, but instead, she inhales deeply, shakes her head, and steps out of the car.

Malcolm immediately notices Brielle's outfit and contains his smirk, but Genevieve can't hide her confusion.

"Mal, Viv," I say, giving each of them a hug. "I'd like you to meet my girlfriend, Brielle Antonova. Brielle, these are my friends, Malcolm and Genevieve Johnson."

"It's nice to meet you," Brielle says sheepishly. "I did a project in college on MK Holdings. A billionaire by the age of twenty-two."

She shakes her head in awe, and it takes everything in me not to snort out a laugh. Because my wife is fangirling over my best friend— not because he used to play professional football, but because of his business decisions. Could she be any more fucking perfect?

When the hostess clears her throat because we're standing in the doorway, Brielle blushes and takes a step back, nearly bumping into me.

"Sorry," she says. "It's just that your portfolio is so inspiring, and I'm hoping to one day open a Pilates studio of my own. Your marketing plans and investments …"

What? How the hell did I not know that?

Of course you wouldn't know that. The woman can barely stand being in the same room as you. She's not going to willingly share her goals and dreams with you.

"You know," Malcolm says with a small laugh, "MK Holdings isn't all me."

Brielle's brows furrow, and Genevieve laughs.

"It's half mine," I tell my future wife with a smirk. "I'm the *K* in MK."

Brielle's eyes turn into saucers, and I chuckle as I slide my arm over her shoulders.

"It's okay," I whisper into her ear as I guide her into the restaurant. "We still have a lot to learn about each other. For instance, I had no idea you were so into cowboys," I say to remind her how ridiculously dressed she is.

"Oh God," Brielle gasps. "Wait. I can't go in there." She glances up at me and glares. "This is all your fault."

"Mine?" I bark out a laugh. "Nah, that outfit was all you, Princess. Giddyup."

Not wanting Brielle to be completely embarrassed, even though she deserves it, I have the hostess sit us in a private corner on the terrace that overlooks the Atlantic. Brunch goes well, our topics flitting from business to personal. Mal and Viv have moved up to northern

Florida to be closer to her family, so I haven't seen them in several months, and it's nice to catch up with my friends.

"You'll have to come back down for the wedding," I tell them, taking the check and sliding my card inside.

"What? You're getting married?" Genevieve gushes, glancing at Brielle's hand.

While I'm close with them, nobody—besides Brielle's family—knows that our marriage is a farce.

"Not yet," I say, pulling Brielle into my arms. "But she's the one—I can feel it." I kiss her temple and inhale her vanilla scent. "And I fully plan to make her mine sooner rather than later."

Genevieve, ever the romantic, sighs. "I never thought I'd see the day. You were always the perpetual bachelor."

"Guess it was just a matter of finding the right woman."

I tilt Brielle's head back and look into her azure eyes, and I don't know if it's because she's putting on an act, but for the first time since the night we spent together—before she knew who I was—she willingly brings her lips to mine.

Her tongue slips between my parted lips, and the moment I taste her sweetness, I get caught up in everything that is Brielle, wanting and craving more of her.

But I need to be careful because addiction is nothing to fuck with.

My dad was addicted to power.

My mom was addicted to my father.

And Enrique was addicted to revenge.

And look how those situations turned out.

My father is buried six feet under. My mother is heartbroken. And my brother's body is nothing but ash. And if I let my addiction get the better of me, I'll end up like the rest of my family.

FOURTEEN

Brielle

HE'S GOING TO DO IT TONIGHT. I CAN FEEL IT.

Kane is going to propose.

It's been a week since I was forced to move in with him.

Since I came up with the bright idea to infiltrate his bedroom and bathroom with my stuff, thinking it'd overwhelm him, only for him to not even bat an eye.

Not that it should surprise me.

Every game I play, Kane ends up winning.

I dressed like a knockoff cowgirl to go to a business brunch, thinking he'd either tell me to change or I'd be denied admittance to the country club, but he was one step ahead, taking us to his restaurant.

I tried to seduce him, thinking it would lead to getting info out of him, but one kiss, and I threw my plan out the window, unable to handle being that close to him—not if I had any chance of resisting my soon-to-be husband.

I leave my clothes all over the floor like a slob, and they magically end up washed and hung up. I scatter my makeup and lotions all over the his-and-hers sinks and counters, and when I go to wash my face in the evening, it's all neatly placed on my side.

Every morning, I leave for the gym before he gets up to avoid him, and every night, he has dinner on the table when I walk in the door.

The only thing I've managed to avoid is having sex with him. I sleep on my side of the bed, and he sleeps on his, not even attempting anything with me.

I don't know if I'm thankful that he's respecting my wishes or aggravated that I have a man at my disposal who knows how to satisfy me, but doesn't due to my stubbornness.

The way my body currently ignites at his touch as we sit at dinner with my family has me leaning more toward the latter.

We're eating at the country club since my mom loves it here and she picked the place. Both my brothers and their wives are here, and my mom is with her husband. Then there's Kane and me.

We've been seen in public a few times now, and the town is talking. They know we're dating, so it makes sense that he'll propose soon, especially since he has no desire to wait to get married. Once we're legally married, the contract will be signed, and Morgan Enterprises will be an official investor in the South Harbor Point waterfront expansion, just like he wanted.

Kane stands and glances at me, and my stomach riots. All I wanted was to fall in love with a man who wanted to spend his life with me. I wanted the family and children and holidays. After Owen was killed and my baby was ripped from my womb, I should've given up hope, but I didn't. I told myself that if I could get through that horrific time, I would do everything in my power to find the love that Andrey had taken from me. I wouldn't let him win. I wanted a Hallmark love story, but instead, I'm getting the Netflix version.

"Brielle," Kane says, garnering everyone's attention, "when I saw you sitting right here with your friend, complaining about men, I never thought the night would end with me becoming undeniably infatuated with you, but here we are. I've considered where I should propose, but when I was told we were coming here, to the very place it'd all started for us, it's like it was kismet."

He pulls out the ring box and opens it, and my heart cracks

because his words are sweet, the look on his face is sincere, but none of it is real, except the ridiculously obnoxious ring he's about to put on my finger.

"Brielle Antonova, will you marry me?"

I'm thankful he didn't lie and tell me he loved me, but that doesn't mean it hurts any less. To know that when I marry, it will represent everything that I'm against—greed, power, control, and revenge. All I wanted was to marry someone good, to have a normal life with a man who loves me, and instead, once again, I'm being dragged back into the fold, only it was my doing.

"Yes," I tell him simply with a small smile, not wanting to be caught grimacing in any photos that might be taken of us.

The last thing I want is for my family to look like fools, and if anyone found out that Kane had blackmailed me into marriage, we would not only be the laughingstock of Harbor Point, but men who feared the Antonov name would use that to their advantage, thinking they could blackmail and threaten us into doing as they wanted.

Kane slides the huge rock onto my finger, and I chant to myself to keep a smile on my face while my family plays their part, hugging and congratulating us.

"I'm so happy for you," Mom says, enveloping me in a motherly hug.

I glance at Matteo, who looks anything but happy, and shake my head.

I considered telling my mom the truth, but decided not to. She's always been so worried about me, afraid that she failed her children, and if she knew my marriage was fake, she would only feel worse. She's been through enough in her life, and she deserves to be happy.

"It's not too late to take him out," Matteo murmurs as he hugs me tightly.

"No more bloodshed," I remind him.

He sighs but nods in agreement.

Once everyone sits back down, the waiter brings out a special dessert to celebrate our engagement. Kane feeds me a bite, playing up his part as the doting fiancé, but I'm too nauseous to eat any more.

When we get home from dinner, I take a long bath, hoping once I get out, he'll be asleep. Only luck isn't on my side because when I step out of the bathroom, he's sitting against the headboard, typing on his phone.

"What about Valentine's Day?"

"What about it?"

I walk over to the dresser and drop my towel, sliding a pair of panties on. Since Kane has seen me naked more than once, it's pointless to try to hide myself from him.

When he doesn't respond, I glance in the mirror, finding him staring heatedly at me. My lady parts come to life, thinking they're about to get some much-needed attention, and I clench my thighs together to stave off the tension between my legs.

Kane knowingly smirks, and I roll my eyes.

"I'm not having sex with you again … ever."

He laughs. "You really think you can resist having sex for the rest of your life?"

"Who said anything about resisting sex? I just said I'm not having sex with *you*."

Kane growls, and within seconds, he's out of the bed and pressed against my back, his hard length prodding the crack of my ass.

"If you even think about opening those pretty legs for anyone but me, just know that you're signing their death warrant."

He grinds his hips into my backside, and I stifle a groan.

"You can do it too," I choke out. "You can fuck whoever you want."

Kane grips my hips and spins me around, lifting me and setting me on top of the dresser. My legs part, and he steps between them.

"Let's get one thing straight." He thumbs my chin, forcing me to look at him. "I have no desire to fuck anyone but you. You are my fiancée, and on Valentine's Day, you'll become my wife, and you'll be the only woman I spend the rest of my life fucking. I loved my father, but I watched what him living two lives did to my parents, and I will never live that type of life."

"And what if I never have sex with you?" I defiantly jut my chin out of his touch.

"Princess," he coos, gliding his hand from the curve of my hip to the apex of my legs, "if I slid my hand into your panties, I guarantee I'd find them slick with arousal."

He quirks a brow, asking permission, and because he's not wrong, I slam my legs closed on his hand, then shove him back so I can hop down.

"You'd find me dry as a desert," I lie. "But you won't find out because you're never touching me again."

I really need to stop talking because when I give in—and we both know I will eventually—I'm going to be forced to eat my damn words.

"Now, if you don't mind, I'd like to go to bed in peace." I throw on a shirt and cotton shorts and then climb into bed, facing away from Kane.

And then I remember what he said about getting married …

"And getting married on Valentine's Day is kind of perfect," I say, turning around so I can look into his eyes.

They widen in shock and, if I'm not mistaken, a bit of hope, until I speak my next words.

"After all, the legend says that Valentine's Day derived from Saint Valentine, a Roman priest who went against the emperor's ban on marriage—which had been done so men were more agreeable to go to war—and he was brutally executed on February 14. Kind of fitting, right?"

Kane's eyes turn into thin slits, but before he can comment, I flip over so my back is to him.

"Good night, fiancé. Can't wait to spend the rest of our lives together in hell."

"And this is my Barbie, Matilda." I grin at my mother. "She's going to marry Ken." I grab the boy Barbie and show it to her. "And they're going to have babies. And Matilda is going to be a teacher." I beam up at my mother, who smiles softly at me.

"A teacher, huh?" she says.

"Yep. Just like me. When I get older, I'm going to go to college and be a teacher, just like Mrs. Stone. She's my favorite teacher and—"

"Enough!" a masculine voice booms, making me jump.

My father stalks in and swipes the Barbies off the table while I shake in fear. He was supposed to be out of town for another day. It's the only time I'm allowed to play with my Barbies. But he must've gotten home early.

"What did I tell you about letting her play with this shit?" my father yells at my mother, yanking on her hair and dragging her off the couch. "I told you she's not allowed to fill her head with this nonsense!"

"Andrey, please!" my mother cries. "I'm sorry. I—"

"I warned you," he says, snatching up my Barbies off the floor.

"Please, Daddy!" I cry as he carries them into the kitchen.

He lifts the lid of the trash, and when he throws my Barbies inside, it feels like he also threw away all of my hopes and dreams.

When I try to reach and grab them, he shoves me so hard that I fly onto the ground and hit my head against the cabinet.

Before I can get up, he lifts me off the floor and gets into my face. "Your only job is to marry Anthony Rothschild. And if I see you playing pretend again, I'll—"

"Let go of her!" Matteo yells.

My eyes fly open, and I suck in a gulp of air, struggling to breathe.

I glance back at Kane, who's sleeping, and I quietly climb out of bed, needing a moment.

I pace the hallway, trying to calm my racing heart, but when my memories hit, it's hard to calm myself down. I never knew you could have a panic attack while you were asleep, but I've learned firsthand that it's possible, and unfortunately for me, it happens often.

When it feels like the walls are closing in, I pad down the stairs, turn off the alarm, and head out the back door. The moment the salty air hits my senses, I release a shaky breath.

There's just something about the beach that calms me.

I don't know what time it is, but the moon is high in the sky, and the waves are crashing against the sand. There's nobody around. It's just me and the ocean.

It's chilly outside, but I welcome the coolness. When my panic attacks hit, the increase in my blood pressure causes me to become overheated and sweat.

I step to where the water meets the sand and have a seat, allowing my toes to dig into the wet sand. And then I inhale another calming breath.

As the waves roll in and out, I can't help but think about the nightmare I just had.

Wanting to be a teacher was only one of the jobs I dreamed of. Yet, when I was allowed to go to college, I chose to major in accounting. According to Andrey, it didn't matter what my major was because my only future involved marrying Anthony. But I picked accounting, hoping that maybe, one day, Andrey would see that I was more than a bargaining chip. I was young and naive, and I thought if he saw my worth, he would view me as an equal.

My thoughts go back to conversations with Kane …

"Didn't you go to college?"

"… you're bored with your life."

He isn't wrong. I might not have wanted to major in

accounting, but I still had hopes and dreams. And what have I done to make them come true?

I wanted to fall in love and get married and have a family, and that's out of the question, thanks to Kane. But there's more to life than that.

I've been back in Harbor Point for almost a year, and what do I have to show for it?

Tons of clothes and shoes and a Pilates membership?

The waves roll back in, bringing more shells with it. I spot a pretty pink one, but when I reach for it, my eyes go to my engagement ring, and a choked sob bubbles out, the devastation at the way my life is unraveling too much to hold in any longer.

I yank the ring off my finger, and I consider throwing it into the ocean when a shadow appears, making me jump to my feet.

"You shouldn't be out here by yourself," Kane says, sounding like he gives a shit about my well-being.

"What's the worst that will happen?" I scoff, trying to hide my fragile state from him. "I'm taken and forced into a marriage with someone I despise?" I laugh humorlessly. "Oh, wait. That already happened."

Since I don't want to talk to him about why I'm out here, I walk back up to the house with him following. Then I go to the bathroom and take a quick shower to rinse the sweat and saltwater and raw emotions off me.

Only when I hear Kane softly snoring through the door do I leave the bathroom and climb back into bed. But between my nightmare and my thoughts on the beach, I can't sleep, so instead, I grab my phone off the nightstand and unlock it.

I pull up Google and type, *What's involved in owning a Pilates studio?*

I might not be able to marry for love, and I'll probably never be a mother like I dreamed of, but that doesn't mean I can't have something for myself.

"Good morning, Brielle. What can I get you?" the perky barista at Lattes and Words asks.

I glance up at the specials board and huff when I see that they're out of almond milk.

Guess oat milk it is.

"I'll take an oat milk honey latte and an almond muffin, please."

"Sure thing." She inputs it into the computer, and the total pops up.

I reach for my phone, but it's not in my leggings pocket, like it usually is.

I'm patting the sides of my thighs, trying to locate it so I can pay since I never bring my wallet with me to the Pilates studio, when Nicole appears from out of nowhere, shrieking, "Oh my God!" She grabs my left hand. "You're engaged? How did I talk to you several times this weekend and you forgot to mention that?" She moves my fingers up and down and laughs. "How do you even lift your hand? It's so heavy."

I yank my hand back with a groan. "Ugh, stop. It's ostentatious and nothing like one I would've picked out. Men who buy rings this size"—I lift my hand to emphasize my point—"have something to prove."

Nicole's eyes go big, and she covers her mouth, stifling what I assume is a laugh. When I look at her in confusion, she nods over my shoulder, and I slowly turn around, coming face-to-face with Kane.

"And what is it that I have to prove?" he drawls, crossing his arms over his chest.

When I was running out the door this morning, he said he was going into the office, so I'm not sure when he followed me here, but, oh well, it's not like I didn't say anything I didn't mean.

"I don't know." I shrug. "You tell me."

His jaw tics, and I know I got to him.

Men have such fragile egos, and him knowing that I despise the ring he spent hundreds of thousands on has to irk him.

"You left your phone at home," he says, handing it to me. "Figured you might need it."

I take it from him, almost feeling bad that I hurt his feelings.

I scan my phone to pay for my coffee and muffin and then step to the side so the line can keep moving.

"So, when's the big day?" Nicole asks, trying to ease the tension.

"Valentine's Day," I tell her.

"Oh, that's sweet," she coos. "Have you decided where you'll be having it?"

When I glance at Kane, waiting for him to answer, he says, "That's up to Brielle."

"Me?" I scoff. "What do I have to do with it?"

Nicole snorts out a laugh, and Kane glares.

"You're the one planning it," he says.

"Oh, great," I hiss. "Not only are you forcing me to marry you, but you're also making me plan the damn thing? Would you like me to pay for it as well?"

He reaches into his jacket pocket and pulls out a black card. "Put everything on there."

"Oh!" Nicole squeals. "This will be so much fun. We should book the Mayfair House Garden and—"

I love Nicole, but the woman cannot read a room to save her life.

"You know this is a fake marriage, right?" I whisper so no one will overhear. "We don't need to do anything special."

Nicole pouts. "But remember how much fun you had planning Dani and Matteo's wedding? And as your maid of honor, it's my job to make sure you're a pampered bride. We can do a spa day ... manis and pedis. It will be so much fun. Plus"—she glances at Kane, still holding his card between his fingers—"he's paying"—she waggles her brows—"so why not give yourself the wedding of your dreams?"

"Maybe because the wedding of my dreams was supposed to

be with the *man* of my dreams," I blurt out. *Or at the very least, with a man who loves me,* I think to myself.

Nicole's gaze turns sympathetic, and I instantly regret voicing my thoughts. I don't want anyone to pity me.

When I sneak a glance at Kane, knowing he must have heard what I said, he shows zero emotion, and for some reason, that annoys me. He knows he's hurting me by forcing me to marry him, yet he doesn't give a shit. He has one goal in mind, and I'm nothing more than a stepping stone to get him to where he wants to be.

Well, fuck him.

"Whatever." I pluck the card out of his fingers. "In that case, let's go shopping. I need to buy my maid of honor a special gift."

Nicole grins, and Kane remains stoic.

We'll see how stoic he is when I max out his card and show him what he's getting himself into by marrying me.

Hell, maybe if I spend enough, he'll realize I'm not worth the hassle and call the whole damn thing off.

"C'mon, bestie," I say, grabbing my coffee and muffin with one hand and Nicole's hand with the other. "We have a wedding to plan."

FIFTEEN

Kane

"MAYBE BECAUSE THE WEDDING OF MY DREAMS WAS supposed to be with the man of my dreams."

I'm in the middle of a meeting with Ena Odell, my tech consultant, at the restaurant in the country club, discussing how to take Morgan Enterprises to the next level, but the only thing I can focus on is Brielle. It wasn't just what she said, but how she looked when she said it, like she genuinely wanted to marry her dream man and that couldn't possibly be me.

Who says I can't be her dream fucking man?

My thoughts go back to when Brielle and I spent the night together. She was looking for the perfect balance of control.

Her dumbass ex had given in to her every whim, which was why he bored her. But with me, while I gave her the control she craved, I also set boundaries she needed.

"You might've given me the control that night, but the next day, you took it away."

That night was supposed to be just that—one night. But like the deadliest spider, she spun me into her web, and rather than risking being caught and killed, I pulled her out and dragged her down with me. Because the thought of never being with her again was unfathomable.

The problem is, forcing Brielle to marry me meant taking away her control …

"Mr. Morgan," Jack, my assistant, says, tearing me from my thoughts. "I need to take this call."

I nod and then focus my attention on Ena, who goes back to discussing how purchasing a new program that just came onto the market would improve operations and increase efficiency.

"If you look at line four on page six …"

I flip through the portfolio she gave me, but can't find what she's talking about, so she leans in.

"Right—"

"Does Brielle know you're having lunch with another woman?" a voice cuts in.

Theodore DeSantis.

"Excuse me?" I quirk a brow, daring him to fuck with me.

"You went through all the trouble to steal her from me, and now you're out with another woman," he accuses. "Brielle deserves better."

How old is this guy? Fourteen?

"Steal her from you?" I scoff, standing and towering over him, having had enough of his bullshit.

"That cocktease was mine fir—"

"You'd better watch what you say," I warn him, backing him against the edge of the bar. "Brielle is mine, and I'm protective of what's mine."

"Yours? No way." He scoffs, refusing to believe it. "I heard you're working with the Antonovs, and Brielle said she wouldn't be with anyone associated with them."

"Hmm … well, she's living under *my* roof"—I chuckle mirthlessly just as I spot Matteo and Lorenzo walking over—"sleeping in *my* bed. Seems like she's mine to me."

"It doesn't make any sense," Theo whines. "I spent months with that bitch playing hard to get …"

Matteo's jaw flexes as he steps forward, but Lorenzo holds him back.

"She's wearing my engagement ring," I add, making Theo's eyes go wide.

"What? No." He shakes his head.

I pull my phone out, opening it to the pictures that Brielle's mom took the night I proposed. And the second Theo sees them, it's like a switch flips.

"Fuck her then," he sneers. "I knew I shouldn't have fucked with that bitch. She wasn't even good in bed … wanting all that weird shit, like for me to—"

The second his words are out, I connect my fist with his pretty face, refusing to let him finish his thought. His head snaps to the side, and he groans in pain.

"Talk about my future wife like that again, and I'll fucking bury you." Another hit, and blood flies out of his mouth. "If I so much as hear that you spoke her name, you're done."

I'm about to hit him again when Matteo steps in between us.

"He's not worth it," he says. "As much as I appreciate you standing up for my sister, he's a little bitch, and he'll press charges. The last thing we need is more heat on us."

I release a harsh breath and step back as Theo covers his mouth with his hands.

"I'm calling the cops," he mutters, doing exactly as Matteo predicted.

Matteo chuckles darkly. "No, you're not because everyone in this room will tell them that you tripped and fell on your ugly fucking face. Leave, DeSantis, now."

Theo glares from Matteo to me, and then like the little bitch he is, he scurries away.

"What the fuck was Bri thinking, dating that guy?" Lorenzo asks once Theo is gone.

"She was thinking that he was her chance at a normal life," Matteo says, emotion thick in his tone.

I'm about to respond when my phone rings. I pull it out to make sure it's not Brielle, but when I don't recognize the number, I hold up a finger, telling them to give me a minute, and answer the call. With my mom out of town, I always answer in case of an emergency.

"Hello?"

"Good afternoon. This is Patty with American Express. I'm calling for Kane Morgan."

"This is he."

The woman walks me through verifying my identity, and the entire time, I'm wondering why she's calling, until she says, "Generally, we don't call to approve a purchase since you're a loyal customer, but due to the amount being so high, we need to confirm your card wasn't stolen."

I reach into my pocket, grab my wallet, and open it to make sure I have my card on me. Only it's not there … because I gave it to Brielle.

"What is the purchase for?" I ask.

"A vehicle, sir. A Nissan GT-R Nismo. Total cost is two hundred twenty-one thousand dollars. A woman by the name of Brielle Antonov is making the purchase, but since she's not an authorized user …"

"My card hasn't been stolen," I say with a chuckle. "My fiancée is trying to prove that she's in control."

"Excuse me?" Patty asks in confusion.

"Nothing." I shake my head, realizing I'm going about this entire thing wrong.

I knew the type of person Brielle was from the first night I met her. She needs to be in control, and if I want her to be on board with this marriage, she has to feel like she's not being forced, even though she is.

I could easily end the engagement. Dominick already agreed to the waterfront expansion deal. And truth be told, I already veered from my original plan to destroy the Antonovs and Russos when I chose to make the deal—putting business above revenge.

But I've gotten a taste of Brielle, so I know how fucking sweet she is underneath all that sour. My mom has always chastised me about having a sweet tooth, and she's not wrong. The woman has me addicted, and there's no way I'm giving up her sweetness that easily.

Which leaves me no choice.

I have to get her to fall in love with me.

"Approve the purchase," I say. "My fiancée has approval to buy whatever she wants."

I hang up, and Matteo quirks a brow.

"Your sister used my card to buy a two-hundred-thousand-dollar car."

Matteo laughs. "She's fucking nuts."

"Yeah," I agree. "But I kind of like her that way."

Brielle might think she's won this battle, but I'm about to win the war.

The rest of lunch goes smoothly, and once we're done and I've agreed to move forward with the new program, I pay the bill.

I'm walking Ena out when I notice Lorenzo is sitting at the bar, alone, with an entire bottle of whiskey in front of him.

It's not my business, but if I'm going to win Brielle over, I need to play nice with her family, and Lorenzo, while not by blood, is part of her family.

After seeing Ena off, I let Jack know I'll meet him back at the office and then head back inside, finding Lorenzo still sitting in the same spot, pouring himself another glass of whiskey.

"Day drinking?" I say, sliding onto the stool next to him.

"When your ex shows up on your front step with a baby, claiming he's yours, it calls for a drink … or five."

"Shit. Please tell me you're having a paternity test done."

"Of course." He side-eyes me. "The results are due back anytime now." He downs what's left of his drink and pours himself another.

"And I'd appreciate it if you didn't tell anyone, including Brielle. I haven't told anyone yet."

"Not even Matteo?"

Anyone who's been around their family knows that Lorenzo and Matteo are close. Hell, Matteo is even married to Lorenzo's sister, Daniella.

He shakes his head. "They've been busy getting ready for their baby and living in wedded bliss. And … fuck!" he barks, downing the drink in one gulp and slamming it on the bar top. "They warned me about her, and I didn't listen. She told me she was on birth control. I saw the fucking pills, but she obviously lied."

My thoughts go to Brielle. When I saw her shit all over the bathroom counter, there was a packet of birth control pills there. I don't know if she takes them regularly, but I'll need to check.

Wonder if she'll willingly stop them so I can knock her up.

The image of her swollen with my baby is much more appealing than I ever thought it would be. I always thought after Enrique died, our bloodline and name would end with me. And when I mentioned wanting an heir, it was only to fuck with the Antonovs since that had been the original deal our families had in place.

But now … the idea of filling Brielle with my cum and putting a baby in her sounds more and more appealing.

"Not that it should surprise me," Lorenzo goes on. "She's a professional fucking liar." He glances over at me. "She worked with your brother to fuck me over."

"Enrique?"

I think about who he worked with. While I didn't agree with his tactic, I kept tabs on him in an attempt to keep him under control. Then he spiraled, and it all went downhill fast.

"Yeah," he says. "Her name is Hillary Sparks. He paid her to seduce me for info about my company when he was trying to take it down, and like an idiot, I fell for it."

He pours two more fingers and throws it back, and I slide the bottle away and lift my finger for the bartender to come over.

"A bottle of water for this guy, please."

The bartender nods and grabs one, setting it on the bar top with a glass of ice.

"And where is your possible baby mama now?" I ask, curious.

"At my house, making herself comfortable, I'm sure."

"Fuck."

"Yeah," he agrees with a sigh.

"And if the baby is yours?"

"She wants to raise him together."

"Doesn't mean you have to be with her," I point out.

"I don't trust her. I'd rather have her in my house than living somewhere else." He takes a sip of his water. "I've always wanted to get married and have kids, but this isn't how I wanted it to go down. My parents were from an arranged marriage …" He looks at me. "Though I guess you probably know that."

I did know that.

My father and his were best friends. But one night, Maria—Anthony's mom—seduced my dad. Giuseppe—Lorenzo's dad—was in love with her and heartbroken when he learned of her betrayal. By the time they learned of Maria's pregnancy, thanks to her hiding it for as long as possible, my dad had already met my mom and fallen in love with her.

But because Maria was pregnant, Giuseppe called off the engagement with her, and she was forced to marry my father. A year later, Giuseppe's dad arranged a marriage between him and Lorenzo's mom, Tanya.

"I know my parents loved each other," Lorenzo says. "But my father … he always loved Maria. I caught him talking to her once, and he played it off, but I don't think he ever got over her."

"I get it," I tell him. "My dad never loved Maria, only stuck it out with her because of Anthony. He was in love with my mom, but he put the business first."

Lorenzo shakes his head. "I don't want that … to be married

because of a baby. I know I sound like a little bitch for saying this, but I want to marry for love."

I think about my views on marriage before I met Brielle. Business has always come first, which is why I never planned to marry, not wanting to put a woman in the same position my mom had been in. My dad might've loved her, but she was always second to his business.

"Brielle deserves better."

Theo's words swirl around in my head.

She does deserve better—she deserves everything. And I'm going to make sure she has it. I was close with my father, but I'm smart enough to learn from his mistakes.

"Why *are you* pushing this whole thing with Bri?" Lorenzo asks.

For a second, I wonder if I spoke my thoughts out loud.

"You're a smart businessman. Some of the deals you've made …" He whistles lowly. "The TechCorp deal? Fucking genius. And Avalon …"

"You stalking me, Russo?" I smirk.

He chuckles. "Any good businessman knows who he's getting into bed with. But honestly, I knew who you were before you showed up here. Your father might've run the business into the ground—"

"No," I correct, my blood boiling at the false accusation. "He didn't run the business into the ground. Your father and Andrey pushed him out. They threatened investors to pull out, cut him out of deals he should've been a part of. He had millions invested, and they took his money and then threw him to the wolves, leading to his downfall."

"I get that," he concedes, "but you revived the company and brought it back to life better than your dad had ever run it. You don't need us or Bri. You've created a reputation for yourself that stands on its own."

"Thanks," I say, trying to play off the compliment like it's not a big deal when the truth is, that's all I wanted. To make my father's company successful. It's all he wanted, and he died, trying to do so.

"But that doesn't change the fact that my father lived and breathed for that company and put your fathers on a pedestal. He gave them everything until his last breath, so I owe it to him to right the wrongs, which includes a Rothschild marrying an Antonov."

I might've changed my last name from Rothschild to Morgan—my mom's last name—to ensure I'd stay under the radar, but at the end of the day, I'm still my father's son.

"Shit." Lorenzo looks down at his phone. "Results are in."

He taps on the screen and stares at it for several seconds while I drag the bottle back over.

"So … are we toasting or drinking the rest of the bottle?"

"No fucking clue," he says, "but the baby is mine." He swallows thickly. "I'm a father."

"Cheers," I say, pouring us each two fingers of whiskey. "To fatherhood."

We clink glasses, and as I drink mine, I picture what Brielle would look like, carrying my baby. Lorenzo might be devastated that he's stuck with Hillary as the mother of his child, but I want nothing more than for Brielle to have my babies … sooner rather than later.

SIXTEEN

Brielle

I SAUNTER INTO THE HOUSE, PRETENDING LIKE I DON'T HAVE a care in the world, even though, deep down, I kind of feel guilty for buying Nicole a new car with Kane's credit card.

The idea popped into my head when we left to go shopping and Nicole mentioned that her father had taken her car back, stating that her choosing not to fall in line with his expectations meant she needed to do it all on her own.

I commend her for doing what she wants, regardless of the consequences. I wish I were as strong as she is. She knows what she wants, and she's going after it—hence her following her dream of opening a coffee shop and bookstore.

In Harbor Point, you need a vehicle. We don't have public transportation, like the big cities do, and getting a rideshare is ridiculous. So, rather than go to the boutiques to buy more clothes neither of us needed, I asked her what car she loved and then took her to the dealership to buy it for her. She argued, but I was persistent, and when the dealership said they had to get approval, I figured Kane would refuse, but when he approved the purchase, I told Nicole even Kane wanted her to have the new car.

She cried, and I was glad to have given her something she needed—not that she needed a two hundred-thousand-dollar car, but now, at least when her shitty father sees her, it'll be a slap in his face because fuck him for trying to screw over my best friend.

"Good evening," Kane says calmly, making me jump.

He's changed out of his suit into a pair of gray sweats and a T-shirt, and I hate that he looks just as hot dressed down as he does dressed up.

When I glance behind him, the table is set up for two, complete with candles in the center.

"What's this for?" I ask carefully, trying to gauge what kind of trap I'm walking into.

"Dinner." He grins. "I'd like to say I made it, but I'm not the best cook, so I had the chef from The Terrace make it since you'd seemed to enjoy the food there."

"Why?" I blurt out.

Kane quirks a brow. "Can't I have a romantic dinner with my future wife?"

He steps over to the chair and pulls it out for me, and I walk over. Since I haven't eaten dinner, I give in and have a seat, letting him push my chair in.

"Would you like a glass of wine?" Kane asks, lifting the bottle.

"Is it poisoned?"

"No." He chuckles. "Not unless you consider a bottle of 2009 Château Lafite Rothschild poison."

He pours us each a glass and then takes a sip to prove I won't keel over if I drink it.

"So, how was your day?" he asks, lifting the metal lid off his food.

It's filet and lobster with risotto and it looks mouthwatering.

"It was good," I tell him, playing along.

I'm starved, and I'd like to eat this delicious meal before we ruin it with an argument.

"What did you do?"

I glare his way, and he chuckles.

"Fair enough. You bought a new car. Though I'm surprised you bought a Nissan when you love your Porsche."

"It wasn't for me," I admit, preparing for an argument. "I told you I was buying Nicole a maid-of-honor gift."

Kane glances at me, his fork stilling. "You bought that car for Nicole?"

"Yep, she didn't have a car, thanks to her asshole dad taking hers back, so I bought her one."

A small smile graces Kane's face. "That was very nice of you."

He takes a bite of his food, and I balk at him in confusion.

"That's it? That's all you're going to say? That was nice of me? I spent a quarter of a million on a car, and you're not upset?"

"Princess," he drawls, "I'm a rich man. I don't give a shit what you spend my money on. If the credit card company hadn't contacted me, I wouldn't have even noticed. But the fact that you bought it for your friend, who needed a vehicle, instead of yourself shows me the type of person you are. You're a good friend to Nicole."

Uncomfortable with his compliment, I simply nod and start eating, unsure how to respond to him. He's acting different tonight, and I don't know what to make of it.

"Did you do anything else today?" he asks between bites.

"We, um … we looked at a wedding venue, at Nicole's insistence, and then we went to Pilates."

"One day, I'll have to tag along and see what Pilates is all about," Kane says conversationally.

"Why?"

"What do you mean, why?" Kane tilts his head to the side. "You attend classes almost daily and clearly love it, so I'd like to know what it entails."

I swallow a large sip of my wine, taken aback. Theodore never once took an interest in my love of Pilates. He just thought it was something rich, bored women did during the day.

"I have actually thought about owning my own studio," I admit, unsure why I'm confiding in Kane. But since he's here and—from what my brothers have mentioned—a good businessman, maybe he can help guide me in the right direction. "The Pilates studio I go to is for sale. When I reached out to the management company this morning, they told me they were accepting offers, so I had my attorney draw up a contract, not wanting to chance someone else buying it first. But this afternoon, they called to tell me it was no longer available."

Sure, I can open my own, but having two Pilates studios in the same town would make it difficult, especially since the one I go to has such a good reputation.

"Did they counter?" Kane asks.

"No." I take a bite of my filet, and it practically melts in my mouth. I wash it down with a sip of the wine, which is equally good. "They just said that they were no longer interested in selling it to me. I looked, and it's still on the market, so maybe they realized who I was—that I was related to the Antonov brothers—and changed their mind." As much as I love my brothers, sometimes, being linked to them kind of sucks.

"Have you spoken to them?"

"I was trying to buy it on my own, without their help."

Kane hums and then says, "Can you forward me the info? I'll look at it for you. See if there are any red flags."

"Really?" I ask. "Why would you do that?"

Kane locks eyes with me. "I could be wrong, but part of being married means having each other's back. Besides, if that body is from Pilates, the last thing I want is for you to give it up."

I roll my eyes, but deep down, butterflies attack my belly. I love that Kane sees the hard work I've put into making a healthier version of myself.

"Now, about that venue," he says. "Is it available for Valentine's Day?"

"Yes, it's available, and it has been booked."

"Good." He nods. "I'll handle the engagement party."

The rest of the meal is spent enjoying our food. And afterward, Kane insists the housekeeper will do the dishes, so I go upstairs to shower.

I'm looking for my leave-in conditioner in the cabinet under the sink when I notice a pharmacy bag. I open it and find my birth control refills in there.

"Huh." I don't remember picking these up, but it's been a crazy month, so I'm not surprised that my brain is foggy.

Since my pills are set to run out tomorrow, I grab a packet from the bag and set it on the counter, then take two more packets and stow them away in my makeup bag. I close the pharmacy bag that contains the other four months' worth of birth control pills and place them in the cabinet.

Kane hasn't brought up me getting pregnant, and I'm glad for that. I might be marrying the man, but there's no way I'm having his babies. I'd rather never have children than have them with a man who will never love me.

"Please," I beg, unsure if anyone can even hear me. "Please don't take my baby."

"You did this," Andrey hisses, coming into view.

He towers over me, a look of disgust marring his features. "You're a whore who chose to spread her legs, and now I'm forced to fix the problem you created."

"Please," I say again. "I'm sorry. The baby might be Anthony's—"

"Enough!" he barks and then leans in close to my face. "No daughter of mine will have a bastard born out of wedlock. It's bad enough you're now damaged goods."

"He … he raped me," I whisper.

"Because you'd spread your legs for another man!" His hand connects with my cheek, and I choke out a sob. "You're a disgrace to this family, and when they're done taking the bastard out of you, you're coming home."

I close my eyes and blink back my tears, not wanting to give him any more of myself. Only when I open them, rather than the doctor standing over me, it's Kane.

"Come back to me, Princess. Whatever's going on in that head of yours, it's not real. You're having a nightmare."

My hand flies to my stomach. *Is this real? Am I still pregnant?*

"Brielle … Brielle, wake up, baby."

My eyes snap open, and instead of lying in a medical clinic, I'm in Kane's arms, nestled against his chest.

Instinctually, my hand goes to my belly, but it's flat. I'm not pregnant. Because Andrey took my baby from me.

My heart is pounding in my chest, and when I suck in a harsh breath, I'm met with resistance. I'm having another panic attack.

"Shh, it's okay," Kane says, his words soothing. "Focus on your breathing."

With me still in his arms, he manages to turn on the tub water and pour bubbles into the water. The lavender scent fills the room, and I snuggle closer into his hold.

He should be the last person I turn to for comfort, but I'm drowning in the past, and he's the only life raft I have.

"Here you go," he says, lowering me into the tub. "This should help."

"No, please," I beg, not caring how needy I sound.

Every time I have a nightmare, I handle it alone. Body sweating, heart racing. It takes hours to compose myself. But in his arms, my body is already calming, and I don't want him to let go of me.

I expect him to get annoyed, but instead, he steps into the tub, still dressed in his sweats, and holds me, like I'm precious to him and not the woman he's forcing to marry him to help his agenda. Between his warmth, the hot water, and the calming scent, within minutes, my heart rate slows down significantly.

I'm so exhausted from the nightmare that I can't keep my eyes open, so I let them fall closed, doing something I haven't done in a long time—trusting someone to keep me safe.

When I wake up, I'm back in bed, under the covers, with Kane's arms protectively wrapped around me from behind. His hard chest is pressed up against my back, and his face is nuzzled into the crook of my neck.

The last man I was this close to was Owen—

"I know you're awake," Kane rasps. "Your breathing changes, and your body tenses up." Instead of rolling me onto my back, he rolls onto his and pulls me with him so I'm spread across his body. "Wanna tell me what happened?"

Unable to make eye contact, I lay my head on his chest, using the rhythm of his heartbeat to steady mine.

A part of me wants to tell him what happened, but another part of me doesn't want to give him any more of myself than I'm being forced to.

Not fighting Andrey harder was the biggest mistake of my life. I'll always wonder if I had fought harder, screamed louder, found a way to run faster, if my baby—and possibly Owen—would be alive. And when I think about it or talk about it, I feel like a stupid, weak little girl all over again.

"It was just a nightmare," I mutter.

"It was more than that," he says, seeing through my half-truth. "After my father was murdered and my mother almost died, she'd wake up the same way, having a panic attack from her nightmares."

"Did she take a bath to calm herself down?"

"Yeah." He glides his hand along the curves of my body, and for some reason, his touch helps to relax me further. "She said the warm water would soothe her."

"Where is she?" I ask, wondering why I haven't met her yet.

"I sent her on vacation while I figure things out. I didn't want to risk your brothers going after her. I'm hoping once we're married, she'll move here and live in the in-law suite in the back."

My body tenses, and Kane notices. Palming my cheek, he lifts my face so I'll look at him.

"What's wrong?" he asks. "Do you not want my mom to live in the back? I can get her a condo somewhere—"

"No." I shake my head. "I just figure she won't like me since I'm an Antonov and all."

"She doesn't agree with my marrying you," he admits with a shrug. "But she doesn't have an issue with you. She knows you're nothing more than a casualty in this war of life, just like she was."

Kane runs his fingers gently through my tresses, and I lay my head back down on his chest.

For a little while, I pretend like I'm in bed with a man who genuinely loves me and wants to marry me. It's not forced. He courted me for months, and when the time was right, he picked out the perfect ring and told me he wanted to spend his life with me, that he couldn't imagine going another day without making me his wife.

When the sun starts to shine through the blinds, I pretend like this is how our life is supposed to be. Cuddled in bed because he needs to be close to me. Only, instead of me awkwardly climbing out of bed, he makes love to me and then carries me to the bathroom, wanting to start his day buried deep inside me.

But once I'm in the shower alone, the pretend morphs into reality.

I'm alone. And the man who's going to marry me doesn't love me—and never will.

SEVENTEEN

Kane

S HE LIED TO ME.
I can feel it deep in my bones.

That nightmare stemmed from a truth. The pained look in her eyes, the way her heart pounded behind her rib cage. I couldn't understand what she was saying, but I could feel it. Whatever she was dreaming about was real.

But she wouldn't tell me.

Because she doesn't trust me.

Which means I need to gain her trust.

And that starts with helping her pave her future.

Brielle loves Pilates and wants to open her own studio. The studio she goes to is for sale, yet for some crazy reason, they won't sell it to her.

I had my assistant make an appointment with the management company under a false name, just in case I'm linked to Brielle, and I'm going to get to the bottom of this.

"Good afternoon," I say to the woman sitting at the receptionist desk. The plaque reads *Dana Willis*. "I have a meeting with Mr. Hyatt. My name is Michael Kors." I smile charmingly while cursing my assistant to hell for thinking he's funny, giving me a dumbass fake name.

"Mr. Kors," Dana says, "Mr. Hyatt had a family emergency, but Mr. DeSantis will take the meeting with you in his place."

Mr. DeSantis …

Well, this just got interesting.

"What's his first name?" I ask.

She glances at me in confusion, and I mentally take a deep breath, having no patience for stupid people.

"Mr. DeSantis," I clarify. "What's his first name? I like to be prepared, and since I was planning to meet with Mr. Hyatt, I just want to make sure I know who I'm meeting with."

"Oh, yes, of course. His name is Evan, and he's Mr. Hyatt's business partner."

"Huh. Any relation to Theodore DeSantis?"

She suspiciously quirks a brow, and I take back calling her stupid.

"We go way back." I grin.

"He's his cousin," she says, standing and walking me down the hall while I put the pieces together, almost positive I know how this puzzle is going to look.

She knocks on the door and then opens it. "Mr. DeSantis, your one o'clock is here. Oh, sorry," she says, backtracking. "I wasn't aware you were still having lunch. Should we—"

Before she can finish her sentence, I step past her, locking eyes with Theodore DeSantis, who's sitting across from who I assume is his cousin.

The left side of his face is still swollen from when I hit him, and I chuckle darkly as I wonder if I'll have the opportunity to make the right side of his face match.

"I'll take it from here," I tell her, pushing her out and closing the door behind me.

"What the hell are you doing here?" Theo hisses, standing.

"I'd ask you the same thing, but I have a feeling I already know. Let me guess. You found out Brielle was trying to purchase the

Pilates studio, and since you're pissed off that she dumped your ass for me, you had your cousin refuse to sell it to her."

"They have the right to refuse—"

I cut across the room and connect my fist with his face, sending him flying onto the desk. Papers fly, and a laptop hits the floor. I punch him again and again, knocking him onto the ground.

I obviously underestimated this fool, but that won't be happening again.

"What the hell?!" his cousin shrieks like a little bitch.

"You want to be next?" I threaten, leaving Theo laid out on the floor.

Evan raises his hands and shakes his head, taking a step back, just as his secretary opens the door, concern etched in her features.

"Leave," I tell her. "You don't want to be a part of this."

She nods and scurries out, closing the door behind her.

"Let me tell you how this is going to go," I say to them. "You are going to sell Brielle Antonova that Pilates studio for not a cent over market value, and if either of you does anything to prolong or fuck up the deal, I'm going to come after you both."

I say to Evan, "In case you don't know who I am, my name is Kane Morgan, and I own Morgan Enterprises. If you so much as think about fucking with my future wife, I will dismantle your companies, piece by piece, until there's nothing left. Am I understood?"

Evan swallows thickly and nods.

"I need to hear the fucking words."

"Yes," Evan chokes out, "I understand."

"Good." I nod and grin. "Send the paperwork over to me by the end of the day so I can have my legal team look over it before I give it to Brielle to sign." I walk over to the door and open it. "Nice doing business with you, Evan."

I glance down at Theodore, who's still on the floor, holding his face. "And, Theo, this is strike two. Three strikes, and you're out."

EIGHTEEN

Brielle

Two hundred people are here.

I don't even know that many people.

Hell, I can count on one hand how many people I would've invited—zero.

"Is this how many people we're inviting to the wedding?" I ask Kane, a bit overwhelmed.

When he said he'd handle the engagement party, I didn't ask questions, but maybe I should've.

"Yes," he says, sliding his arm around my back and guiding me over to the next group of people we need to greet. "It would be rude not to."

While we're chatting with a few of his employees who made the move with him to Harbor Point, I notice my family standing on the other side of the room. Matteo has his arm slung over Dani, who is hella pregnant and looks absolutely adorable. Dominick has his arms wrapped around Peyton's waist, glancing down at her like she's his entire world. My mom is looking at her husband like he hung the damn moon.

I glance at Kane, who's chatting about something work-related, and he looks over at me, granting me a small smile. I wonder if this is as good as it's going to get for me—getting a smile from a man who will never love me the way my brothers love their wives.

The thought is both heartbreaking and depressing.

"Excuse me," I choke out. "I need to use the ladies' room."

Kane's brows furrow in confusion, but before he can question me, I slip out of his hold and go in search of the restrooms.

The engagement party is being held at Ocean Blue, a hotel that Kane's company owns. It's located just outside of Harbor Point, on the water, and I must admit, it's a beautiful property.

After going to the bathroom and reapplying my lipstick, I head back out, but I must make a wrong turn somewhere because rather than end up back at the party, I find myself opening the door that leads to the beach.

The ocean breeze sends chills throughout my body, but I revel in the rare cool evening since South Florida doesn't have enough of these types of nights.

I step out onto the deck and lean against the railing, inhaling the salty air. I close my eyes, and I'm taking a calming breath when a strong pair of arms wraps around me from behind, making me jump.

"Shh, it's just me," Kane says. "You seemed upset in there, and when I went in search of you and couldn't find you, I got worried."

"Don't worry." I chuckle humorlessly. "I'm not going anywhere. I have nowhere to go."

Kane spins me around and looks down at me, his eyes trying to read me.

"What's the matter?" he asks when he doesn't find whatever it is he was looking for.

"Noth—"

"Don't lie to me."

His tone sounds like he actually wants the truth, so I decide to give it to him.

"I'm a closet romantic," I admit with a small laugh. "I love weddings and romance books. I always thought when I got married, it would be for love. When I was little and my dad locked me in my room for being bad, I would play with my Barbies—the ones I kept hidden so my dad wouldn't find them—pretending she met the man of her dreams and he swept her off her feet. They would fall in love and get married on the beach. It would be an intimate wedding with a red-and-black theme because I loved red roses. And only their closest friends and family would be there to witness them vow to love each other forever.

"Then, after a few years of traveling and enjoying each other's company, they would have a half-dozen babies and live in a house on the beach, and he would love her more than anything in this world."

My eyes fill with tears, and I turn away from Kane, not wanting him to see me so vulnerable. Thankfully, he lets me, and for the next few minutes, I quietly cry as I accept that my life will never be like my Barbies.

"I got you an engagement present," he says.

"Another gigantic ring?" I half joke.

"No," he says dryly. "The Pilates studio is yours."

I spin around in shock. "What?" I gasp. "What do you mean, it's mine?"

He pulls an envelope out of his tuxedo coat and hands it to me. "I had my legal team look over the contract, and the papers are ready to be signed, if this is what you want."

I slowly take the envelope out of his hand and open it, and inside is a contract between me and the seller for North Harbor Point Pilates.

"You bought me the Pilates studio?" I whisper.

"No." He shakes his head. "I made it to where *you* can buy it with your money."

I choke on a sob.

Most women would want a man to buy it for them, but Kane knew I needed this for myself. I need to purchase it with my own money, so it's something no one can take away from me. It's why I didn't go to my brothers. They would've bulldozed right over me, buying it as their company and giving it to me to run. Their hearts would've been in the right place, but that's not want I wanted … what I needed.

"Thank you," I tell him, my hands trembling with emotion. "This … this means so much to me."

"I know you have your brothers, but if you need any help while you're figuring it all out, I'm here," Kane says. "I might not be your dream husband, but I'd like to think I'm a knowledgeable businessman."

He hits me with a lopsided grin, and for the first time, I wonder if maybe it's possible to have everything I dreamed of with Kane.

He might not love me the way my brothers love their wives, but what he just did for me speaks volumes. I shared my dreams with him, and instead of telling me I was stupid—like Andrey would've done to my mom—he not only listened, but he made one of them come true.

"Thank you," I say again, reaching up and palming his cheek. "This is the best present I've ever been given."

I press my lips to his to give him a quick kiss. Only the moment our mouths connect, I crave more. Later, I'm going to blame my sexual desperation on the lack of connection I've had recently mixed with my emotions being in hyperdrive, thanks to Kane's selfless gift. But right now, my only thought is how soft yet strong his lips feel against mine.

His hand comes up, and his fingers delve into my hair as he deepens the kiss, and I part my lips, welcoming it.

Our lips curl around one another, and when mine part, his tongue slides in, finding mine. He tastes like whiskey and control, and before I can stop it, a moan escapes from the back of my throat.

Kane once said that even though I hated him, I couldn't help but want him, and he's not wrong. I want Kane Morgan more than I'd ever admit.

My hands come up, and I claw at his chest, needing more. And without breaking our kiss, he lifts me onto the edge of the wooden rail and parts my legs.

"Tell me you want me to make you come," he murmurs against my mouth, once again giving me the control I crave.

"Make me come."

The words aren't even completely out of my mouth before Kane's mouth is back on mine. His fingers tighten in my hair, and his other hand slides beneath my silky dress and panties, expertly parting my folds and finding my clit. The juices between my legs are flowing, and he uses them to create friction as he rubs delicious circles along my clit.

I'm wound so tight that it only takes a few strokes before I'm moaning into his mouth as I come all over his fingers.

The last time this happened, I pushed him away, told him it would never happen again, but this time, I don't bother with the lies because we both know it'll happen again and again. Because I can't stay away from Kane. And I would be lying if I said I wasn't falling for him.

He pulls his fingers out from between my legs and breaks the kiss. "Always so fucking responsive for me." He lifts his fingers to my mouth and swipes my arousal across my lips. "Taste yourself. Taste how much you want me."

Without thought, I glide my tongue along the seam of my lips, and Kane grins a wolfish grin, loving that I listened to him. I want to tell him to go fuck himself, but the taste of myself has me squirming in my spot, wanting more than just a quick orgasm.

As if he can hear my thoughts, he says, "Soon, Princess. Soon, I'll give you everything you need." He takes his fingers and brings them to his own mouth, making a show of licking each digit. "So damn good."

He presses his lips to mine in a soft kiss that isn't as emotionally charged as the last one, but is filled with so much reverence that an outsider would think the man kissing me actually loves me.

Looks can be deceiving.

"Why not now?" I breathe out, wanting him to fuck me right here, not caring who could possibly see. My pussy is in need of a good fucking, and that orgasm was only a tease.

"Because, as I told you before …" He gives me one more chaste kiss and then lifts me off the railing and onto the ground. "The next time I fuck you, you'll be so desperate for it that you'll beg me for it. And I don't think you're quite there yet."

I am … I am totally there, but I don't tell him that. Instead, I nod and take his hand, letting him guide me back to the party, where we spend the rest of the evening celebrating our engagement. For some reason, when people congratulate us, rather than me forcing a reaction, I find myself genuinely smiling at the thought of marrying Kane.

Kane

This woman is fucking with my head.

I had a plan.

Destroy the waterfront deal, which would not only burn the Antonovs' and Russos' connections, but it would cost them millions.

Then I spent the night with Brielle and let a woman guide my emotions.

I should've learned from my father's mistakes.

But here I am, making them.

It started with the marriage. I convinced myself I was righting the wrongs of the past.

Then I threw in an heir.

Again, it's what's owed to my family.

I told myself I would keep my heart out of it. Treat it like a business deal.

But the more I'm around her, the harder it's becoming to keep my heart locked away.

I reach under the sink and grab the pharmacy bag.

I thought it was a good idea at the time, but now I'm second-guessing myself.

Fuck! I've become weak.

I put the bag back. Stare down at it. Grab it again.

"Hey, Kane … can you—" Brielle opens the bathroom door and glances at me curiously. "What's in the pharmacy bag?"

"An out-of-date prescription," I lie. "Found it when I was making room for your stuff and forgot to throw it away. What's up?" I ask, changing the subject.

She looks like she wants to question me, but instead, she turns around and lifts her blonde tresses, exposing her flawless back. "Can you unzip me, please?"

"Of course." I fold up the bag and shove it into my tux jacket and then walk over to her.

As my fingers run down her back, lowering the zipper, Brielle outwardly shivers, and I grin, loving the way my touch affects her.

"There you go," I say once it's undone. "And in case I forgot to mention it, you looked beautiful tonight."

I lay a soft kiss on her flesh, and then I leave her in the bathroom to finish getting undressed. I consider throwing the bag in the garbage, but doing so will mean admitting I've gone completely soft for this woman. So, instead, I head to my office and place the bag in my drawer, locking it for safekeeping.

It's just a slight deviation from my plan, I tell myself.

But my goal is still the same.

NINETEEN

Brielle

"Oh my God. This feels so good."

I glance at my pregnant sister-in-law, whose eyes are rolling up to the gods, and laugh. I might not have wanted to do anything that involved *celebrating* my upcoming marriage, but spending the day at the spa with Nicole, Dani, Peyton, and my mom has been nice.

When I first moved back, I tried to keep in touch with some old friends, but I quickly learned how fake they were, trying to use me to get to my brothers, and once they were both off the market, I barely heard from them. So, when Nicole asked me who I wanted to join us, my family and Nicole were the only people that popped into my head.

"Be careful," I say to Dani. "It might get back to Matteo that someone else is getting you off, and he'll kill 'em."

Dani snorts out a laugh, but then quickly sobers. "You're right. He probably would. Although, the closer I get to popping this little one out, the more he gives in to my every whim. I could bat my lashes and ask him not to kill anyone, and he'd listen."

Everyone laughs, and I join in, but my focus is on her belly, wishing I could push my envy away but wanting so badly what she has.

"So, when does the studio officially become yours?" Nicole asks, shaking me from my thoughts.

"Wait, what studio?" Peyton asks.

"North Harbor Point Pilates," I say with a grin. "I didn't want to jinx it until it went through … but the contract has been signed, and once the funds have cleared, the studio is all mine."

"Oh, Bri!" Dani exclaims. "That's so awesome."

"It all happened so quickly," I admit.

One minute, I was googling purchasing the studio, and the next, the contract was signed.

"Congratulations, honey," my mom says with a sniffle.

"Mom, why are you crying?" I laugh. "It's a good thing."

"These aren't tears of sadness," Mom clarifies. "They're from joy." She smiles warmly at me and then glances at Peyton and Dani. "All I wanted was for my kids to find love and happiness, and I'm so glad they have."

Dani glances at me with a soft, sympathetic smile, knowing what my mom doesn't know—that I haven't found love. But I shake my head, silently telling her to let it go.

"Kane's actually the one who got it for me," I admit, unsure why I feel the need to say that. "Apparently, Theo was butthurt that I'd broken things off with him, and he tried to ruin the deal I was working on with the investment company. But Kane found out and handled it."

Nicole smirks. "Look at him go. Not even married yet, and he's husband goals."

I roll my eyes and lean my head back, ignoring her remark. Every day this week, Kane has joined me for breakfast at Nicole's coffee shop before we part ways—me to the Pilates studio and him to work. And every day, once he's gone, Nicole tells me that my husband is in love with me. And it didn't help that, one morning, when I was running late, he got in line for me, and when the person in front of him bought the last strawberry muffin—after I told him I was dying for one—he gave them a hundred dollars to order a different muffin. Apparently, that was enough to have her crossing over to Team Kane.

Once our pedicures are done, we follow Leslie, the spa owner, back to the luncheon room, where we're having afternoon tea. The room is decorated in different shades of pink with a banner across the top that reads *Bridal Shower*.

There are adorable four-tier stands that hold layers of sandwiches and snacks and so many sweets. Nicole once told me her favorite place to travel as a teenager was to the UK, and I now understand why.

"This is so cute!" Dani gushes. "I need to take a picture." She pulls out her phone, but then drops it, clutching her belly.

"Are you okay?" I ask just as a loud scream pierces the air from somewhere outside of the room we're in.

Immediately on alert, I run toward the door and slam it closed, locking it behind me. I don't know what the hell is going on, but I'm not going to make it easy for whoever it is on the other side.

"We need to hide," I tell everyone as I glance around the room, confirming there are no other doors.

"I don't know what's happening," Leslie cries in panic as the screams continue.

"You guys," Dani whispers, "I think my water broke."

I look down, and sure enough, there's water dripping down the insides of her legs.

"Okay, we have to—" I begin, but my words are cut off when the doorknob jiggles, giving me flashbacks to when my nephew was taken by Anthony and Peyton and I had to chase him down.

"Peyton, Dani, text my brothers. There should've been guards out there, which means they either came in without them knowing or they took them out."

A loud bang makes everyone shriek, and I know we only have a few moments until the door is either broken down or they lose their patience and shoot their way in.

"Everyone, in," I say, opening the closet door.

It's a tight fit, especially with Dani heavily pregnant, but they're all in.

"Wait, Bri, what are you doing?" Mom asks when she realizes I'm not joining them.

"If they get to the closet, they'll take us all out," I rush out. "Hopefully, before that happens, Dominick or Matteo will get here."

I slam the door before anyone can argue and then run over to the other door, situating myself so I'm behind it.

A second later, the door swings open, and a man with a black ski mask stalks into the room.

"It's empty," he barks.

"Check the other door," another guy demands. "We need to find the girl."

"Looking for me?" I shout, needing to get his attention.

He turns around, and before he can focus, I slam my foot into his crotch, hopefully pushing his dick into his stomach.

He groans and, shocked by my move, drops his gun.

I snatch it up, and without thinking, I shoot him in the chest.

"Put the gun down!" the other man barks just as I turn around and shoot him as well.

It hits his shoulder, sending him stumbling back a few steps. He raises his gun, determined to get a shot in, but I pull the trigger, hitting him in the neck. Blood spurts out everywhere, and he drops to the floor.

"What the hell is—"

Before I can shoot the third man, he points and shoots at me. I drop to the ground, trying to get a shot in, but when he aims his gun at me, I know it's over. He has the perfect shot, and if he knows what he's doing, it will end my life.

As I look into his cold, lifeless eyes, all I can think about is how little I've lived, and now, I'll never get the chance to, thanks to being forced to marry a man who doesn't love me.

I close my eyes, praying that someone arrives before he gets to the closet, and then the gun goes off. Only a few seconds later, the pain I should've felt doesn't come.

"Fuck, Princess, come here."

My eyes fling open, and Kane lifts me into his arms.

"Was I shot?" I ask, wondering if maybe I'm in shock.

"No, I was a few doors down at a business lunch when Dominick texted an alert that you guys were being attacked. Thankfully, I had been added to the group chat, and I ran over."

He tightens his hold on me. "Fuck, I could've lost you."

He carries me over to the table and gently places me on it.

"You saved my life," I whisper.

"I'm just glad I got here in time."

"Where is she?" Matteo yells, storming inside. "Where's Dani?"

"In the closet," I tell him. "And she's in labor."

Matteo runs over to the closet, yanking it open, and the women file out. My mom and Nicole rush over to me, and Peyton stays with Dani, who is groaning in pain.

"We need to get her to the hospital soon," Peyton says. "Her contractions are appearing closer together."

"Boss," Kaleb, one of Matteo's men, calls out, "this one's not dead yet."

Matteo stalks over to the guy and lifts him by the collar of his shirt. "Who sent you?" he barks. "And before you think about lying or telling me you aren't saying, I'll bring a doctor in and keep you alive so I can torture it out of you until you wish you were dead."

"Carlos Santiago," the guy breathes out, having trouble catching his breath.

"Who's that?" I rasp. "Who the hell is Carlos Santiago?"

Matteo glances at me, looking like he's seen a ghost, but it isn't him who answers—it's our mom.

"Carlos Santiago was a business associate of your father's. He trafficked women into the port. But he died years ago, shortly after your father."

"Who killed him?" I ask.

"I did," Dominick says, standing in the doorway. "And unless dead men can make orders, there's no way he's the one doing all this."

Doing all this ...

What he's referring to is whoever has been tormenting our family for the last year and a half. We thought it was Anthony, but after I killed him, it continued with shipments being stolen and my brothers' men getting arrested for distribution. Then Dani was taken the night The Underground was ambushed during my brother Matteo's fight. We thought it was Enrique, until Matteo took him out, and the bullshit continued with them leaving Matteo a note on his wedding day, implying that he wouldn't live long enough to be a husband and a dad because they wanted Harbor Point and they wouldn't walk away from it.

"Oh my God!" I hiss, hopping off the table and walking over to the guy Matteo is standing over. "Who were you coming after?" I ask. "You said, 'We need to find the girl.' Who is the girl?"

"Nicole," he chokes out. "Nicole Vanderbilt."

Before I can ask him why, he starts coughing, and then blood dribbles out of his mouth. Within seconds, his eyes, which are still open, are lifeless while we all glance at my best friend, wondering why the hell they were coming for her. Until it hits me.

"The mayor," I whisper. "He's connected to all this."

"You're shaking."

"I'm okay," I insist as I run around the room, grabbing a change of clothes.

"No, you're not," Kane argues. "Come here."

I ignore him, but when he pulls me into his arms, I go willingly.

My heart is thumping, and I'm close to hyperventilating. During the ride home, I felt okay, but the second we were through the door, the events of today started to hit me.

"It's your adrenaline," he says, as if he can hear my thoughts. "It's coming down, and you're going to crash. You were attacked, shot at, and killed multiple men. Give yourself a minute to calm down."

He envelops me in his strong arms, and a threatening sob releases as I bury my face in his chest. His cologne is woodsy with a hint of spice, and I'm coming to associate his scent with comfort—something I'll most likely regret when this farce of a marriage blows up in our faces. And how could it not? It's built on revenge and lies. And the worst part is that I'm doing exactly what I never wanted to do—I'm marrying a man who's part of the underworld.

When it becomes harder for me to breathe, Kane lifts me into his arms and carries me to the bathroom, once again turning the tub on and pouring the calming bubble bath into the water.

"I have to get to the hospital," I mutter, the fight in me nowhere to be found.

"Right now, my only concern is you."

He undresses me and sets my phone on the edge of the tub, and when he's about to step in, still in his clothes, I shake my head, wanting to be skin to skin with him.

It's stupid and crazy, and I know I'm setting myself up for heartbreak, but I don't want anything between Kane and me right now.

He gently sets me in the tub, and I sigh as the warm water surrounds me, watching as he unbuttons his shirt and then takes it off, exposing his perfectly sculpted chest and torso.

"You should come to Pilates with me," I note.

"Or"—he unbuttons and unzips his pants and pulls them down, along with his briefs, shucking them to the side—"you could give me a private class."

His cock bobs between his legs, and even soft, it's a sight to behold.

I probably shouldn't be thinking about sex right now. I'm still in shock over what happened today, but as I stare at my fiancé, all I can think about is how he's the perfect distraction. All hard lines and toned muscle. Even his cock is thick …

"My eyes are up here, Miss Antonova."

He smirks, and I blush at having been caught ogling him.

"True, but your cock is prettier than your eyes." I lean over the edge, splashing a bit of water over the sides, and wrap my fingers around his shaft.

Kane steps back, and I pout when I lose access to one of his best features.

"As much as I'd enjoy you giving my cock attention, not now, Princess." He nods for me to shift forward and slides in behind me. "You've been through a lot today, and having sex with me would only be putting a bandage over the wounds."

I sigh into him, knowing he's right. As much as I want him—and if I'm being honest, I do most of the damn time—my head is all over the place.

I've just closed my eyes when my phone goes off with a text message. Kane reaches over and hands it to me, and I find a group message from Matteo.

> Alba Tanya Antonov is here!
> 21.5 inches
> 7lbs 6oz
> <attached picture>
> Dani and Alba are doing well. Come visit anytime.
> Room 226

"Dani had her baby," I choke out, emotion clogging my throat.

It's been six years, but every time I see a baby, I can't help but wonder what my baby would've looked like.

I raise the phone to show Kane the picture, and he stiffens behind me.

I'm about to ask him what's wrong when he says, "I need … to make a phone call."

"Now?" I ask in confusion.

"Yes, now," he barks as he clambers out of the tub and leaves me to wonder what the hell just happened.

I get out and rinse off and then get dressed in a simple sundress since it's been hot out the past several days. I bought a baby gift a couple of weeks ago, so I grab it and go in search of Kane, who's dressed and sitting at his desk, his head in his hands.

"Everything okay?" I ask.

He looks up at me, and for the first time since the baby shower, when he demanded I marry him, he looks like he hates me.

"Did you need something?" he snaps, his words like a slap to the face.

"No. I'm going to the hospital to see the baby," I tell him, my head still a bit fuzzy from the earlier attack. This is the second time I've been forced to take someone's life, and it doesn't get easier—even if he deserved it. "I just came to see if you wanted to go."

Kane chuckles darkly. "Sure." He stands. "I should probably go see my niece. Since her father will never be able to."

Oh God. I didn't think about that.

Dani's baby is biologically Enrique's.

Who's dead.

Which makes Kane her biological uncle.

"I'm sorry," I tell him, dropping the gift bag and cutting across the room and around the desk. "You're right. You are her uncle …"

I try to slide onto his lap, but Kane shakes his head.

"Not now. I just … I need some time. I know my brother did some beyond fucked-up shit, but …"

"But he's still your brother," I finish because I get it.

My brothers are far from perfect. They're criminals who deal in arms and drugs, and they have played God with too many lives to count.

But they're still my brothers, and I love them.

And Kane loved his brother, despite the horrible choices he made while he was alive.

"Fuck!" Kane stands, grabs a paperweight from the desk, and chucks it. "I just keep thinking, *What if I had stepped in?*" He stalks over to the other side of the room and leans against the wall. "He was my brother, and I just stood by and watched him spiral."

"You couldn't have done anything," I tell him honestly, walking over to where he is. "He was committed to his plan, to getting his revenge."

Just like Kane is, I think but push that to the side.

"He has a daughter," he chokes out. "A little girl he'll never get to meet or hold. Not that he deserves to. What he did to Daniella is unforgivable. But … I haven't even told my mom," he admits. "If she knew …" His red-rimmed eyes meet mine. "Fuck, it'd break her heart if she knew there was someone out there with our blood flowing through their veins who she'd never be allowed to call family."

"You never know. Maybe Dani and Matteo will—"

"Give me a fucking break." Kane barks out a mirthless laugh. "Matteo would kill my mom and me before he let us anywhere near his daughter. And I don't blame him because if I were in the same position, I would do everything in my power to protect our child."

Our child.

A baby created from a part of me and a part of Kane.

The idea should scare me, but instead, I find myself bridging the gap between us and framing his face in my hands, wanting to comfort him the same way he comforted me not too long ago.

"Brielle, not now," he rasps. "I can't do this right now."

"Please, let me in," I implore. "When I had my nightmare, you were there for me. After the attack, you took care of me. Let me be here for you. Tell me what you need."

His eyes lock with mine, and he stares at me for several seconds. And just when I think he's going to push me away again, he wraps his hand around my neck and pulls me into him for a bruising kiss.

His fingers slide up my nape and delve into my hair as he sucks my bottom lip into his mouth and then bites down on it … hard.

I yelp as the taste of copper fills my senses and attempt to back away, but Kane deepens the kiss, pulling me closer by tightening his hold on the back of my head.

Pain radiates through my scalp, and I find myself pushing away from him as flashbacks of Anthony forcing himself on me hit me.

The act must cause him to snap out of it because he opens his eyes, looking distraught.

"Fuck, Princess, I'm sorry." He reaches out and gently runs the pad of his thumb across my bleeding lip. "This is why I walked away … why I told you I needed some time. I don't ever want to hurt you, and right now, I'm not capable of being in control of my emotions."

"Then let me take control," I tell him, threading our fingers together and kissing the top of his knuckles. "Let me help you forget."

TWENTY

Kane

"LET ME HELP YOU FORGET."

I knew Daniella Antonova was having my brother's baby. I did my research. I found out her due date and pieced it together—hence me showing up at her baby shower to drop my bomb.

And then I shoved the information aside, focusing on my own agenda.

Righting the wrongs that were owed to my family.

But tonight, when Brielle showed me the picture of the baby and she looked so much like my brother, it reminded me all over again of the domino effect that the Antonovs and Russos had set off that ended with my father buried six feet under—and nearly taking my mother down with him.

After my father's death, when the Antonovs froze his company out, I didn't argue. I knew I wasn't equipped to battle them in court. So, I bided my time. I created a new brand. Started from the ground up and played it smart. I told myself that I wouldn't make the same mistakes my father and brother had made. To be successful in my line of work, it's all about being patient and playing the long game. I did everything I was supposed to do …

Yet here I am, letting a woman control my emotions.

"Kane," Brielle says, her brows furrowed in concern, "please, let me help you forget."

I should tell her that what I need is to remember what her family did to mine, the years it took to rebuild from the destruction they'd left behind, that my brother lost his head while trying to avenge our father's death and raped Daniella Antonov—and that's why I have a niece who will never know we're related.

I should remember that Brielle was supposed to be nothing more than revenge.

Only I don't want to remember any of it.

Because I've fallen in love with the one woman who was off-limits. Despite the pain our families have caused each other. Even though she'll most likely never return my feelings. I can't stop myself.

From the moment I brought her up to my hotel room, I didn't stand a chance.

"Okay," I tell her. "Make me forget."

I follow her upstairs to our bedroom, and when we enter, I wait for her to tell me what to do. Like the night in the hotel, I'm giving her complete control.

"Lie on the bed," she says, her voice confident.

Lying on my back, I prop my head up with the pillow so I can watch her as she disappears into the closet and comes back out, holding one of my ties.

"This is my favorite tie of yours," she says, sauntering over to the side of the bed. "It reminds me of the color of your eyes." She climbs onto the bed and straddles my torso. "Lift your arms."

Once they're above my head, she goes about tying my hands together and then attaching them to the headboard.

"Should I be concerned at how easily you just did that?" I ask, making her laugh.

"Too late now."

She wiggles her ass, and I clench my jaw, hating that I can't smack it.

Taking the hem of her dress, she pulls it over her head and tosses it onto the floor, leaving her in only her pink lace bra and panties. I've learned that Brielle doesn't like things simple. Even her undergarments are expensive and feminine. She loves nice shit, and since I get the pleasure of seeing her in it, I'm not going to complain.

"Hmm, what should I do first?" she says, scooting down until she's situated on my cock, giving me the perfect view of her body.

She drags her perfectly manicured finger down my bare chest and along the happy trail, stopping when she gets to the waistband of my sweats.

"You should suck my dick," I tell her since I've been imagining her mouth wrapped around my shaft for weeks. "That would definitely help me forget."

She grins and nods, and then surprisingly, she pulls my pants down my legs, exposing my hard length. She wraps her fingers around my shaft and leans over, pressing a teasing kiss to the crown. The swells of her breasts spill out of the top of her bra cups, and instinctually, I try to reach for her, wanting to touch her, only to be met with resistance.

Fucking tie.

"Kane," she chides, glancing up at me through her thick lashes. "Be a good boy and don't fight it, and I'll make sure you forget about everything but me."

Fuck, this woman. She's going to be the death of me, I swear.

She licks the tip and makes a show of moaning when she gets a taste of pre-cum. And then, like the fucking minx she is, she opens her mouth and takes me all the way down her throat. My cock swells beneath her touch, and I force myself to think of shit other than her warm, wet mouth wrapped around my cock so I don't blow my load.

Talk to Dominick about the mayor.

The deal with Jenkins industries.

That property I need to—

The tip of my cock hits the back of her throat, and every thought but Brielle sucking my dick fades away. She slurps and sucks, and in my position, I have the perfect view of the saliva that drips out of the sides of her mouth as she bobs her head up and down.

"Fuck!" I moan, tugging at my wrists, needing her to slow down. "Baby, I'm going to—"

She pops off my dick, and a string of saliva stretches from my shaft to her mouth, making me groan.

"Come here," I command, needing to taste her lips.

She quirks a brow. "I don't think you're in any place to make demands."

"Princess, you are the only fucking thing I'm thinking about. Now, get your ass over here so I can kiss you."

She smiles softly, a light tinge of pink tinting her cheeks, and I fully understand why wars have been started over women. The way Brielle is looking at me, with her eyes wide in excitement and her lips puffy from sucking my dick, I would give this woman anything she asked for.

She shifts forward, her material-clad pussy rubbing along my shaft, and leans in, pressing her lips to mine. I want to pull her closer, rip those fucking panties off her, and thrust up inside her, but since I can't do shit, I simply kiss her. My tongue slides between her lips, and I revel in the taste of her.

"Baby, take your bra off," I murmur against her lips. "And then put those perfect tits in my face."

She moans at my command and reaches around, unlatching her bra. Her breasts drop slightly, and when the cool air hits her nipples, they harden into twin peaks.

"Now, Princess," I growl, needing her nipple in my mouth.

"Who's in charge?" she sasses, contradicting her words as she moves closer, taking her breast into her hand and guiding it toward my mouth.

I lean in as far as the binds will allow and suck the hardened tip into my mouth. I bite down on it, then swirl my tongue around it to soothe the pain.

"Oh God," Brielle breathes. "Don't stop, Kane."

She shoves her tits in my face, and I give each one the attention they deserve. Licking and sucking, I don't stop until she's writhing against my cock, the wetness between her legs soaking my shaft.

"That's it, baby. Use me for your pleasure," I tell her. "Slide that wet cunt along my cock."

She picks up speed, grinding herself harder along my hard length. Her pussy is fucking soaked, her lower lips enveloping my shaft. She's so fucking close. I can feel it.

I pull her nipple into my mouth, sucking it as hard as I can, and when I bite down on it again, she flies over the edge, coming hard and loud.

"Oh my God, Kane," she hisses, dropping her forehead into the crook of my neck.

"I want another one, Bri. Take those goddamn panties off and come sit on my face, baby."

I slide down so my head is a bit lower as she lifts and pulls the material down one leg and then the other.

When I glance down at her neatly trimmed pussy, my cock swells. But I want that pussy on my mouth before I have it wrapped around my dick.

"Come here," I tell her, nodding to emphasize my command. "Sit on my face."

With lust-filled eyes, she climbs up me and situates herself on either side of my face, her pussy directly hovering over my mouth.

"Sit," I growl, and she drops down, giving me exactly what I want.

It's a bit harder without any hands, but I nudge her lips apart with my nose and quickly find her clit. As I lick her delicious cunt, she grinds her pussy against my face, using it to bring her closer to her orgasm.

"I'm so close," she moans. "Right—"

I latch on to her clit, and she screams my name as her orgasm rips through her, soaking my face with her juices. I lap at them, swallowing every drop I can get, until she's pushing back because she's too sensitive.

"Do you have any idea how good you eat pussy?" she mutters,

her lids starting to droop from her multiple orgasms. "I think part of your vows should be that you'll eat my pussy every day for the rest of our lives."

I bark out a laugh, ignoring the twinge in my chest at the fact that she just implied we'll be married until we die. "I can do that, but right now, I need that pussy wrapped around my cock. I need to come in your tight cunt."

She glances around, as if she's looking for something, and I lose my patience.

"Now, baby. Stick my dick in that pussy."

"I … I need a condom."

I growl, and she glances down at me in shock.

"You're mine, and I don't want anything between us. Now, sit on my fucking cock."

She reaches between us, wrapping her delicate fingers around my shaft, and then she lifts and slowly eases her way all the way down, sucking every inch of my dick into her warmth.

And then she starts to ride me. Working her hips in a hypnotizing rhythm.

I try to reach for her, but I'm denied by the fucking tie.

"Kiss me!" I grit through clenched teeth.

Her lips crash over mine, and we kiss one another in frenzied desperation. And when she comes again, I swallow down her screams and take over, thrusting into her from the bottom.

Her walls choke me as another orgasm hits her, this time taking me along with her. And as I fill her with my seed, I think about the bag of placebos I removed from under her cabinet, wishing I had switched out her pills with them, because I want this woman pregnant with my baby as soon as possible.

She's mine. Till death do us part.

TWENTY-ONE

Brielle

TOLD MYSELF THAT THE FIRST NIGHT I'D SPENT WITH KANE was a one-off. The chemistry between us wasn't something that could be re-created. I even convinced myself that because I had been so starved for attention that I made it better than what it was.

I was wrong on all accounts.

Sex with Kane isn't like anything I've experienced. He takes charge while giving me control. The chemistry between us is off the charts. Hell, I actually orgasm when I'm with him. But it's more than that. Being with him has me feeling things I haven't felt in years. Wanting things I was too scared to want.

He's asleep next to me, and I can't help imagining what it would be like to be with him for the rest of my life. When he insisted that I marry him, a part of me figured we would get married, and then once he got what he had come to Harbor Point for, he would leave, and I would start my life all over again. But now, the thought of him leaving has me feeling shit I don't want to feel.

I glance down at his strong arms wrapped around me, and my heart races in my chest. The life I've lived means that my body knows what a threat looks like, and Kane is not only a threat to my mental well-being, but to my heart.

I need to distance myself.

Clear my head and remember who this man is.

I slide out from under him, careful not to wake him. Grabbing my phone, I quietly pad to the bathroom, texting Nicole that we're going shopping this morning. Unless she's short an employee, Sunday is usually her day off, so I'm not surprised when she texts that she's down.

After some good retail therapy, I'll take her with me to see Matteo, Dani, and the baby. Because she gave birth naturally, they're only in the hospital for a couple of days before they go home.

I shower, do my makeup and hair, and then get dressed. I assume Kane is still in bed since I haven't heard anything coming from the room, so I nearly jump out of my skin when I step out of the walk-in closet and find him leaning against the edge of the bed in nothing but the boxer briefs he fell asleep in, his arms crossed over his chest and his brown hair messy from sleep.

"Going somewhere?"

"Um, yeah. I'm meeting Nicole."

He quirks a brow.

"We're going shopping."

"Why?" He pushes off the bed and stalks toward me. "Do you need something?"

"No," I reply defensively. "We're just going for fun."

"You mean, you're sneaking out to go shopping so you can escape your feelings after what happened last night."

Damn him for calling me out.

"I don't know what the hell you're talking about," I lie, trying to move around him to get away. But of course, he sees it coming and pushes me against the wall.

"Since you want to play dumb this morning, let me break it down for you. We had sex last night—"

"We've had sex before."

"Not like last night," he notes, lifting my chin when I look away. "Last night was more. We both felt it, and now you're freaking out, and instead of facing your feelings, you're trying to escape them by doing what you do best when you need a distraction—shop."

"You don't know shit," I hiss, despite him hitting the nail on the head.

"Okay." He steps back. "But just know that when you come home later with all the clothes and shit you bought, you're still going to feel just as confused as you do now because you won't have addressed your feelings like a big girl," he mocks.

"I hate you."

"No, you don't." He steps toward me and cups the side of my face, forcing me to meet his whiskey eyes. "And that scares the shit out of you."

He slides his hands down my body and clasps my ass, lifting me and carrying me over to the dresser, where he sets me down and spreads my legs, stepping between them. Our faces are so close that I can feel his cool breath mingling with mine.

"I'm not going to enable you while you run from your feelings, Princess. Now, talk to me. Tell me what's going through your head."

I swallow thickly, debating whether to tell him the truth. That I'm falling for the man who's forcing me to marry him. But instead, I go with a partial truth.

"Shopping is my escape," I admit. "But it's not just the shopping. It's what I buy, what it all represents. My entire life, I was the perfectly groomed Antonov princess. It was expected that I wore the most expensive brands, that my hair and makeup were done to perfection because our family had an image to uphold. Andrey Antonov owned this town, had people eating out of his dirty-ass hand. On the inside, we were living in hell, but to the outside world, we were picture-perfect. The rich looked up to him, wanting to be richer. And the poor believed that by trusting him, they could one day become just like him."

I snort out a mirthless laugh. "We didn't talk in my family. My father gave orders, and we obeyed them. If we stepped out of line …" I shake my head, hating to even think about my childhood. "I might've been dressed like the perfect Antonov daughter, but the Gucci and Chanel only hid the scars underneath."

Kane reaches up and frames my face, and there's just something about the way he holds me that always makes me feel heard and safe. Like I can tell him anything, no matter how bad it is, and he'll listen.

"I understand needing to uphold a certain image," he tells me. "My father hid us away, partly because he didn't want us exposed to what people would say if they found out he had an entire other family with his mistress, but also because he didn't want to taint his image. But inside these walls, we talk. We don't hide or escape. You're too strong for that, Brielle."

Warmth spreads through my veins, and I nod, wanting that type of relationship with him. I've been lonely for years, and I don't want to go back to taking on the world by myself. And something tells me that Kane would make a great ally.

But then the other part of what he said has me thinking …

"I don't want to live two lives."

He raises a brow in confusion.

"Your dad was married to one woman while he was with another. I know this marriage isn't real, but—"

"Fuck that," he says. "I will never cheat on you. And if you so much as look at another man, I'll be forced to take out the competition. So, be careful who you give your attention to. I warned you before that I don't share, and I meant it. You're mine, baby."

He lifts me into his arms, and I shriek in shock.

"What are you doing?"

"Taking you back to bed." He drops me onto the mattress and hovers over me, nuzzling his face into the crook of my neck. "And then I'm going to eat you for breakfast."

"What about me?" I laugh as his facial hair tickles my face. "I'm hungry too."

He pulls back and gives me a wolfish grin. "Oh, Princess, I've got plenty for you to eat."

"I have to go visit my brother and Dani."

I hold my breath, waiting for Kane's reaction.

We've spent the past couple of hours in bed, getting lost in each other. When Nicole called to see where I was, I was in the middle of giving Kane head, so of course, he used the opportunity to text her that I was having breakfast with him and I needed a rain check.

When we're within these walls and it's just us, it feels safe. But the thought of leaving them, of dealing with reality, is another story. Everything about us is complicated, and then add the outside distractors, like Dani giving birth to Kane's niece and the girls and me being attacked during our spa day due to some psycho bitch—at least Dani thinks it's a woman—coming after my family because she thinks we should hand Harbor Point over to her, and I don't want to leave.

But it's inevitable.

"Would you like me to go with you?" Kane asks, rubbing circles along my hips.

We're still in bed, both of us naked and tangled around each other.

"I don't want you to do anything that will make you uncomfortable, but"—I clear my throat—"if we're getting married soon, then you're about to become family, and my family is around a lot."

"Then we'll go." He slides closer to me and kisses my lips softly. "But first, I'm pretty sure it's almost lunch, and I'm starving."

He waggles his brows, and his cock thickens against my leg.

"Okay," I agree. "First, lunch, and then we'll go to the hospital."

"Oh, Dani," I coo, taking the sweet little girl into my arms. "She's absolutely perfect," I choke out, leaning in and closing my eyes and inhaling her baby scent.

The last babies I held were Dominick and Peyton's twin boys, and they smelled similar—like perfection and innocence, mixed with baby powder. I wonder if all babies smell like this … and then my thoughts go to my unborn baby. Would he or she have smelled the same way?

I open my eyes, blinking back the tears that are threatening to come, and Dani meets my gaze with knowing eyes. I shake my head, not wanting to go there, and she nods in understanding.

"Welcome to the world, Alba Antonov," I say softly. "You are so loved." I press a kiss to her forehead and take a calming breath. I should be past my abortion by now. It's been years, and I was barely even pregnant, but that doesn't stop my heart from mourning the loss.

"And you're going to be so spoiled by your auntie Bri," I add to lighten the mood. "Starting with this …"

Holding her carefully, I go to bend down to grab the gift bag, but Kane beats me to it, handing it to Dani.

"Thank you," I murmur.

Dani opens the bag and then cracks up laughing, holding up the Burberry onesie with a built-in pleated skirt over it.

"You didn't," Dani says with a laugh.

"My niece will be the most stylish baby there is," I say with a grin, but I can't help but think about Kane's and my conversation earlier. About how my expensive clothes are a cover for the scars I hide underneath. And as I stare at my niece, rocking her gently, I say a silent prayer that she never needs expensive clothes to hide her scars.

"So, when do they let you go home?" I ask, bringing Alba back over to Dani.

"Tomorrow."

"Well, be prepared because I'll be stopping by often to get my fill of this precious little girl," I say, handing her to her mom.

"You're welcome anytime," Matteo says.

"Would you like to hold her?" Dani asks.

I look at her in confusion because I already held her, but then I follow her line of sight over to Kane, who's back to standing against the wall.

"Dani," Matteo murmurs, the warning in his tone clear.

"He's family," Dani says softly to Matteo, then turns her attention back to Kane. "What your brother did was horrific, but"—she sniffles back a sob—"she's your niece."

Matteo growls, and Dani glances at him, silently begging him not to lose his shit. He doesn't say a word, but he plucks the baby out of her arms and protectively holds her to his chest.

Kane's jaw clenches like he's pissed, but his eyes are filled with a myriad of emotions. I'm about to say something to save him from this moment, but before I can, he speaks.

"She might be biologically related to me, but she's your family, not mine."

Matteo's eyes shoot to Kane's in what looks like appreciation.

"Well, a child can never have too much family," Dani says. "And with you marrying Bri soon … you are family."

Kane doesn't hold the baby, but after that, the tension eases in the room. We spend the next several minutes talking about the labor and delivery and how she's breastfeeding but is also pumping because Matteo wants to be able to feed the baby as well.

When Alba starts to fuss, we say our goodbye so she can breastfeed in private, and then we head out to lunch—since we never ate, choosing sex over sustenance—where I tell him about my plans to have North Harbor Point Pilates renovated.

"There's just so much potential," I tell him, taking a bite of my chicken salad sandwich. "I'm bringing in a Pilates expert, and we're going to go over what the ideal studio would look like. Then, I'll get it all put together and submit the plans for bids from contractors."

Kane looks at me with a smile, and I squirm in my seat.

"What?"

"Nothing." He shakes his head. "I just love to see the passion in your eyes. I'm not an expert on Pilates, but if you need anything, let me know."

"Thank you." I glance over at Daniil standing in the corner of the restaurant and throw my napkin onto my plate, stuffed. "Hopefully, my brothers will figure out who this asshole is so we can go back to our normal lives."

Because of the attack, Dominick has put his family on lockdown, and once Dani is home from the hospital, she's promised Matteo she won't leave until they figure out who has been terrorizing our families.

"Speaking of your brothers," Kane says, pulling his credit card out of his wallet and handing it to the waitress, "after lunch, I want to go by Dominick's house to talk to him about all this."

My brows shoot to my forehead at the thought of Kane and Dominick working together. "Do you want me to go with you?"

"No. I want you to go home and focus on your Pilates studio. And once I'm done, I was thinking you could give me a private class in the gym."

He waggles his brows playfully, and I bark out a laugh.

"It's your funeral."

He quirks a brow. "Going to see your brother or the Pilates class?"

"You're a dead man regardless." I laugh. "If Dominick doesn't kill you, Pilates will."

TWENTY-TWO

Kane

"I DON'T HAVE TIME TO BULLSHIT RIGHT NOW," Dominick says, walking out his front door and toward his SUV. "The mayor is hiding out at his house, and I'm going to pay him a visit."

"Then it's perfect timing." I walk around to the passenger side of his vehicle. "I was here to ask what we're doing about this bitch who went after our women."

Dominick stops and stares at me. "Our women?"

"Brielle was there."

"I know, but I wasn't aware she was *your woman*."

"In a week's time, she'll be my wife. She's every bit my fucking woman, and I'm not going to sit back while some crazy bitch keeps going after her."

"Get in," he says. Once we're in and he turns the car on, he adds, "I see Brielle has you believing it's a woman as well."

"I'm not an expert on relationships, but I've learned over the years that women tend to be smarter than men, so if they believe it's a woman, I'm not going to count it out."

"Your brother ever mention working with a woman?"

"Only woman I knew he was working with was Hillary, but he didn't tell me. I was keeping tabs on him, trying to make sure he didn't do anything stupid. Not that it did much good once he lost his shit."

"Fucking cunt," he mutters. "I can't believe she sank her claws into Lorenzo. Thank God he got away from that bitch."

I chuckle but keep my thoughts to myself since Lorenzo obviously hasn't told anyone about Hillary showing up and forcing him into an insta-family.

"Anything on Carlos Santiago?" I ask, changing the subject.

I looked him up, but everything regarding him has been wiped from the internet.

"Only that he had a son named Emmanual who took over the business after Carlos died. Looks like he went legit and then died a few years back in a car accident."

"Any children?"

"Two daughters—Leysa died in the car accident with her father and Laura is in school."

"Wife?"

"Remarried and, from what we've seen, doesn't give a shit about her dead husband's business."

"Well, someone does."

"Yeah, and I'm hoping Mr. Mayor will know who."

Dominick pulls up to the gated community, and I'm expecting him to be stopped, but the moment the guard sees him, he lets us through.

"Matteo meeting us?" I ask when we pull into what I assume is the mayor's driveway.

"No. He's with Dani and their daughter. I told him I'd handle it."

We get out, and it's then I notice two more vehicles pulling up. They park, and six men get out, a few I recognize as Dominick's men.

"Not taking any chances," he says. "I'm adding another guard on Brielle since she's insistent on going about her life instead of staying inside."

I chuckle, imagining that conversation.

"She's strong-minded." I shrug.

Dominick side-eyes me. "I see she's got you wrapped around her finger."

I don't confirm or deny even though we both know he's not wrong.

Rather than knocking on the door, one of Dominick's men quickly picks the lock, and another one disarms the alarm when it goes off.

Ilene, the mayor's wife, appears first to see what's going on. When she sees who's in her home, she screams, and one of the men pulls her to the side as I follow Dominick's lead and head straight to the mayor's office, where he's scrambling to grab his shit and run.

"Going somewhere?" Dominick asks, closing the door behind us.

"It wasn't me!" Eric yells. "You don't understand." He glances from Dominick to me, his eyes wide in fear.

"So, make us understand," Dominick says calmly, having a seat in the chair in front of the desk.

Eric shakes his head, his eyes going to the door, as if he's calculating if he could make it.

"Sit your ass down," I command, sitting next to Dominick. "Your wife is being detained until we have this conversation, and if you try to run, you'll be met with several more men who will consider you a threat and kill you on the spot."

"My hands are tied," Eric cries, falling into his chair in defeat.

"And who tied them?" Dominick asks.

"I can't say. He'll kill me. I messed up. I got into bed with the wrong guy, and he's out to get you. If you're smart, you'll move, sell the port, and find a new place to run your businesses."

"This is our city," Dominick says. "You have two options—tell me who you're working with, or I'll slit your throat." His tone is calm, smooth, like he's telling the corrupt mayor about the weather, but anyone who knows Dominick Antonov knows that he doesn't make threats unless he can back them up.

"Carlos Santiago," Eric hisses. "That's all I know."

"And you've seen him?" Dominick asks, remaining calm.

"No." Eric shakes his head. "He donated to my campaign in exchange for me agreeing that I'd push you out."

Dominick barks out a laugh. "That wasn't very smart."

"I know," he whines. "But I was desperate. I made some bad choices. I needed the money to stay afloat."

"Hmm." I chuckle. "Must be why they were going after your daughter."

The mayor swallows thickly. "I can help you. I'll help you find him. He texts me sometimes … and I'll set up a meeting. If you can just protect me, please."

Dominick snorts out a laugh and stands, so I follow since I'm just along for the ride. "I think I'll wait and see how this plays out. Have a good day, Mayor."

"It could be a woman," I note once we're back in his SUV.

"It could be *any-fucking-one*. Hell, it could be you."

"You know damn well that shit isn't my style," I drawl. "You don't think I know you had me looked into? The moment my name was pinged, my IT guy sent me everything."

Dominick nods and then hits a button on his steering wheel. "Call Eddy."

"Boss," the guy says once he answers.

"I need you to dig deeper on Carlos Santiago. The mayor said he's working with him as well."

"He's dead," Eddy says dumbly.

"I know he's fucking dead!" Dominick barks. "I killed him with my bare hands, but someone is fucking with my family, and two people have mentioned this asshole's name."

"Unless whoever it is was aware of your connection to Carlos Santiago and is using his name to fuck with you," I point out.

"Who's that?" Eddy asks.

"The dipshit who's forcing my sister to marry him," Dominick notes, reminding me that while we might be allies, we're not on the same team either.

"Ahh, Kane Morgan," Eddy says over the line. "I see your mom is enjoying the mountains."

I stiffen at his words, and Dominick smirks.

"You didn't think we'd find where she was, right? Eddy here is the best hacker on the East Coast."

"Finding her was child's play," Eddy adds with a chuckle.

"I need you to find everything you can on Carlos," Dominick says, shifting the conversation.

"And the mayor?" Eddy asks.

"We've bugged his office. Hopefully, he talks before he has it searched. My guess is, he has a burner phone stashed somewhere. My men are looking for it as we speak."

"You got it," Eddy says before he hangs up.

"If you knew where my mom was this entire time, why didn't you go after her?"

"One, we don't go after women if it can be helped. And two …" Dominick sighs. "My sister asked us not to. She doesn't want bloodshed, and she's been through a lot. Daniil said she's been happy lately. Bought a gym—"

"Pilates studio," I correct.

"Yeah," he says. "Heard what you did to Theo, and you're a good businessman. The investors for the waterfront expansion were more than happy to have you on board. And since I'm trying to go as legit as possible …" He shrugs, then glances at me. "But, Kane, if you hurt my sister, I promise that I will do more than shed blood."

The threat should piss me off, but the only thought that occurs to me is that if someone hurt Brielle, I would tear this fucking town apart.

Speaking of which …

"I'm going to have security installed in the house," I say,

changing gears. "Can I use your contact to ensure it's done right? I don't know what this fucker is capable of, and I want to make sure Brielle is safe when she's at home."

"You're not afraid we'll bug your place?" He smirks.

"I have nothing to hide," I tell him. "You wanna listen to me fuck your sister all over the house, go for it."

Dominick whips his head around to glare at me. "And to think, I was actually starting to tolerate you, Morgan."

TWENTY-THREE

Today is the day. I dreamed of this day when I was younger too many times to count. The elegant white dress that would make me feel no less than a queen. Dominick walking me down the aisle—because, in my dreams, Andrey was dead—and giving me away. My friends and family would be in attendance, watching as the man of my dreams vowed to love me till death did us part.

My wedding dress is gorgeous.

My brother is walking me down the aisle.

My friends and family—and hundreds of people I don't know or care about—are in attendance.

But the man I'm about to marry doesn't love me. And our vows won't mean anything.

Sure, he's attracted to me, and the sex is off the charts. I've never been so satisfied in my life. With Owen, we were young and learning what our bodies were capable of. And with Theo, I was bored out of my mind. But Kane knows how to please me. And when we're together, it feels real. Like I'm not part of his vendetta and he's not forcing me to marry him.

But standing in front of the floor-length mirror, I can't help but be reminded that while the orgasms are real, the feelings aren't. At least not on Kane's end.

I wish I could say that I was unaffected. Falling for the man who's forcing me to marry him makes me sound weak. And in our world, the last thing a woman wants is to feel weak.

But I can't help it.

The way he gives me his undivided attention.

When I wake up from my nightmares, he comforts me.

He went out of his way to ensure I could buy the Pilates studio.

When we have sex, it feels like we're making love.

And afterward, he holds me like I mean the world to him.

"You look beautiful," Dani says.

"I still can't believe you're here." I reach over and gently run my hand over her baby girl's head.

"And miss my sister's wedding?" She scoffs. "Not happening. Besides, this little one has her days and nights mixed up, so she'll sleep through the entire thing, I'm sure."

Peyton groans. "That's the worst."

"There's a reason why they make babies so cute," Mom says, giving Alba a kiss on the crown of her head. "For all the sleepless nights we have to endure." She turns toward me, a soft smile on her face. "You look like a princess, Brielle. I'm so happy you found your one."

I nod, my emotions getting clogged in my throat, and hug my mom, ignoring the looks of sympathy Peyton, Nicole, and Dani are giving me.

I've accepted this is my future. I've made peace with it. And I'm not going to live my life full of resentment. I might not be marrying a man who loves me, but I have a good life.

Kane

"You look handsome."

I turn around, shocked to find my mom standing in the doorway.

Her brown hair has been straightened, and she's dressed for the occasion in a cream-colored floral dress.

"Mom, you're here."

"I might not agree with your choices, but I couldn't miss my son's wedding."

She steps into the room and pulls me into her embrace. "We're all we have now that your father and brother are gone. I really wish you would reconsider, but since you're hell-bent on marrying this woman, I'm going to have to accept your decision."

"Thank you," I tell her.

"I'm assuming by the empty room, your future in-laws aren't keen on your decision either?"

Lorenzo actually came in earlier to wish me luck, along with Dominick, who glared at me and then excused himself to go find his sister since the service is about to start. I heard Matteo is in attendance, but I haven't seen him, and my assistant, Jack, went out to find a seat. My good friend Malcolm and his wife are also here.

But the truth is, while I have a lot of acquaintances—both college and business associates—I've mostly kept to myself since my father died, focusing on building the company from the ground up while taking care of my mom, who was shot and almost died.

"This is what Dad wanted," I tell her. "He made this deal with the Antonovs and Russos and—"

"And it was a bullshit deal," she hisses. "Arranged marriages are not how business should be done." She shakes her head and then sighs. "It's not too late, Kane. You can change your mind and do the right thing. You did the impossible. You built your father's company back up and made it more successful than he was capable of accomplishing."

"Kane, it's time," Lorenzo says, poking his head in.

"Thanks. I'll be right there."

I walk out with my mom, and she finds an empty seat, giving me one last glance, silently begging me to do the right thing.

And for a moment, I consider it. But then the music starts, and

Brielle walks out with her arm in Dominick's, and every thought flies out the window. Because even though this started as a way to get back at their family for their part in my father's demise, being with her is no longer about that. I've fallen in love with my soon-to-be wife, and I have no intention of letting her go.

She might resent me for forcing this marriage on her, but she can't deny the chemistry between us. No one makes her orgasm like I do. And she might not admit it, but she's happy. So, no, I'm not going to call off the wedding, but I will vow to make her happy every day for the rest of our lives.

When Dominick hands Brielle over to me, I shake his hand and then take hers in mine.

"You look breathtaking," I tell her.

She smiles softly, and the most beautiful shade of pink tinges her cheeks.

We step up to the altar, and the priest goes about welcoming everyone. He shares a couple of Bible verses about love, and then it's time for our vows.

Brielle mentioned that we'd be doing the traditional *repeat after me* vows, but when the priest looks at me for me to go first, I stop him before he can start, and Brielle glances at me in confusion.

"Brielle," I say, taking her hands in mine, "the way we met was untraditional."

She snorts out a laugh, and I grin when she covers her mouth in embarrassment.

"But I wouldn't have it any other way. You bewitched me the moment I saw you at the country club. Your independence, determination, and motivation are only a few of the qualities that drew me to you. And as your husband, I vow to stand by your side, nurturing and supporting your hopes and dreams, every day for the rest of our lives."

I pull the wedding band out of my pocket and slide it onto her finger. "Till death do us part."

Brielle looks down at the ring and then up at me with glassy eyes.

A tear escapes, tracking down her cheek, and I reach out, catching it with my thumb. And then she surprises me when she leans into my touch and grins at me—reinforcing my earlier thoughts that I'm making the right choice by marrying this woman.

"Miss Antonov, it's your turn," the priest says. "Would you like to say a few words?"

"No," she chokes out. "I'll … I'll stick to the traditional vows."

She averts her gaze from mine, but I lift her chin, wanting to look into her beautiful eyes as she repeats the priest's words.

When she finishes, he tells her she can place the ring on my finger, and she looks up at me in horror. And that's when it hits me— she didn't get me a ring. And why would she? I'm forcing the woman into marriage. After she picked the venue, I had a wedding planner take over because Brielle wasn't keen on planning the wedding.

"I'm sorry," she whispers, her eyes darting between me and the guests in embarrassment. My woman doesn't like to be vulnerable in public, and not bringing my ring will have everyone questioning our relationship and her character. "I … I didn't even …" She shakes her head.

"It's okay," I tell her. Then, to the priest, I say, "You can continue."

He pronounces us husband and wife, and I step toward Brielle, framing her face in my hands.

"I know I'm not the man of your dreams and this isn't how you planned to get married, but I want you to know I meant every word of my vows. Till death do us part."

Without giving her a chance to reply, I tilt her face up and press my lips to hers, kissing her for the first time as my wife.

"Let's go celebrate, wife. And then after, I plan to take you home and spend the rest of the night inside you."

TWENTY-FOUR

Brielle

"**Y**OU BEWITCHED ME THE MOMENT I SAW YOU AT THE country club. Your independence, determination, and motivation are only a few of the qualities that drew me to you. And as your husband, I vow to stand by your side, nurturing and supporting your hopes and dreams, every day for the rest of our lives."

Kane's words threw me off-kilter. We'd agreed to traditional vows, but then he veered off course and spoke the words I had longed to hear. All I'd ever wanted was a husband who saw me as an equal. And when I finally got the words, it was from a man who could give me everything I'd ever wanted … except his heart.

"I can't wait to peel this dress off you later," Kane murmurs, reminding me that we're on the dance floor, having our first dance.

After I picked out the venue, I told him I didn't want to plan the wedding, that I had too much going on. The truth was, I just didn't want to go through the motions for a loveless wedding.

I expected him to be an asshole about it. But he simply nodded and said he'd handle it. And he did. While it's not on the beach with only our family and friends, like I would've wanted, the wedding and reception are beautiful and classy.

"Kane"—I glance up at him—"I really am sorry that I forgot

about the ring." I had one job—to get a wedding band for him—and it completely slipped my mind.

"You didn't ask for this," he says, smiling down at me, but unlike when he usually smiles at me, it's pained. "But I meant my vows. Every word of them. I never planned to get married, wasn't looking for it. But from the moment I saw you, I knew I needed to make you mine."

"Because of the deal my family made with yours …"

"No." He wraps his fingers around the side of my neck and meets my eyes. "Because, despite the designer clothes and makeup and ice-queen facade you put on for the public, I see you, Princess, and I want to spend the rest of my life making you happy."

"Kane," I choke out, confused by his words and unsure what to say to that.

This is an arranged marriage gone wrong.

A forced marriage.

So, why does he sound like he wants it to be more?

Before I can ask him, the song ends, and everyone claps. The deejay welcomes everyone onto the dance floor, and since I need a minute to collect my thoughts, I excuse myself to the restroom. But before I can get away, a beautiful woman who looks just like Kane approaches.

"Mom, this is Brielle. Brielle, this is Silvia Morgan, my mom."

"It's nice to meet you, Ms. Morgan," I say politely.

"Please, call me Silvia. You look beautiful."

"Thank you. I didn't know you would be in town. Will you be staying?"

Silvia glances between Kane and me. "I think I'm going to stick around for a little while, spend some time with my son, and I would love to get to know you as well. I've rented a condo downtown …"

"What?" Kane asks. "We have the in-law suite behind the house."

"I know, and I appreciate that. But I'd imagine, with you being newlyweds, you'll want your privacy."

She winks playfully, and my stomach drops because, like my mom, she doesn't know the marriage is a farce.

"I have to use the restroom," I tell them both and then take off.

"You okay?" Nicole asks when she walks into the restroom immediately after me.

"He said he meant his vows," I whisper. "I just don't understand."

"A lot of people who get married the way you did end up having feelings."

"Not me," I choke out, even though we both know I'm lying. "He forced me to marry him, the same way the men in my life have forced their wants and needs and demands on me my entire life. I might be attracted to him, but I can never love Kane."

I look in the mirror and make a silent vow to never let Kane in. "He might have pretty words, but this relationship isn't real. And it never will be."

"I'm tired," I say a few hours later when we walk into the empty house.

Kane frowns but nods in understanding. "Do you need help taking the dress off?"

"No, I got it," I say, my tone harsh.

I head inside the bathroom, slamming the door behind me, and when I can't get the dress undone, I rip it so I can get it off. It doesn't matter. I have no intention of saving the dress. It's just another reminder that our marriage is bullshit. Kane might've meant his vows, but does it matter if they're not accompanied by his heart?

Underneath the dress, I'm wearing a white lace bridal set that I will not be putting to use. I take them off, tossing it into the pile with my dress, and then I grab my makeup remover and start washing my face. When my eyes catch a glimpse of my rings, I pull the gaudy one off my finger and set it in the soap dish, only leaving the wedding band.

I shower, and when I go out to the bedroom, Kane isn't there. So, I get dressed, and then I slide into bed, where I refuse to cry myself to sleep. All these men have taken enough from me. I'm not going to let them have my tears too.

TWENTY-FIVE

"**M**ORNING," BRIELLE MUTTERS, JOINING ME IN THE bathroom.

When I came back to the room last night and found her asleep, I went down to my office and worked for a while, giving her some space.

I don't know what happened last night, but it feels like all the progress we'd made was wiped out.

"Morning," I say back, sticking my toothbrush in my mouth.

I'm not shocked to see her in here with me since she joins me every morning to shower and get ready for the day, but I am surprised she's doing it after the way she pushed me away last night.

Maybe she was just tired?

She grabs the toothpaste, applies some onto the brush, and when she drops the tube, my eye catches her engagement ring in the soap dish.

She took it off.

"You're not wearing the engagement ring?" I ask.

She glances down at it and flinches. It's so quick that if I wasn't watching her, I wouldn't have caught it—but I was, and I did.

"I'm sure a lot of women would love the ring," she blurts out, not looking at me. "But it's just not for me. I always imagined when I was proposed to, it would be because the man I was with loved me, and the ring would symbolize that love." She shrugs. "This ring is huge, and like I said before, it just looks like it's trying to make a point." Her eyes finally meet mine. "And I don't like the point it's trying to make."

The point it's trying to make.

The forced marriage.

I open my mouth to tell her that my feelings have changed, that I'm falling in love with her, but I stop myself, worried that I'll scare her away. I tried to tell her through my vows yesterday, and then she shut me out. Maybe she's not ready to hear it yet.

"What are you up to today?" I ask instead, like a fucking coward. "I was thinking we could—"

"I have plans," she says, cutting me off. "Have a good day."

And just like that, I've been dismissed.

"If you love her, just tell her."

"It's not that easy," I say to my mom over the phone. "I tried to tell her with my vows, and I think I spooked her."

"So, talk to her," Mom insists. "I've never been married, but one of the most important things in a relationship is having open communication."

Fuck, she's right. I need to talk to her.

We hang up, and since Brielle just left, I get in my car to follow her. She always goes to the coffee shop, so I'm not surprised to find her there. Only, before I can get out to join her, she's walking out with her coffee in hand and heading to her car like she's in a rush.

She's also not dressed in her usual workout gear.

She takes off down the street, and since I'm a nosy bastard, I follow her. She flies through the streets in her cherry-red Porsche, not stopping until she arrives at … the Humane Society?

She gets out, drinks the last of her coffee, tosses it in the trash, and then walks inside. Since she clearly didn't want me to know what she was doing, I drive away, letting her do her thing.

I have nothing else going on, so I head to the office to get some work done. When there's nothing else to do, I go to the country club to get lunch, where I find Lorenzo sitting at the bar with a whiskey in his hand.

"A little early to be drinking?" I say lightly, sliding onto the seat next to him.

"Getting drunk is the only way to survive living with that bitch." He swallows the rest of his drink in one go and gestures for the bartender to bring him another.

I order a drink as well as a chicken Cobb salad and then glance at Lorenzo. "You okay?"

We don't know each other, but anyone can see how defeated the guy is.

"Leo is barely three months old, and I don't know how I'm going to spend the next several years with this woman. She's driving me fucking nuts."

"I'm assuming Leo is your son?"

"Yeah." The bartender sets our drinks down, and he takes a sip of his. "Leonardo Sparks. She didn't even give him my last name, yet she's acting like she's in love with me. Says she wants to be a family. She's up to something. She has to be. She always is."

"Well, while you figure it out, at least you have your son under your roof, and once you find out the game she's playing, you can plan your next move. Have you told Dominick and Matteo yet?"

Lorenzo shakes his head. "Not yet. They'll want to *remove* her from the situation, and maybe it makes me soft, but I don't really want to kill the mother of my child, even if she's a conniving bitch."

He sighs. "I've always tried to do the right thing. Be a good guy. My dad taught me to be respectful to women. Even though my mom wasn't his first choice as a partner, he was always good to her. But I swear to God, if I find out this bitch is fucking with me, I'm going to make her regret showing up on my doorstep."

"Nah." I shake my head as the bartender places my salad in front of me. "You won't make her regret showing up because, without her doing so, you wouldn't have known you had a son. You'll make her regret not handing him over to you and walking away."

I glance at Lorenzo, and he nods in agreement.

"Let me find out she's fucking with me, and I'll make sure she regrets ever coming to Harbor Point to begin with."

After lunch, I go home, and the house is quiet. After getting a workout in and swimming a few laps in the pool, I heat up dinner, but Brielle says she's busy, so I save her some and eat alone, wondering if this is how our marriage is going to be.

And this continues every day for the next week. When she's home, she pretends I don't exist. She refuses to eat the leftovers I save her, and when she leaves, she doesn't say where she's going, and she no longer hangs out at the coffee shop so I can't corner her there.

The following Sunday, since I have nothing else going on, I follow her to the coffee shop, hoping to put an end to this bullshit. I get she's upset that I forced her to marry me, but we both know she still wants me. She might glare daggers at me to my face, but when she thinks I'm not looking, I see the lust and longing in her eyes.

Like last Sunday, when I pull up, she's already got her coffee in hand, heading back to her car. And like last Sunday, when I follow her, we end up at the Humane Society. But instead of driving away, I park and follow her inside, only to be stopped by her standing in the doorway with her arms crossed over her chest.

"Daniil said you were following me. Why?"

Shit, I forgot about her guard. At least that means he's doing his job.

"Why are you here?" I ask, ignoring her question.

"Brielle!" an elderly woman says, coming around the desk. "I missed you last week."

"How was your trip to visit your kids?" Brielle asks, giving the woman a hug.

"Cold!" The woman laughs. "But it was a good visit. I was surprised to see that you volunteered the day after your wedding. No honeymoon?"

Brielle smiles sheepishly at the woman, and I curse myself for not considering she might've wanted to go on a honeymoon. She barely wanted anything to do with the wedding, so I figured a honeymoon was out of the question.

Jesus, my mom was right. We really do need to talk.

And then the woman's words hit me.

"You volunteer here?"

Brielle glances at me and nods.

"Is this your husband?" the woman asks, extending her hand. "I'm Jude, the manager here. Brielle has been volunteering here for a long time now. And her donations have saved so many animals."

"I'm Kane."

"It's wonderful to meet you. Brielle, why don't you show him around? I know a certain someone will be excited to see you."

The woman winks, and Brielle forces a smile.

I get a visitor badge, and Brielle takes me into the back, where all the animals are, saying hello to several of them along the way.

"I love animals, especially cats," she says after a few minutes. "I found one once when I was little." She opens the door to a decent-sized room, and the cats lift their heads to acknowledge us. "I snuck him into our house and named him Pebbles because I loved Fruity Pebbles."

She laughs softly and kneels in front of a cat toy. A brown and black striped cat pokes its head out and starts to meow, climbing into her lap like they've been friends for years.

"I used my money to get him a litter box and food, and since I was only thirteen at the time, I carried it all back myself. My dad had said no pets, and when he found out that I had one hiding in my room, he threw it out, and it got hit by a car and died."

She snuggles her face into the crook of the cat's neck, and it purrs loudly.

"I always said that when I finally got out from under Andrey's thumb, I would have a house full of cats." She laughs, and it's the first real laugh I've heard from her since we got married.

"But I moved in with Dominick, and since Peyton is allergic to cats, I started volunteering here." She smiles down at the cat. "I get to give them all the love they deserve. Don't I?" she says to the cat she's still holding. "This is Molly. She was found on the streets, and she had gotten into a fight of some sort, so her ear had to be stitched. When we called the owner, they said they didn't have time for a pet and we could keep her. She's a bit older at three years old, so she hasn't been adopted yet. Everyone wants the cute kittens, not the older, damaged cats." She rubs the tip of her ear lovingly.

She introduces me to several of the cats, but it's clear Molly is her favorite, and once I head out, leaving her to volunteer, I know what I need to do.

Just like the cat, Brielle wants to be loved. And that's exactly what I'm going to do—I'm going to love the hell out of her.

TWENTY-SIX

Brielle

"**M**OLLY, WHERE ARE YOU?"

It's the end of my shift, and I always come back to say bye to Molly, but I can't find her. I check in the cat house she loves to lie in, but she's not in there.

"Hey, Bri," Sandra, one of the other volunteers, says, stepping inside and giving me a sympathetic smile. "Molly was adopted."

I freeze in place. "What? When?"

I was only gone for a couple of hours, feeding and cleaning all the other cat rooms and cages. How the hell did she get adopted without me knowing?

"A little bit ago. They were preapproved, so it was a quick process."

"Oh, okay." My nose stings, and tears prick my eyes. "I wish I had gotten to say goodbye, but I'm glad she got to go to a good home."

"She did." Sandra grins. "You heading out?"

"Yeah, all the rooms and cages are clean. I'll see you in a few days."

"See you then."

Since I have nothing else going on today, I stop by Dani and Matteo's to see them and their adorable baby, and then I go over to the Pilates studio to get a workout in.

It's going to take about thirty days for the sale to go through, and once it does, I'll be closing it down for renovations.

Since this is my first time owning a small business, I've hired an accountant who's familiar with businesses like mine to walk me through everything, and the studio manager has agreed to stay on. She's pregnant and due soon, so it was perfect timing. She should be ready to come back around the same time the studio is ready to reopen.

When I get out of my class, I shower and change out of the workout outfit I keep here, and then I check my phone, finding a text from Kane, asking when I'll be home. I consider coming up with an excuse to stay out longer, but when I can't think of one, I text back that I'll be there soon.

I pull in and park in the garage and then head in through the mudroom, which leads into the kitchen, where I find Kane cooking dinner.

"Smells good."

"I would hope so. It's one of your favorites." He lifts the lid, and the spices permeate the air, making my stomach growl in hunger.

"Cajun seafood pasta. How did you know?"

"Nicole." He smirks. "She seems to be Team Kane."

I roll my eyes. "She's a romantic. You make this yourself?" I ask, quirking a brow.

Since I've moved in, all the complex meals are made and delivered by the chef he hired.

"I'm heating it up myself." He smirks, making me laugh.

I stick my finger in the sauce and bring it to my lips, moaning at how good it is. I'm about to dip my finger in for another taste when I hear a meow, making me stop in my place.

"Did you hear that?"

"What?"

Another meow, and then Molly prances into the kitchen.

"Molly!" I bend down and scoop her into my arms.

She nuzzles into my neck, and tears prick my eyes as it hits me what Kane did.

"You adopted her for me," I choke out, holding her closer to my chest.

Kane glances at me and smiles softly. "I'm starting to realize I would do pretty much anything for you. But, no, I didn't adopt her …"

My heart sinks at the thought of having to give her back.

"You did," he says, moving the pan off the burner and turning it off. "She's yours. You were already approved from volunteering there. I just filled out the paperwork so I could surprise you. Her litter box and crap are in the guest bathroom, and they gave me the food they feed her so you have some until you decide on what you want to feed her."

"Kane," I breathe, tears sliding down my cheeks, "you're making it really hard for me to hate you."

His mouth curves into a playful grin as he steps toward me. "Good, because you've made it really hard for me to hate you."

I stare at him for several seconds, and Molly squirms to get down, so I let her go, leaving nothing between Kane and me. He takes another step so our bodies are flush.

"You're an Antonov, so by default, you're supposed to be the enemy." He clasps my jaw. "But I can't find it in me to hate a single thing about you."

"I don't think I hate you either," I admit.

Kane's eyes descend to my mouth, and my heart lurches in my chest when I think he's going to kiss me.

But instead of doing so, he tightens his hold on the side of my neck and murmurs, "Tell me I can kiss you, Princess," once again proving how well he already knows me. He doesn't even know what I've been through, yet he understands the control I crave.

"Kiss me."

The words aren't even all the way out of my mouth before Kane's mouth is on mine. A whimper escapes me, and he lifts me into his arms, carrying me over to the counter and spreading my legs. And then we're all teeth and tongues and hands as we quickly remove each other's clothes.

"Fuck," he groans, wrapping his fingers around the base of my throat and then peppering kisses along my sensitive flesh.

"Do you have any idea what this body does to me?" He palms my breast with one hand while keeping his other wrapped around my throat and then sucks my nipple into his mouth.

"Harder," I breathe out.

Kane glances up at me, and it takes everything in me not to shy away in embarrassment for what I'm asking.

"You're going to have to be more specific," he says, his gaze filled with lust. "You want me to choke you or suck that pretty nipple harder?"

"Choke me," I blurt out.

He stares at me for several seconds, and I'm about to tell him never mind when he nods and says, "We need a safe word."

"What? Why?"

"Because if I'm going to do anything that could hurt you, even if you want it, we need to make sure it's done safely. I'm not an expert on BDSM, but I know enough to know that we need a safe word."

"Okay, um …" I glance around, unsure what to use as a safe word. I've read about them in articles when I was researching my craving for rough sex after being raped, but I never considered I would be in the position to make one. And then I remember that one article suggested you pick a word you'd easily remember but wouldn't use on a regular basis. "Roses."

It's my favorite type of flower, and I'll easily remember it.

"Roses," Kane confirms.

"Yeah. Roses."

Kane nods and then tightens his hold around my throat, crashing his mouth against mine. His tongue sweeps across the seam of my lips, and I open, giving him full access to taste and devour me.

"Tell me it again," he murmurs against my lips.

"Roses."

"Good girl."

His lips connect with mine once again, and his hand glides up my thigh and delves between my parted legs. He thrusts his fingers into my core, and I moan into his mouth at the delicious intrusion.

He takes my noises as his cue to thrust back in harder, and I clench around his fingers, already close to coming.

His skilled mouth devours mine while he squeezes my throat, slowly cutting off my air supply little by little as he fingers me. When my orgasm starts to creep up, Kane senses it and applies more pressure around my neck, heightening my senses.

"That's it, baby. Come all over my fingers."

At his command, I fly over the edge, pleasure tearing through my body. He tightens his grip around my neck a bit more, and fireworks shoot off behind my lids as I come long and hard around his hand.

While I'm mid-orgasm, Kane yanks his fingers out of me and pulls me off the counter, flipping me onto my stomach so I'm leaning against the edge, and thrusts into me from behind. One orgasm rolls into two, and I scream out his name as he grips the curve of my hip with one hand and shoves his fingers into my mouth with the other, forcing me to taste my arousal.

"Goddamn, you're perfect," he groans.

His movements turn erratic, desperate, and then he sinks his teeth into the delicate flesh of my shoulder. Another wave of pleasure rolls through me as Kane drains every drop of his orgasm into me.

As we work to catch our breath, an easy calmness settles over us as it hits me—Kane isn't the man I wanted to marry, but he's quickly becoming the man I want to be married to.

And that scares the hell out of me.

"Isn't she just the cutest?"

I snuggle Molly into my chest, and she purrs softly.

After our delicious dinner, Kane showed me Molly's bathroom—yes, I've deemed it hers, and I'm already planning on how to decorate it and make it fit for the little princess she is. Then

I assumed we'd go our separate ways, like we do most nights, so I was a bit taken aback when he asked if I wanted to watch a movie—and even more shocked when I agreed.

While we were scrolling, I saw *Gossip Girl* and made him click on it when he said he'd never even heard of it. We're two episodes in, and Molly is cuddling between us, happy to finally have a home.

"She's adorable," he says dryly.

"Having rescuer's remorse already?"

"No, but she's a total cockblock," he complains. "Every time I think about touching you, I swear she glares at me."

"You should've thought about that when you decided to use her to bribe me back into your good graces."

I quirk a knowing brow, and he shrugs.

"It worked. I just didn't realize how needy cats were."

"Just because she wants to be cuddled and loved doesn't make her needy." I lift her up and give her kisses. "I'm going to order you a custom collar," I say to her. "I bet Gucci or Versace sells them. Which do you prefer?"

Kane chuckles. "Do you think—" His words are cut off by the sound of his phone ringing. "It's Dominick."

"Put it on speaker."

He clicks Accept. "Dominick, what's up?"

"We're in the middle of watching *Gossip Girl*," I add. "So, it'd better be important."

"We have a problem," Dominick says, his tone serious. "A body's been found at the construction site down at the waterfront property."

Kane's eyes meet mine. "Do they know who it is?"

"No, but I have to ask—"

"It wasn't me," Kane says, his gaze never leaving mine. "I want this expansion to be a success the same way you do. And in case you forgot, I have millions invested as well."

Dominick curses under his breath. "I have our legal team on

it. They're in connection with our source inside the police station, and I'm hoping we'll have more answers soon. In the meantime, we're meeting at my office tomorrow morning, eight a.m."

"I'll be there."

Dominick hangs up, and Kane exhales heavily.

"It has to be whoever is messing with your family."

Molly uncurls, and Kane reaches over to pet her belly.

"Yeah, but the problem is, we're no closer to finding out who that is. The mayor's house has been bugged, but he hasn't given shit away. We know it has something to do with Carlos Santiago since two people have mentioned his name, but that's all we've got.

"Have you combed through your brother's things? He might've been working with whoever it was. We can't prove it, but we think Anthony was working with them because he didn't have the money or resources to do some of the things he did."

"I have." Kane leans back and scrubs his face in frustration. "Enrique was smart and wiped his devices before he died."

"I hate to say this, but maybe someone should reach out to Hillary and see if she knows anything."

Kane glances at me for several seconds and then smirks. "If I tell you something, you have to swear not to tell anyone."

"What?" I ask nervously.

"You have to swear. It's not my place to say anything, so if you open your mouth, Lorenzo will know I told you."

"Tell me!"

"Lorenzo has been in touch with Hillary."

"What?" I shriek. "Why? Oh my God, don't tell me he's back together with her."

"Worse," Kane says dryly. "She showed up at his house with a baby."

"No!"

"Yep. He had a paternity test done, and the baby is his."

"And he told you and not my brothers?"

"I was at the country club when he was getting shit-faced while he was waiting for the test results."

"Poor Lorenzo. He's stuck with her for life now."

"That's part of why he doesn't want to tell your brothers. He's afraid they'll take her out."

I snort out a laugh because he's not wrong. Matteo loves Lorenzo like a brother, and he would definitely consider killing her if he thought it was for the best for Lorenzo and the baby.

"He hasn't told them yet, but he told me that he asked Hillary if she knew anything about Carlos Santiago, and she said Enrique didn't tell her anything."

"Ugh, I can't believe she's back in his life. Lorenzo is such a good guy, and to be forced to live with that gold-digging bitch is cruel."

"He's not being forced to do anything," Kane says, glancing at me. "She had his baby, and he wants them under his roof."

"He might as well have been forced." I scoff. "It's that or let her crazy ass live somewhere else with his baby. There's no way I would leave her with my baby. He's doing what he has to do."

"Speaking of babies …" Kane hits me with a gorgeous smirk and runs his hand up my leg to the top of my thigh.

Since I changed into my pajamas to watch TV, I'm in a tiny cotton tank and shorts, so his fingers easily slide underneath, finding my core quickly.

"Fuck, no panties," he mutters, his whiskey-colored eyes filled with heat.

I part my legs to give him better access, and he pushes a single finger into me.

"Still full of my cum, I see."

Ah, so this is where he's going with his *speaking of babies* comment …

"I'm on birth control," I point out. "Feel free to fill me with your cum."

I can't stand the way it drips out of me for hours afterward, but sex without a condom is way better than with one.

"You could get off it."

"I could make you pull out every time."

He chuckles. "I'm just saying, if you wanted to get off your birth control, I wouldn't be opposed to you getting pregnant. I saw the way you looked at Dani and Matteo's baby. You can't tell me you don't want one."

Emotion clogs my throat as I think about what it would feel like to be able to carry a baby to term. To give birth to him or her and love them for the rest of my life.

But then I think about the way Matteo looked at Dani, and my heart sinks.

"I don't want to have a baby," I tell Kane. "I know you said it was part of the deal, but ..."

"Ever?" he asks, his brows tightening in confusion.

"I don't know." I shift so his hand slides out of my shorts and stand, taking Molly with me. "Maybe one day, but not now."

Not when my husband doesn't love me.

When he only wants a baby to secure an heir and intertwine our families' blood.

He might be a savvy businessman, dressed in a designer business suit, but he's still the son of Joseph Rothschild—who was part of one of the most notorious crime families on the East Coast. And if I've learned one thing from growing up around men like him, it's that business always comes first.

"I'm tired. I'm going to bed."

I barely make it a few feet away before Kane's on me, wrapping his arms around my torso and resting his chin on my shoulder.

Molly, the damn traitor, jumps out of my arms, leaving the two of us alone in the living room.

"If you don't want to get off birth control, you don't have to." Kane turns me around and pulls my gaze up to meet his. "But that doesn't mean every time I come in your tight little pussy, I won't be hoping my swimmers are strong enough to get past whatever barrier those pills provide."

He captures my mouth with his and then lifts me into his arms. And since I can't stay away from my husband, I wrap my arms around his neck and let him walk us to the room, where he tests the effectiveness of my birth control several times.

TWENTY-SEVEN

Kane

"WHAT THE FUCK DO YOU MEAN, IT'S MY DAD?"
When I arrived at Dominick's office this morning to meet with him, Matteo, and Lorenzo to discuss the dead-body incident, the last thing I expected was to be told that the body they'd found was my father's.

"They were able to run the DNA through their database, and it's your dad. They also found this note." Dominick hands me a folded piece of paper. "I'm assuming it's to you since you're the only one invested in the waterfront expansion with multiple brothers."

Sides were chosen. Your brothers chose mine. Too bad you didn't make the same choice. Now, you and your wife will pay.

"Quite the poet." I drop the paper onto the desk and sit back in my seat.

"She's fucking nuts," Matteo says.

"And if we've learned anything, it's that the crazy ones shouldn't be taken lightly," Lorenzo adds, no doubt referring to the woman he's cohabitating with—and still hasn't told his friends about.

Which reminds me …

I pull out my phone and dial Daniil's number.

"You have eyes on Bri?" I ask him when he answers on the first ring.

"Yeah. She's—" His words are cut off by the sound of chaos on the other line, and my heart drops.

"Daniil!" I yell. "What the fuck is happening?"

When he doesn't answer, I look up at the guys, who are staring at me with a mixture of concern and confusion.

"Something just went down." I pull up the tracking app I have on Brielle's phone. "Make sure your wives are locked down. I need to get to Bri."

I rush out of the office and down the stairs, not wanting to wait for the elevator, while I call Brielle repeatedly.

With each nonanswer, my heart rate picks up. I know something is wrong.

I jump into my car, and I'm about to take off when Matteo slides into the passenger seat.

"Dani and Alba are safe. I have the condo secured with four guards on them. Let's go."

The drive to the Pilates studio feels like it takes hours instead of minutes, and when we arrive, there are already cops and firefighters at the scene.

"Where is she?" I ask Nicole the moment I see her standing with the officer.

"There was a fire next door, and when we walked out, a water main burst," she cries. "I was so focused on everything that was going on that I didn't notice that she was being taken. I'm so sorry."

"Fuck," Matteo hisses.

I follow his line of sight and see Daniil's lifeless body on the ground. A few feet away is Josh, the other guard assigned to Brielle— also dead.

"Did you see anything?" I ask her. "A certain color car? Was it a man or a woman who took her? Anything that could help?"

She shakes her head, trying to remember, when it hits me.

"I have another tracker on her."

I pull out my phone and go to the tracking app I recently had installed. "They're heading south on I-95. Let's go."

"How are you tracking my sister?" Matteo asks as we get back into my car.

"Her wedding band. I installed a tracker in it, just in case." I click the screen so I can follow it on my dashboard. "With all this shit going on, I wanted to make sure I had another way to track her in case something like this happened."

"That's fucking smart," Matteo says, putting his phone to his ear.

He calls Dominick first, letting him know about Daniil and Josh so he can handle it. Then he calls one of his men, relaying the direction we're heading in so they can meet us there.

"They've stopped at the port," he says. "Same fucking place they brought Dani last year."

He calls his men working at the port and tells them to shoot first, but to make sure Brielle is safe.

"There has to be a reason they brought her there." I increase my speed, flying around the cars that are going slower. If a cop wants to pull me over, he can do so once I've got Bri in my fucking arms.

"Yeah, whoever it is, is trying to send a message," Matteo says slowly. "Carlos Santiago trafficked women before my brother shut him down. They held Dani in a cargo crate. They fucked with several of our shipments. And now they're taking Bri to the fucking port. Fuck, why didn't we put the pieces together before?" He slams his fist against the dashboard and then calls Eddy, asking him to pull the footage from the cameras in front of the studio and at the port so we can try to see who's responsible.

There's an accident on I-95, and I almost consider getting out and running to the port, but we're too far, and it will take too long.

"The guys are saying they don't see anyone there."

Finally, the traffic picks back up, and I weave in and out of the vehicles on the road.

As we're pulling in, Matteo's phone rings, and he puts it on speaker.

"Boss," his guy yells, "the cargo ship just crashed into the dock. Containers are everywhere, but we don't see Brielle anywhere."

"Don't worry about the containers," Matteo yells, jumping out of the car and running toward the docks. "Watch for my fucking sister! She has to be here somewhere."

We get to the docks, and I glance around, trying to figure out where the hell she is. The dot shows she's around here somewhere … and then my gaze lands on the other cargo ship leaving.

"Motherfucker," I hiss, realizing the crash was another goddamn distraction. "She's on that ship!" I yell at Matteo as I take off running down the dock.

They can't leave without the port pilot guiding them out, so my only hope is to get on the pilot ship. Matteo catches up to me and hands me a gun. Then we both jump onto the pilot ship, along with three other men.

"Remember," Matteo says as the pilot ship heads toward the side of the cargo ship, "my sister is on board. Shoot to kill, but make sure she's safe."

Brielle

My walls were down.

Everything had been going well lately.

For the first time in years, I looked forward to going home and spending my evening curled up with a man.

He might not love me, but it's clear he cares about me. It's in the way he hugs and kisses me and gives me affection. He stocks my favorite protein shakes in the fridge. He orders my coffee and breakfast ahead to ensure I get the pastry I want. When we have sex, he makes sure I'm taken care of and always lets me take control. I could talk to him about the Pilates studio for hours, and he'd listen attentively the entire time. And he brought Molly home.

So, I let my guard down.

And when the fire alarm went off next door, causing the one in the Pilates studio to go off as well, I walked outside without thinking.

There was smoke coming out of the store, and the water main had burst. My only thought was that I was going to lose the studio I'd just closed on.

Because I'd let my guard down.

And then I was snatched up.

I watched Daniil and Josh lose their lives when they tried to save me.

And before I could call for help, my phone was snatched out of my hand and thrown into the street.

The only good thing was that Nicole wasn't taken.

I was shoved into the trunk of a vehicle and brought to the port, where my wrists were bound and I was forced into a cargo ship.

They didn't bother to cover my eyes, which told me I was going to die.

And my only hope at this point is that they make it quick.

But when two huge men corner me with malice in their eyes, it hits me that they're going to torture me before I die.

"We were told to send a message," one of the guys says, his accent thick, slicing the ropes on my wrists because he obviously doesn't see me as a threat.

I'm not sure where they're from, but when he speaks to the other man, it's clear they're Hispanic. Because I was raised to be a good trophy wife, Andrey made me learn Spanish, Italian, and Russian, so I understand every word they're saying in Spanish.

"I get her first. Then you can have her next."

"Fine. Then we'll kill her."

"He didn't say to kill her. Only to send a message."

"Killing her will send a message."

They both laugh, and I close my eyes, mentally preparing for what's about to come.

The first guy advances on me, and I scream even though it's

futile. I claw at his arms and neck and face, refusing to go down without a fight.

He yells at the other guy to hold me down.

I kick and scream and attack him until my wrists are twisted behind my back, and my shoes, yoga pants, and underwear are ripped from my body.

I try to turn off my brain, to think happy thoughts to help me mentally escape.

My precious cat, Molly.

Working out at the Pilates studio.

Coffee with Nicole.

Spending time with my niece and nephews.

Cooking Sunday meals with my mom.

Kane and I cuddling on the couch and watching TV.

But still, visions of Anthony forcing himself on me hit me hard, and it's like I'm in my apartment all over again with no control.

Tears prick my eyes as the monster in front of me forces my legs open, but I refuse to give him anything more than he's going to take without my permission.

"You little cunt," he spits, unbuckling his belt. "I'm gonna tear you—"

He doesn't finish his thought, falling to the ground as blood pours out of his head. Before the other guy can run, a bullet hits him in the forehead, taking him out as well.

"Fuck!" my brother shouts, lowering his gun and averting his eyes from my naked body, while Kane scoops up my clothes and helps me get dressed.

"You saved me," I mutter, nuzzling my face into Kane's neck as he scoops me into his arms and carries me out of the container.

My entire body is shaking, and I'm struggling to catch my breath. But I'm okay. Kane saved me before that nasty asshole could rape me.

"Matteo killed the men," Kane corrects, snapping me out of my thoughts. "He's got damn good aim."

Matteo's glassy eyes meet mine, and I'm momentarily taken

aback by the raw emotion shining in them. But then I remember how much guilt he felt when he found out I had been raped before. Matteo's always been the brother hell-bent on protecting me, and it nearly killed him to know he hadn't protected me when I was younger.

For years, I thought my brothers knew what Anthony and Andrey had done to me, but I should've known that they never would've gone along with that. They might be driven by their business, but they've proven repeatedly how much they love me and would do anything to protect me.

"Thank you for saving me," I choke out.

Matteo nods once and then closes his eyes, and when he re-opens them, he's back to the normal Matteo—the one who hides his emotions.

"I might've killed them, but Kane had the tracker on you and knew where to find you," Matteo notes. "Another minute, and we wouldn't have been able to get onto the pilot ship to get to you."

"Wow, am I dreaming, or are my husband and brother getting along?" I half joke to lighten the mood.

Kane chuckles and kisses my forehead. "I'm glad you're okay, Princess. Do we need to take you to the hospital?"

"No." I burrow closer into his chest. "You got to me before they could do anything."

It takes a little while for the ship to dock back at the port, but the entire time, Kane never lets go of me. When we get off the ship, Matteo insists Kane take me home while he stays to deal with the bodies.

"They said they were supposed to be sending a message," I tell Matteo before we leave.

He nods. "I know you want to be independent, but …"

"I know. I'll lie low for a while. And I'd like to cover the funeral costs for Daniil and Josh," I choke out.

It hits me that Daniil is gone. Paying for their funerals won't make up for the fact that they died, trying to save me, but it's the least I can do. I didn't know Josh well, but Daniil had become like a big brother to me, and it guts me that his life is over, all because of some bullshit fight over territory.

"C'mon, wife," Kane says, setting me into the passenger seat of the car. "Let's get you home."

I go to reach for my phone to check on Nicole when I remember I don't have it. "Hey, Kane … how did you track me when they threw my phone?"

"Your ring," he says, tapping on the wedding band. "I had a tracker put in it when it was custom-designed. After everything I'd seen, growing up, like walking in on my mom almost bleeding out on the floor, I wasn't going to risk not having a way to find you." He takes my hand in his and squeezes it. "I'll always find you, Princess."

My heart swells in my chest.

His words shouldn't affect me the way they do.

But I can't help it.

I'm falling in love with my husband.

And I think I'm actually okay with that.

TWENTY-EIGHT

Brielle

"YOU THOUGHT YOU COULD GET AWAY WITH THIS?" ANTHONY shouts as he holds my hands down. "This body was supposed to be mine!"

"Brielle, baby, wake up."

My eyes pop open, and I suck in a harsh breath, taking in my surroundings.

I'm in Kane's home—safe.

"Fuck, Bri." Kane pulls my trembling body into his arms. "Please talk to me. There's no way these are random nightmares."

He strokes my sweaty hair back, and my heart rate starts to slow.

I've been having this same nightmare every night for the past week, ever since I was taken and almost raped, and every night, Kane gently wakes me up and holds me, telling me that I'm okay, and comforts me until I'm calm enough to go back to sleep.

"If you won't talk to me, maybe you could talk to someone else, like a therapist."

His eyes meet mine, filled with concern, and I shock myself when my first thought is that I want to let him in.

"I was raped," I admit softly.

His brows tighten. "At the port … I thought you said—"

"No. Years ago. But the attack at the port brought back the memories and nightmares. My senior year of college, I was in my apartment, studying, and …" I take a deep breath and then say the words that never get any easier to say. "I was raped."

"Fuck," Kane breathes out, holding me tighter. "What do you need from me? How the hell do I make this better? Is he still alive? I'll fucking kill him."

My heart squeezes in my chest at how easily my husband would take someone's life for me. But that's not what I need. I've actually been doing a lot of research about rape victims since the nightmares returned, and something someone mentioned in a forum for sexual assault victims caught my eye.

"He's gone," I tell him. "But there is something you could do for me …"

"Anything."

"I want you to try to rape me."

When Kane flinches, I realize how bad that sounded.

"What I mean is, I read that many abuse victims will try to re-enact their abuse in order to try and gain control over the damage and pain they feel with someone they trust …" I lock eyes with him. "And I trust you."

I wait to regret my words.

To feel the need to take them back.

But I don't because it's the truth.

My relationship with Kane might've started unconventionally, but what I feel for him is real.

"Princess," Kane drawls, "you have no idea what that means to me, but what you're asking …" He shakes his head. "The last thing I want to do is hurt you."

"You wouldn't," I choke out. "I've read about this. You would attack me, and I would finally get to fight back and be in control. The night I was raped, I fought back, but I couldn't stop him. And when those assholes kidnapped me last week, again, I fought back, but you saved me. I think the loss of control is what eats away at me. But maybe if we re-create it and it ends differently, that's what I'll think about instead."

Kane nods and continues to stroke my hair, and after a while, I prepare for him to tell me he can't do it or that he doesn't think it'll work.

But once again, he shocks me when he says, "Okay, I'll think about it. But you need to tell me what happened. I can't re-create it if I don't know what you went through."

"Really?" I breathe out. "You'll do it?"

"I don't think you get it," he says, looking into my eyes. "I'd do anything for you, Princess."

Butterflies attack my chest, and I reach out, cupping his nape and pulling his face toward mine for a kiss. "Thank you," I murmur against his lips.

"Don't thank me yet. I said I'll consider it, but not in our home. This is where I want you to feel safe, and if it doesn't work, I don't want you to associate it with what you went through. I need to re-search it myself first and make sure it's the right decision. And if it is, then I'll figure out the specifics … when and where."

"Okay, I understand." Just the fact that he's considering it means the world to me.

"Now, tell me what happened. Every detail you can handle."

While I relay the second-worst night of my life, Kane holds me tightly and listens to everything I say. Without telling him who raped me—because I'm not ready to admit that it was his flesh and blood—I give him all the details I can recall.

"I was studying for my accounting exam when he broke into my apartment and cornered me on my bed. He yelled at me, calling me a slut and a tease, as I fought back the best I could. He pinned me down and then raped me as I cried and begged him to stop. And once he was done with me, he spit in my face and told me I'd got-ten what I deserved."

When I'm done, Kane runs his knuckles down my cheek, wip-ing the tears I didn't know had fallen, and then lifts the back of my head, bringing my mouth up to his for a sweet kiss.

"Thank you for telling me. For trusting me with your horrid past."

His sweet words are like a balm to my soul.

"I want you," I whisper against his mouth, wanting to replace the raw memories with ones filled with Kane.

It's been a week since I've felt Kane between my legs. After I was attacked in the cargo container, he refused to do anything more than hold me.

"Not now, baby." He shakes his head. "Not after what you just shared with me."

"Kane, please," I beg, shifting so I'm straddling his thighs. "I can't help what happened to me, but this is my life, and I want to be with my husband. Don't turn me away, please."

"Fuck, Bri," he groans, "when you say shit like that, you know I can't say no."

I pull my nightie over my head, exposing my bare breasts, and Kane's eyes light up with need.

"Then don't say no."

I reach between us and pull his hard shaft out of its confines.

Then, without any foreplay, I push my panties to the side and guide him inside me, moaning as he fills me perfectly.

His hands palm my breasts, his thumbs and forefingers pinching and pulling my pebbled nipples. And as I ride my husband, I think about what he said about his sperm being so strong that it breaks through the barrier of my birth control.

And for the first time, a part of me wishes that would happen.

Because the thought of having Kane's baby doesn't seem so bad anymore.

"I'm so glad we're doing Sunday brunch," Mom says, giving me a two-cheek kiss, when we walk into Dominick and Peyton's house.

"Your brother told me what happened with those assholes at the port. How are you doing?" she asks softly.

"I'm okay," I tell her honestly. "Kane has been amazing."

Nobody knows about my nightmares, including my mom. I don't know if it's because I feel like it's a sign of weakness to let what Anthony and Andrey did get to me, but I've never told anyone … until Kane.

"Good. He seems like a decent man," she says. "I was thinking since Walter and I are home for a little while, you should show me this Pilates studio you love so much that you bought it."

"Mom, you're going to do Pilates?" I laugh.

"All this traveling has me putting on a few pounds. And nobody can deny how gorgeous and fit your body is." She waggles her brows.

"I agree." Kane comes up behind me and wraps his arms around me, leaning over and kissing the sensitive area below my ear. "My wife has a banging body. I've asked her for a private session several times, but she's yet to give it to me."

"Oh my God. Stop!" I playfully slap his shoulder.

"We should all do it," Dani says, joining us with her precious daughter in her arms. "I doubt Pilates will turn this body"—she waves down her front—"into that"—she nods toward my body—"but it can't hurt, right?"

"Your body is perfect the way it is," Matteo growls, pulling her into his arms. "You get rid of a single curve, and I'll be pissed."

I smile at my brother and sister-in-law, but for the first time, rather than feeling envious of what they have, I can relate because Kane tells me and shows me every day how attracted he is to me.

"I'm down," Peyton agrees. "After having three babies, I can definitely benefit from working out."

"It'll be a waste of time," Dominick says with a smirk. "You'll be pregnant soon."

My mom gasps. "You're having another baby?"

"No." Peyton glares at her husband. "We are not having any more babies. You want to hold a newborn? Hold Alba."

Dominick pouts, and Peyton rolls her eyes, completely unaffected.

"You know," Kane murmurs into my ear, "I bet there are a lot of positions we could try out if you gave me a private session."

"That's yoga." I laugh, turning to face him. "But nice try." I peck his lips and then walk around him so I can get my baby fix in with Alba.

Dani hands her over, and I inhale her baby scent.

My gaze meets Kane's, and the heated look he gives me has my thighs clenching.

"Jesus," Dani mumbles. "He's not even looking at me, and I swear I just got pregnant."

I bark out a laugh, startling the baby, and shake my head, soothing her before she cries. "Yeah, it's a good thing I'm on birth control because I have no doubt that he'd succeed in knocking me up."

"Umm, there's something I need to tell everyone," Lorenzo announces, making everyone stop what they're doing and look at him.

When he doesn't say anything right away, Matteo sighs. "Just say it, man. Hillary showed up with your fucking baby and is living with you."

Lorenzo's eyes go wide. "What? How did you know?"

"You're my best friend," Matteo tells him. "You don't think I know what goes on in this town? The minute she got here, my men told me. But you obviously weren't ready to talk about it, so I kept my mouth shut."

"And then, when we were trying to piece shit together and you told us that Hillary didn't know anything, I was going to have someone check on her," Dominick adds. "But Matteo said not to bother because she was staying at your house."

"Damn, so everyone knew?" Lorenzo glances around at everyone.

"I didn't," Mom says with a pout. "But nobody ever tells me anything."

Matteo chuckles. "That's because you're usually in another country." He steps toward Lorenzo. "I hate that bitch for what she did, but I know how it feels to become a father, so I'm not going to touch her. But if she fucks with you in any way, I'm going to take her ass out and make you a single dad."

Lorenzo nods in understanding.

"Welcome to fatherhood." Matteo gives Lorenzo a hug.

"I can't wait to meet my nephew," Dani adds, giving him a hug as well.

"You know it's a boy?" Lorenzo shakes his head. "Of course you do. You probably even know his blood type."

"A-negative." Matteo shrugs. "And the paternity test wasn't fucked with. Leonardo really is your son."

Lorenzo snorts out a laugh and gives my brother another hug. "Thank you for always having my back."

While we enjoy brunch, the conversation is kept kid-friendly—the men refuse to talk business in front of the kids—but afterward, the guys go to Dominick's office while the women and Walter hang out in the living room, playing with the kids.

From what Kane's told me, Matteo is having someone go to Colombia to look into the Santiago family because it's clear they're missing a piece of the puzzle.

The county has put up red tape, halting the waterfront expansion, thanks to Kane's dad's body being found on the property—which was obviously a setup since the police received an anonymous tip. But Kane isn't worried. He was more upset about his father's body being dug up to send a message than anything else.

When the guys come out, Kane's eyes find me, causing butterflies to take off in my belly.

He saunters over to me and pulls me into his arms. "Let's go away."

"What?" I pull back slightly. "Go away where?"

"Wherever you want. We never had a honeymoon, and I have a private plane that can be fueled and ready at any moment. Name the place, and we'll go. Just you and me."

The idea of going away with Kane is tempting, but …

"What about Molly?"

"Of course she's coming," he says matter-of-factly. "What do you say?"

I try to think of a reason why we shouldn't go away, but the truth is, aside from my studio, which is now closed for renovations, there's nothing keeping me here.

"Hmm … I mean, we have the beach here, so … how about we go skiing?"

Kane grins. "You ski?"

"Of course." I laugh. "We used to go all the time when I was growing up. I have two older brothers who taught me how to ski and snowboard."

"And she's actually decent," Matteo adds, butting into our conversation.

"That doesn't surprise me," Kane says. "She conquers everything she puts her mind to."

The affection in his words has me falling harder for this man.

"Let's do it," Kane says. "I have a cabin in upstate New York we can stay at, so we can bring Molly without issue. But be warned …" Kane smirks. "You might be good, but I'm the ski master."

I snort out a laugh. "Would you like to place a wager on it?"

"Sure." He leans in so only I can hear when he says, "If I outski you, you have to let me in the back door."

I freeze at his words and then quickly shake it off.

The truth is, nobody has been back there since the night Anthony attacked me. Kane has hinted at it a few times, but I played it off, not wanting to go there.

"Fine," I say. "But if I win, you have to let me in the back door."

Kane's eyes go wide in horror, and it takes everything in me to hold back my laugh.

"Fine." He copies my response.

"Fine?"

"It doesn't matter what you bet." He smirks. "Because there's no way you're outskiing me."

TWENTY-NINE

Brielle

"**F**UCK, BABY. YOU'RE SOAKING WET."

Kane peppers kisses along my flesh while he massages my clit, and I squirm against the bed, so turned on that I'm afraid I'm going to soak the sheets before I even come.

"Kane," I moan, pushing against his hand. "Please."

"Soon, Princess," he coos as he slides his hand over my backside and circles my puckered hole with the tip of his finger. "First, tell me I can take this tight ass."

I'd like to say I outskied Kane, but the fact is, while I'm a damn good skier, Kane is better. We've been at his beautiful cabin for six days, and we've been on the slopes almost the entire time, and every time, he outdoes me in both skiing and snowboarding.

But that's okay because when we aren't skiing or snowboarding, we're in his hot tub or bed, tangled around one another.

Every night, I go to bed, sated from the numerous orgasms Kane has given me, and every morning, I wake up to him giving me even more.

And this morning is no different. Except he's apparently calling in the bet that we made—and he won.

His thumb leaves my clit, and I whine at the loss of contact.

"Kane, please," I beg. "I was so close."

"And you know I'll get you there … eventually."

He moves behind me and spreads my cheeks, and I stiffen at the motion, torn between wanting to give him what he wants and not wanting to be taken out of the moment by my past.

I glance back, needing to see him, to remind myself that it's Kane I'm with and he would never do anything I didn't agree to.

Even right now, as he leans over and licks along my ass crack, he doesn't take it any further because I haven't verbally agreed.

Kane's eyes meet mine. "Tell me I can fuck this ass."

"I'm scared," I admit, making his brows furrow in concern. "I don't want it to hurt."

I don't tell him that when I was raped, Anthony sodomized me, and it hurt more than anything I'd ever experienced.

"Bri, do you think I would do anything that would hurt you?"

Without having to think about it, I give him my honest answer. "No."

And it's the truth. Maybe I shouldn't, but I trust Kane. Our relationship might've started out unconventional, and I swore I'd never love him, but somewhere along the way, it turned into so much more than I'd ever thought it would.

I've fallen in love with my husband, and I want to give him every part of me, including this. Not just because he wants it, but because I want it too. I haven't told him everything that I went through yet, but I plan to soon. I should've already done so, and then he wouldn't be thinking that my reluctance has anything to do with him.

But a part of me worries that once I tell him, he'll never look at me the same again. Not that I don't trust him with my past, but because I remember how Dominick and Matteo reacted after they learned what had happened to me. They looked at me softer, spoke to me gentler. Like I was an expensive vase on the verge of shattering and they had to handle me with kid gloves.

Kane doesn't treat me like I'm fragile, and I'm afraid once he knows the whole truth, that'll change. He'll want to put me in a bubble and protect me from the world. And I like the way Kane looks at me now.

"Okay," I tell him, hoping he doesn't catch the crack in that one word.

But of course, Kane is too observant, especially when it comes to me, and the second he hears the hesitation in my answer, he pulls me into his arms.

My back is to his front, and my ass is pressed against his hard shaft.

"Look at me," he says, turning my face toward him. "If you don't want this, we don't have to do it."

"I do," I admit. "It's just that I had a bad experience, and I'm nervous it's going to hurt."

I'm also nervous that flashbacks will hit me and it will ruin the moment. And the last thing I want is my past tainting a single moment with Kane.

"What's your safe word?"

"Roses."

"If I do anything that you're uncomfortable with, you say the word, and I'll stop."

"Okay," I breathe out.

With one hand, he tightens his hold on my head and then brings his mouth down to meet mine, kissing me with such raw passion that I melt into his touch, not realizing that his finger is back to circling my hole. He slides his finger between my legs and then, using my juices, slowly pushes it past the rim, making me groan into his mouth.

He repeats the process several times—pulling it out, gathering my juices, and then sliding it into my ass—and every time, when he pushes it into me, the pleasure intensifies. When he does it again, instinctually, I push back, wanting his finger to go deeper.

"Does it feel good?" he murmurs against my lips. "My finger in your ass?"

"Yes," I pant, needing more.

He pulls it out, and I whine at the emptiness. But like all the times before, he dips it back into my juices and then sinks not one, but two fingers into my ass.

"Oh God," I mutter, feeling so full.

"That's it, baby," he says. "I want you to fuck my fingers like a good girl."

At his words, I thrust my ass back, and his fingers slide deeper into me. There's a bite of pain from him adding a second finger, but it quickly morphs into pleasure as I fuck his fingers.

The hand that's not busy fucking my ass reaches around and circles my clit, and within seconds, I come completely undone, screaming out his name as I climax all over his fingers.

"I want your cock in my ass," I beg, shocking myself when he removes his fingers from inside me.

He chuckles and tilts my face back, kissing me quick but hard. "I'll be right back. Get on all fours and put that peach of an ass in the air."

He gives it a playful slap and then pads to the bathroom. When he returns, he's gloriously naked, and his cock is glistening with …

"Is that lube?"

"You think I'm going to fuck your ass without it?" He shakes his head. "It's one thing to put a couple of fingers in there. But I promised I wouldn't hurt you, and I meant it."

He comes up behind me, and his hard length rubs against the crack of my ass when he leans over and trails sensual kisses down my spine. When he gets to my ass, he bites my left cheek, making me squeal, and then rubs the sting away.

I can't see what he's doing, but I feel the cold liquid run down my crack, and then Kane rubs it in, making me moan in pleasure.

"What's your safe word?" he asks.

"What?" I breathe out, unable to think clearly with his fingers massaging my ass.

He stops, and I glance back.

"What's your safe word, Princess?"

"Roses. Now, please, fuck my ass."

I never thought I'd be begging for a man to take me in the back door, but here we are, and despite the orgasm he already gave me, I'm too turned on to be self-conscious about it.

Kane lines up the crown of his cock with my entrance, and when he slowly pushes in, pain courses through me.

"Oh shit, it hurts," I mutter, trying to stay in the moment before memories from my past threaten to overtake me.

"Do you need to use your safe word?"

"No," I gasp, shaking my head. "Keep going."

"Push out," he commands gently, and since I don't want this to hurt, I listen.

Slowly, he slides in, and with the inch that enters me, the pain mixes with pleasure.

When he stills, I release a harsh breath.

"You're in?"

"Halfway." He chuckles, and I groan. "Reach beneath you and stroke your clit."

My clit is sensitive, but as I play with it, the pleasure helps distract me from the pain, and before I know it, Kane's all the way in.

"God, baby, if you could see the way your ass is sucking my cock in."

"I don't need to see it. I feel it. Now, for the love of all that's holy, please fuck me."

Kane doesn't have to be told again. He pulls back and then slowly slides in, and within a few strokes, he's worked up a rhythm that has me moaning in pleasure instead of pain.

And then he reaches around and grabs my breast, pulling me up so my back is almost flush with his front, and pinches my nipple. Between his hard length buried deep in my ass, my thumb stroking my clit, and him playing with my nipple, my body grows taut, and then I come completely undone. My body shakes, my legs and pussy trembling as black spots cloud my vision.

I vaguely feel Kane pull out, and then a moment later, warm spurts hit my back. I collapse onto my stomach, completely spent, and Kane disappears and then reappears a minute later, wiping a warm cloth across my overheated flesh to clean me up.

And then I'm in his arms, and he's stroking my hair and face.

"You did so good," he coos. "Did you like it? I want you to be honest."

"I don't think I've ever come so hard in my life," I admit with a yawn, my eyes fluttering shut.

I cuddle into his chest, and he kisses my forehead affectionately.

"Good. All I ever want is to bring you pleasure."

"I have something I need to do tonight," Kane says vaguely when we return from the slopes a few hours later. After we took a nap, we headed down to the main resort for lunch, and then spent the rest of the afternoon skiing. "Do you mind hanging out by yourself for a few hours?"

He hasn't left my side the entire trip, so I'm surprised he's going to now—the day before we leave to go home—but I'm not incapable of entertaining myself.

"Sure. I might check out one of the classes at the gym. As good as the workouts are with you"—I smirk playfully—"I've been wanting to see what the gym has to offer."

His cabin is part of a gorgeous ski resort that has tons of amenities, including a state-of-the-art gym with several different types of classes.

"Have fun … but not too much." He cups my nape and pulls me in for a quick kiss. "I'm going to shower and then head out."

He doesn't ask me to shower with him, which I find odd since I can't recall a time that we haven't showered together this entire trip. But I shrug it off.

Maybe he's just in a rush. Business doesn't stop just because we're on vacation.

After he leaves, I change into my workout attire, and I'm about to head down to the main resort where the gym is located when there's a knock on the door.

Despite us being away from Harbor Point and at a private resort, Kane insisted we bring two guards with us, refusing to take any chances with my life—his words.

So, for someone to be at the door, it means Daniil and Josh allowed them to pass, or they took them out.

I look through the peephole, and my heart squeezes in my chest when I realize what I just thought.

Daniil and Josh …

They're not there because they died, trying to protect me.

It's been weeks, but several times a day, I forget that they're gone. Especially Daniil. He was with me for so long, and we got so close that it's hard to imagine anyone but him protecting me.

Once I open the door, I find Giani and Kiril standing guard, along with another guy, holding a bouquet of flowers.

"Can I help you?" I ask.

"Brielle Morgan?"

"Yes."

"These are for you." He hands me the flowers and then walks away, leaving me standing there, wondering who they're from.

"Don't worry, ma'am," Kiril says. "They've been approved."

I sag in relief. "Thank you."

I close the door and set the bouquet on the table, leaning in to smell the floral scent. They're blood-red roses and gorgeous.

Just like the roses I told him I love.

I turn them around and spot a card with my name scrawled across the front, immediately recognizing it as Kane's handwriting.

Princess,

Kiril and Giani have been instructed to bring you to me tonight at 6 p.m. Wear whatever you want. And remember your safe word—roses.

XO,

Kane

My stomach drops.

Remember your safe word …

Is this it? Is Kane going to go along with my request?

He said he didn't want to do it in our home, so while we're away would be the perfect time to do this.

Since I need a way to release some of my anxiety, I continue with my original plan and head over to the gym, joining their Pilates class. I consider texting Kane several times to ask him what he's up to, but refrain, going along with what he has planned.

Then, I spend the rest of the afternoon getting ready. I shave everything, straighten my hair, and perfect my makeup, giving myself a sultry smoky eye. I go with the dark olive faux leather trench dress I brought, pairing it with my knee-high, stiletto caramel leather Saint Laurent boots.

Since it's cold outside, I throw on my peacoat, put my phone into my clutch, and head out with my guards.

The drive is long, and when we finally arrive, I have no idea where we are.

"Ma'am, Mr. Morgan said to go inside, and you'll be directed where to go from there. We'll be out here."

"Okay."

While I trust Kane, a small part of me is nervous, as I'm unsure what's going on. In our world, it's hard to completely trust anyone, especially the man who forced me to marry him. He might have proven he cares about me, but I can't forget that our marriage is due to his need to avenge his father's death.

I walk up to the door and ring the bell, and a beautiful woman opens it.

"Good evening, Mrs. Morgan. Welcome to Elite."

I step inside, and she guides me down a dark corridor and then into an elevator. Instead of going up, we go down, and once we get off, we head down a long hallway with closed doors on both sides.

"Can I ask what Elite is?"

She turns around and grins. "Elite is New York's premier underground sex club."

Oh God. This is it.

It's happening tonight.

Even knowing what's to come, I can't help the nerves that course through my veins.

I've read up on what to expect—though every article and forum says each victim will react differently. I spoke to a therapist who worked with sexual assault victims, and she confirmed what I wanted to do was common. She even said that the way I was going about it was smart. Some victims will put themselves into horrible situations to re-enact what they went through. But the fact that I'm doing it with someone I trust shows that I'm being responsible about it.

But even after doing my research and speaking to a professional, I'm still nervous about how this will all go down. And what if it doesn't help? What if it only makes it worse?

"Here we are," the woman says, scanning the key card and opening the door. "There are drinks in the mini fridge. Feel free to get comfortable."

I glance around the room and find that, instead of it looking elegant or sexy, it's kind of bland. There's a queen-size bed in the middle of the room with a floral comforter neatly tucked into it. There's a white wicker dresser and two nightstands and a TV hanging in the corner.

On the floor is a blush-colored rug, and on the bed is …

"Oh my God," I gasp.

There are textbooks and pajamas.

Kane is re-creating the scene.

This is supposed to be a teenage girl's room.

She told me to get comfortable.

I run my fingers along the pajamas and then take a deep breath.

I can do this.

I change out of my outfit and into the pajamas and then have a seat on the bed. When nothing happens and Kane doesn't show up, I grab one of the books, curious if he picked them out or if he told an employee to randomly place a few textbooks on the bed to set the scene.

The first one is an accounting textbook. There's no way that can be a coincidence.

I flip through it, remembering all the nights I spent studying. Suddenly, the door clicks open. I glance up, prepared for what's to come. Only nobody enters.

And then I'm grabbed from behind.

I was so focused on the decor that I didn't notice there was another door.

"You fucking bitch," a masculine voice growls, throwing me onto the bed. "You're a fucking tease and a slut!"

He pins my arms to the bed, and my heart pounds in my chest.

This feels too real.

Too raw.

And for a moment, I'm taken back to my college apartment, and instead of Kane holding me down, it's Anthony.

Only this time, I refuse to cry.

I can't change what happened to me back then, but I'm in control now.

"Fuck you!" I bark, pushing against his chest and kneeing him in the balls. "Don't you fucking touch me."

He rolls to the side, groaning, but then he quickly recovers and grabs me by my hips, flipping me onto my stomach.

He's not giving up. And if I don't fight harder, I'm going to be raped again.

I think about what I was taught in the self-defense classes I took, and I lift onto my hands and knees and push back with my butt, getting him away. Then I sit up and fling my head back, hitting him in the face.

He drops onto the floor, and I scramble off the bed, ready to run out of the room, when my eyes land on the man sitting on the floor with blood dripping from his nose.

It's not Anthony.

It's Kane. My husband.

My body sags, and despite the crimson leaking from his nostrils, he catches me, pulling me into his arms.

"Fuck, Princess, you did so good," he rasps.

"I'm so sorry," I cry, letting my emotions pour out of me as I grab the hem of Kane's shirt and bring it up to his nose to stop the bleeding. "I knew it was you, but then … it was like you turned into Anthony and—"

Kane tenses, and I pause, debating whether to backtrack or carry on.

But Kane makes the decision for me when he says, "Anthony … as in Anthony Rothschild?"

"Yes," I choke out. "He raped me."

I stare at Kane's stricken face, but thankfully, he doesn't let me go.

"Jesus, Bri. Please tell me my dad didn't know."

"I don't know," I admit. "Anthony raped me, and then everything spun out of control. Andrey found out I was pregnant and killed my boyfriend and then forced me to have an abortion. My entire world had exploded, and I couldn't handle it, so I went to Russia to live with my grandparents and didn't return until Dominick showed up and forced me to come home after they both passed away."

My cries turn into sobs after I finally tell him the entire truth.

And even though I don't know what this will mean for us, it feels good to tell him everything.

"I'm so sorry, Princess," he murmurs, holding me tight. "I promise no one will ever hurt you again."

I want to tell him that he can't promise that, but the conviction in his words has me almost believing him. As I cry in his arms, with him murmuring comforting words in my ear, my last thought before I fall asleep is that right now, the only person who can hurt me is Kane. Because I've given him my heart, and now I have to hope he doesn't break it.

THIRTY

Kane

BRIELLE WAS RAPED BY MY FLESH AND BLOOD.

And then she was forced to have an abortion.

She had her boyfriend and baby ripped from her.

She fled to Russia and then was forced to come home.

Where she tried to get her life on track.

And then what did I do? I forced her to marry me.

I knew she craved control, had scars that ran deep, but I didn't know how deep they went.

As I watch her sleep, I know what I have to do to make it right …

"I can feel you watching me," she croaks out, a beautiful smile spreading across her face.

Since we re-created the scene and she nearly beat the shit out of me and then told me everything, it's like a weight has been lifted off her, and the darkness that surrounded her has been cracked open, letting the light shine in.

"I can't help it. You look gorgeous when you sleep."

"I bet I'd look even more gorgeous with your cock inside me," she teases, draping a bare leg over mine.

"I have no doubt, but we have to catch our flight."

She pouts, but doesn't argue.

Since I couldn't sleep, I packed up our stuff, so all we have to do is get dressed.

The drive to the private airstrip is quiet. Brielle is working on the Pilates studio renovations with Molly sleeping in her lap while I make plans that I wish I didn't have to make.

When we get home, I tell her I have a work emergency, and even though she looks like she wants to argue, she lets me go.

Only I don't go to my office. I go to Dominick's, where I find him and Matteo.

"Good. You're both here."

I close the door behind me to give us some privacy, not wanting anything regarding Brielle to be overheard. "Want to tell me how you act like you're so protective of your sister, yet you let her get raped and then forced into having an abortion?"

Dominick's eyes go wide, and Matteo's turn hard.

"Did my father know?" I ask without giving them a chance to answer my question since I didn't actually expect an answer.

"We don't know," Dominick says. "The conversation between our fathers wasn't recorded. From what Giuseppe said, your dad and Anthony met with Andrey to discuss the arranged marriage because they didn't want to wait any longer."

"After he fucking raped her?" I bark.

"Yeah," Matteo says, standing and getting in my face. "After *your brother* raped her."

"He's not my fucking brother," I correct. "He was a loose cannon, which is why our father never let him anywhere near the company."

"Do you hear yourself?" Matteo barks. "He wasn't good enough to run the company, but he was good enough to force my sister to marry him." He chuckles darkly. "Guess it runs in the family."

I want to tell him he's wrong, but he's only saying what I've been thinking for the past two days since I found out what Brielle had gone through.

"Regardless," Dominick says, "my guess is that Andrey was pissed that Brielle was not only having sex with her boyfriend when she was supposed to save herself for marriage, but he also took Anthony raping her personally since Andrey viewed Brielle as nothing more than property. So, he forced her to have an abortion."

"And you did nothing to stop this?" I accuse.

"We didn't know," Matteo says. "We were combing the fucking streets, trying to find her."

"We think when Andrey met up with your dad and Anthony, Andrey probably threw the abortion in your dad's and Anthony's faces since the entire purpose of the arranged marriage was to tie the families together through blood, and had the baby been Anthony's, it would've done just that."

"So, my dad got pissed," I say, the pieces all coming together, "and shot your father, and then Giuseppe used Andrey's death as an excuse to go after my father since he never got past the betrayal with Maria."

"Ding, ding, ding." Matteo slow claps. "You win a prize."

Actually, I think to myself, *I just lost the prize.*

THIRTY-ONE

Brielle

"I THINK I'M PREGNANT."

I don't know if it's because my period is late and I can't keep my food down to save my life, or because my husband has been avoiding me since I told him I was raped and forced to have an abortion, but when Kane asked if I'd accompany him to a gala this evening, I broke down in tears the minute he walked out the door and then ran to my mom's house, needing her.

Mom's eyes go comically wide. "Have you told your husband?"

I shake my head. "He's been … distant since we got home from our ski trip," I tell her. "Maybe he's just been busy, and I'm overthinking things, but it's been two weeks since we had sex."

Mom glances at me sympathetically, and I choke out a sob.

"Oh my God," I cry. "I need to fix this."

Tonight, I'm going to seduce my husband and fix whatever is broken between us.

"Oh, honey," she says, pulling me into her arms. "You don't need to *fix* anything. You need to talk to him. Contrary to popular belief, men don't want sex twenty-four/seven, and if he doesn't want to have sex, it probably means he's stressed out or he has a lot on his mind. But you won't know what's going on until you talk to him."

I know she's right, but I'm terrified of what will be said when we do talk.

What if I am pregnant and he no longer wants to be with me? What if him finding out I was raped by his flesh and blood was too much and he sees me differently now?

"I'm scared," I whisper. "I … I love him."

She pulls back, and her brows furrow in confusion. That's when I realize what I said … and what she doesn't know—that our marriage wasn't based on our feelings for each other. Only things have changed, and I've caught feelings for my husband.

But then she nods once and says, "Of course you do, and loving someone can be scary."

I sigh in relief. As much as I want to tell her the truth, I don't want her to worry about me. All she wants is for her kids to be happy and in love, and finding out her only daughter was forced into marriage will upset her.

"After everything you've been through, you deserve to be loved," she continues. "And it's clear that Kane loves you. Let him in, honey." She kisses my forehead.

"Okay," I breathe out. "Tonight, after the gala, I'll talk to him."

"Good." She smiles. "Now, what do you say we do a little retail therapy for the gala tonight to take your mind off everything?"

"Actually," I say, thinking about what Kane said regarding my shopping habits, "if it's okay with you, I'd like to stay here and bake something yummy with you, like we used to. I have plenty of dresses I can wear tonight."

Growing up, I used to cook Sunday dinner with my mom every week, and my favorite part was baking the dessert.

Mom beams. "I would love to bake with you. Any cravings?"

She winks, and I wrap my arms around her, hugging her again, thankful that I have my mom in my life. I missed her so much when I was in Russia, and even when I moved home, I struggled with letting my family in.

"I don't even know if I'm pregnant," I mutter.

"Well, there's only one way to find out …"

"Not yet," I tell her. "Right now, I just want to spend the afternoon with you."

Everything else can be dealt with later.

"You got it," she says. "What do you say we make your favorite dessert—dulce de leche?"

"Now you're talking!"

Mom and I go to the grocery store to buy everything we'll need, and then we spend the rest of the day baking my favorite dessert. Afterward, we go by Dominick and Peyton's and then Dani and Matteo's to deliver them each a dessert since we made one for everyone—where I learn my entire family is also attending the same gala.

At least I'll have the support of my family tonight.

"You got this," I say to myself several hours later, standing in front of the floor-length mirror, forcing a smile on my face as I double-check my appearance.

Tonight, I'm wearing a dress that I bought several months back but have not worn yet. It's a stretchy, off-the-shoulder sky-blue satin dress. It was formfitting when I got it, but when I put it on a few minutes ago, I couldn't ignore the fact that it almost didn't zip up, forcing myself to face the fact that there's a good chance I really am pregnant, which I don't understand because I'm on birth control and I have never missed a single pill.

Kane joked about his sperm breaking through the barrier my pills provide, but it was nothing more than that—a joke.

My hand goes to my belly, and a wave of emotion crosses over me at the thought of being pregnant with his baby. While it was nice to spend the afternoon with my mom, pushing everything else to the side—including the idea that I might be pregnant—now that

I'm back home, with nothing to distract myself, the stress is back to weighing down on me.

It will be different this time, I tell myself, gliding my hand over the area where—if I am pregnant—the baby is growing.

I won't be forced to have an abortion. I'll get to experience every part of my pregnancy. And then I'll give birth to a sweet little baby and become a mom.

I'll have everything I've ever wanted.

The baby.

The family.

A husband who …

I swallow thickly.

He might not love me, despite my mom believing he does, but there's no doubt that he cares deeply for me.

Except for the fact that he hasn't touched you in two weeks.

"Jesus, Princess," Kane says, making me spin around to face him. "You look stunning."

When I was younger, Andrey would force us to attend these types of events, and I loved dressing up, pretending like I was a princess being let out of the castle.

For the first time, I understand where Kane's nickname came from. He's always seen beyond the makeup and clothes to a girl who wanted nothing more than to escape the castle she was imprisoned in.

"Stunning enough that you want to rip this dress off me and fuck me against the wall?" I half joke as I take in my husband, who's dressed to the nines in a sharp black tux with a matching sky-blue tie—he asked me what color I was wearing so he could match me.

Kane smiles, but it's not his usual charming smile. It's filled with longing, and my heart plummets into my stomach.

"I always want to rip your clothes off," he says, bridging the gap between us. "But I don't want to be late."

I tamp down my disappointment and grab my clutch.

When we step outside of our home, a sleek black limo is waiting for us, and that's when it hits me. He never mentioned what the gala was for. And now that I'm thinking about it, neither did anyone in my family.

Kane opens the door for me and helps me slide in, and once he's in, he threads his fingers through mine, bringing our hands up to his lips for a sweet kiss, which causes me to choke up. The way he's been looking at me and touching me is like he's preparing to say goodbye, which can't be right because Kane promised *till death do us part* in his vows.

I want to ask him what's going on, but now isn't the time, so I promise myself I'll do so tonight, after we get home. And then once he confirms that it's all in my head, I'll tell him that I suspect I might be pregnant.

We arrive at the gala a few minutes later, and there's press waiting outside to take our pictures. Kane never lets go of my hand the entire time we stop to talk to the press, where I learn the gala we're attending is to support an organization that works to prevent sexual abuse as well as support victims.

I want to believe it's a coincidence, but the way Kane avoids my glances tells me this was one hundred percent intentional.

Once we're inside, we're met by several powerful businessmen, businesswomen, and politicians, including the mayor, his wife, and Nicole.

"I didn't know you were going to be here," Nicole says, giving me a hug.

"Kane dropped it on me at the last minute," I murmur. "But I'm glad you're here."

Just as we separate, my eyes catch on my family, who are walking over to us.

"Brielle," my mom says, enveloping me in a hug. "You look beautiful."

I give each of my sisters-in-law and brothers a hug, giving Dani an extra-tight hug since she went through something similar to me.

When I stop at Lorenzo, who is standing in the back with none other than Hillary, I give him a brotherly hug, then pull my attention to her.

"Hillary"—I nod toward her, having no desire to touch her—"I'm surprised to see you here."

She smiles condescendingly. "It is for a good cause."

I snort a laugh, mentally noting the irony in her words since she literally helped Enrique kidnap Dani, which led to him sexually assaulting her repeatedly.

While the servers walk throughout the room with hors d'oeuvres, we peruse the items in the silent auction, and I bid on several of them.

When Kane hands me a glass of champagne, I pretend to drink it and then get rid of the glass the first chance I get. Dani notices, tilting her head to the side slightly, and I shake mine, not wanting to discuss the possibility of my pregnancy with anyone other than my mom until I've spoken to Kane.

"Mr. Morgan," a beautiful woman says, interrupting the conversation Kane and Matteo were having with a couple of businessmen, discussing the possibility of a new project they're looking to head up. She's dressed in a white silk dress, making her naturally tan skin look flawless. Her black hair is down in waves, and her chocolate-brown eyes are laser-focused on him.

"I'm so glad to finally meet you in person." She extends her perfectly manicured hand, a flirtatious smile on her face that has my hackles rising. "I've worked with your family in the past, and I would love to discuss the possibility of us working together."

She slides Kane her business card and then excuses herself. Without looking at it, Kane pockets it, and then his attention goes back to the men he was talking to. Something about her rubbed me the wrong way. Maybe it was because she didn't actually introduce herself.

"Oh my God," Dani hisses. "I think that was her."

"Who?" I ask, a shiver racing up my spine.

"The woman who took me last year. Her eyes ... they were so

dark and cold. I would never forget them. And the way she walked … I think that was her."

"What's wrong?" Matteo asks, immediately noticing Dani's distress.

"That woman," Dani whispers, staring into the distance since said woman has already disappeared into the crowd, "the one who gave Kane her card—I think it's *her*."

While Matteo calls someone, barking orders to find the woman in question, I reach into Kane's pocket and pull the card out, gasping when I see what's written on it.

Leysa Santiago

It's not too late to change your mind.

"What were Carlos's daughters' names?" I ask Kane.

He glances down at me, his brows furrowing in confusion.

"His daughters. You said one was killed in an accident and the other was in school," I prompt, referring to the conversation we had one night during dinner when he told me what my brothers found out about the Santiago family when Matteo sent one of his men to find out info on them.

"Leysa and Laura," Matteo answers, despite being on the phone.

"It was her." I hand Matteo the card, and he curses under his breath. "And I don't think she died in that accident after all."

Since we don't want to draw attention, Dominick walks over and insists everyone act normal and stay together. So, as a family, we make our way into the banquet hall, where a five-course dinner is being served.

While the first and second courses are brought out, several people speak about the organization and the good it's accomplished. And then, before the third course is brought out, Kane is called to the podium.

"While Morgan Enterprises has graciously donated five million dollars to the cause, Mr. Morgan has matched the company's donation himself. Kane, please come on up, so we can thank you."

He gives my hand a quick squeeze and then walks up to the podium, shaking the gentleman's hand.

"There are many charities worthy of our donations, and Morgan Enterprises takes great pride in being able to donate and make a difference where we can," Kane begins. "But this cause has recently become personal to me." His eyes briefly meet mine as his words wrap around my heart like a heated blanket, warming it up and melting the ice from it. "Someone close to me went through something life-changing. She's one of the strongest women I've ever known, but her journey hasn't been easy, and my hope is that the donations we've given will help others like her heal."

He smiles at the audience, but it's sad, reminding me of the way he's been looking at me recently. "It wasn't until I did my research that I learned nearly five hundred million people a year are sexually assaulted in the US. One in three women and one in six men experience sexual violence during their lifetime. So, I encourage you to open your hearts and wallets to give to an organization that needs your help."

He shakes the gentleman's hand again and then steps down, walking back over to me. He leans in and kisses the corner of my mouth, and there's so much I want to say, but I'm too choked up to speak.

During the rest of the meal, other donors are recognized for their donations. And after dessert is served, everyone is encouraged to head outside for the fireworks display.

They announce that over fifty million dollars has been raised tonight, and then the fireworks start. I'm surprised when Kane steps up, enveloping me from behind, but rather than question it, I lean back against him and soak up the comfort he provides.

The first firework goes off and then another, and I'm so lost in the beautiful display in front of me that I don't realize when the sound of the fireworks morphs into something else.

"Get down!" Kane yells, not missing a beat.

He gently guides me onto the ground as explosives erupt around us. People scream and cry out of shock and fear, but Kane stays calm, shielding me from the sparks flying every which way. It feels like it goes on forever, and my heart not only aches for those who are hit in the cross fire, but for the charity function that has now been tainted.

Eventually, the fireworks, as well as the explosions, go silent.

"Don't move," Kane murmurs, leaving me on the ground while he assesses the situation.

"Sir, Dominick said all is clear," Giani tells him.

"All right, let's get you into the limo," Kane says, helping me onto my feet.

He wraps his arms around me protectively and guides me to the limo with Giani and Kiril flanking us.

"I hate that fucking bitch," I hiss, pissed that she ruined such an important cause just to send yet another message. "When my brothers find her, I hope they string her up like a hog and torture her."

"She's getting desperate," Kane says, holding me close. "The mayor said she donated to his campaign with the agreement that he'd force your family out of Harbor Point, not realizing that he didn't have the means to do so. So, now she's pissed and lashing out. I don't want you taking any unnecessary risks."

He leans in and kisses my collarbone, and I tilt my head to the side to give him easier access, craving his touch, but rather than taking the hint, he pulls back and takes another piece of my heart right along with him.

"Kane," I choke out, unable to handle another moment of his distance, "when we get home—"

His phone rings, cutting me off, and I sigh in annoyance, wanting to talk to him about what's going on with him. Not too long ago, he said he didn't want any walls between us. What's changed since then?

"Yeah," Kane says to whoever is on the other end. "Okay, let me drop Brielle off and make sure she's safe, and then I'll meet you there."

"You're leaving?" I ask once he hangs up, the hurt in my tone evident.

"Eddy found footage of the guy who had dug up my father's grave and linked him back to Carlos Santiago. Matteo's men found him, and they're holding him at the warehouse."

Since I know this is life or death, I simply nod in understanding.

"What were you saying before?" he asks.

"Nothing. It can wait until you get home."

After Kane ensures I'm inside and the guards are in place, he takes off, leaving me to shower alone. I've just taken off my dress when my phone rings with a number I don't recognize.

"I'm looking for Brielle Antonov-Morgan," the person says on the other line.

"This is she."

"This is Timothy Reynolds. I own the plaza where your studio is located."

"Oh, yes! How can I help you?"

"A vandalism has been reported at your place of business, and we need you to come down to speak to the officer."

"What?" I gasp. "Someone vandalized my studio? Why didn't the alarm go off?"

"Yes, ma'am. Unfortunately, the alarm was down, and we're trying to pull up the footage, but the software is a bit outdated, so we're not sure who is responsible yet, but the police are investigating it. I suggest bringing any insurance paperwork you have so it can be attached to the statement, and then you can start the process of filing a claim in the morning. The damage looks to be pretty bad."

"Okay, thanks," I choke out, feeling like the hits keep coming.

First Kane pushing me away.

Then the gala being ruined.

Now my studio, which was in the process of being renovated, has been destroyed. Not only will it set the timeline back, but I hate that I'm being sucked into my brothers' bullshit. I have nothing to do with their business, yet I'm being dragged into it anyway.

Not bothering to remove my makeup, I throw on a pair of shorts and shirt and then go in search of the insurance documents. Since

Kane was the one who helped me acquire it, he has a folder with all the paperwork. He told me he'd make me copies for my own records, but he hasn't gotten around to it yet.

I look through the folders on his desk, but none of them are it. I consider calling him, but he's probably at the warehouse by now, and I don't want to disturb him. The studio is my baby, and I need to handle it.

I open his side drawer since I've seen him put folders in there and flip through them. I'm about to close it when the label on one of the folders catches my attention—**Divorce Papers.**

My heart drops.

Has Kane been married before? He told me he had no desire to get married until he met me, so that doesn't make any sense.

I pull the file out and set it on the desk when something else catches my eye—a pharmacy bag. I open it, and my heart stops when I see what's inside. Birth control pills.

The same ones I use.

The same ones I took and still ended up pregnant.

Oh God.

I pull the bag out to deal with it later, then open the file. It's a petition for dissolution of marriage. My eyes descend to the names— *Kane Morgan and Brielle Antonov-Morgan.*

My stomach roils, and since there's no way I'm going to make it to the bathroom, I lean over the garbage can next to Kane's desk and throw up everything I ate and drank this evening.

He wants a divorce.

After everything he went through to force me into this marriage. After spending months trying to convince me that he actually cared about me. He wants a divorce.

I look at the date on the paperwork and find it's a few days after he found out I was raped and forced to have an abortion.

"… you're now damaged goods."

A single tear slides down my cheek as my father's words play on repeat in my head.

I'm pregnant with Kane's baby.

And from the pharmacy bag, my guess is, I'm pregnant because he fucked with my birth control.

Against my better judgment, I let him in.

I fell in love with him.

And now he no longer wants me because I'm damaged goods.

"*Meow.*"

I glance down at Molly circling my feet, and I pick her up, holding her close to my chest.

"C'mon, pretty girl," I say through a sob. "We need to pack."

THIRTY-TWO

Kane

The moment I step into my house, I know something is off. For one, the guards aren't manning the door, and it's quiet … too quiet. Brielle usually has music playing or the TV on, and when I walk inside, the cat usually prances to the door to greet me.

"Brielle," I call out.

I pull my phone out and call Giani, not wanting to waste any time. If something happened to her, I'll tear this fucking town apart until I find her. I promised her she'd be safe, and I'm not a liar.

"Sir."

"Where the hell is my wife?" I ask, cutting right to the chase.

"I'm sorry, but I can't say."

I run up the stairs and into our room, but it's empty.

I check the bathroom, and my eyes land on the engagement ring, still in the soap dish, only next to it is also her wedding band.

She left me.

"Can you at least tell me that she's safe?" I rasp, emotion clogging my throat.

"She is," Giani tells me. "We're with her."

"Let me talk to her."

I glance in the closet and find several empty hangers.

She packed a bag and left.

My heart thumps in my chest, the blood flowing through my

veins. She's gone, and I have no way to find her. While I was at the warehouse, interrogating the asshole who dug up my father's body, she was making her escape.

The worst part is that it was a complete waste of time. The only thing that guy could tell us was that he had been paid to dig up the body and put it on the property. This bitch is a master at flying under the radar so she can play her fucking games.

"She doesn't want to speak to you, sir," Giani says after a moment.

"She's my goddamn wife!" I boom. "Tell her I just need to speak to her for a moment."

She can't leave without knowing that I love her, that I've been pushing her away out of guilt for forcing her to marry me. She needs to know that I want to be married to her, but that I need for it to be her choice.

"Umm, sir, she said the divorce papers in your office said all that needed to be said."

Fuck! She found them. But she doesn't understand the context.

She thinks I no longer want to be married to her when that's the furthest thing from the truth.

"Giani …"

"I'm sorry, sir, but I have to hang up now."

The call cuts off, and I lose my shit. I grab the closest thing to me—a lamp—and fling it across the room so it shatters against the wall.

This isn't how it was supposed to go down.

I wanted to talk to her, explain where I was coming from, and show her that I wanted to be a better man for her.

I go to my office, and sure enough, the divorce papers, along with the pharmacy bag, are sitting on the fucking desk.

My phone rings, and I answer it without checking to see who it is, hoping it's Brielle.

"Hey," Dominick says. "I need you to come to my house."

"Is Brielle there?" I choke out.

"No, but her studio was vandalized, so I had Eddy pull the cameras, and we know who did it."

"What?" I bark. "What the fuck do you mean, her studio was vandalized?"

I'm already heading out to my car.

"She got a call tonight from her landlord. Her studio was broken into and destroyed. She asked me to file the insurance claim for her since she's not in a place to do it herself."

Fuck. That's why she was in my office. She was looking for the insurance paperwork.

"I'll handle it," I tell him as I drive out of my garage and head toward his place.

When I arrive at Dominick's house, Matteo's there, glaring daggers at me.

"Don't give me that fucking look," I tell him. "I don't want to divorce her."

"So, you, what? Drew up divorce papers for shits and giggles?" Matteo accuses. "Just when I was starting to actually tolerate your ass."

"I'm not talking to you about this."

"Yes, you are." Matteo gets in my face. "You didn't hear my sister bawling her fucking eyes out because she'd fallen in love with you, only for you to divorce her less than two fucking months later."

"I'm not divorcing her!"

"Keep your voices down," Dominick says, strolling into the room. "I have three kids sleeping, and if you wake them up, you'll be responsible for putting them back to bed."

He hands me his phone, and I click play, watching as Theodore DeSantis walks into Brielle's studio and proceeds to destroy it.

"He's a fucking dead man." I hand the phone back to Dominick. "Now, tell me where my wife is."

Matteo snorts out a laugh. "Tell us why you forced her to marry you, only to draw up divorce papers a couple months later."

"I'll tell *her* once I find her."

I need to have this conversation with Brielle. She's the priority. And I'm not going to gossip about our relationship with her brothers like we're a bunch of teenage girls.

"That's not happening," Dominick says.

"It's a small town. She has to be here somewhere, and I won't stop until I find her."

I stalk toward the front door and open it.

"And Theo's mine!" I yell back, closing it behind me.

She's not in Harbor Point.

I've searched everywhere, turned over every goddamn stone. But she's not here.

It's been a week, and I haven't been able to locate Theo or Brielle. If I didn't know how much she couldn't stand the man, I'd wonder if they were together. But there's no way she'd leave town with the asshole who vandalized her studio.

"Good morning, sir. I'm Sasha. I was working with your wife on the studio. I appreciate you reaching out."

This morning, I'm meeting with the Pilates studio expert Brielle was working with. Rather than filing an insurance claim, which would've taken months, I hired a crew to go in and clean up the studio. I refuse to believe Brielle is gone forever. And once she comes back, she'll want to open the studio, and it will be done the way she dreamed.

I spend the next thirty minutes going over everything Sasha says Brielle wanted while my assistant takes notes. And then I meet with the contractor to ensure he can make it all happen.

"I'd like it done as soon as possible."

"We have one job ahead—"

"I'll pay you double to make this project priority."

The man's eyes shine with dollar signs. "Will do."

I shake his hand and walk him out. "I look forward to doing business with you."

Four weeks.

It's been four damn weeks since my wife disappeared, and I'm no closer to her or the asshole who fucked up her studio.

The contractor is on schedule, and the studio is due to be completed in the next week. But it doesn't matter when my wife isn't here to run it.

"We'll let you know when the last phase is complete so you can come in and do a walk-through," the contractor says.

"I appreciate it."

I leave them to continue working and step onto the sidewalk to text my private investigator to see if he has any updates when I spot none other than Theodore DeSantis walking out of the restaurant across the street.

"Jack, I'll meet you back at the office," I tell my assistant, pocketing my phone.

Theo gets into his car, and I follow him into the parking garage near where he works. He drives up three floors and then parks.

> Me: I need Magnolia Parking Garage dark. I have a meeting with Theo.

> Dominick: Done.

I swing into a parking spot and get out while he takes his sweet time doing whatever he's doing in his car.

When he steps out, I don't give him a chance to notice that I'm here before I grab him by the front of his dress shirt and shove him against the wall.

"You thought you were slick, turning the security cameras off so you could fuck up my wife's studio?" I rear back and punch him in the face—once, twice. "I warned you not to touch what's mine."

I punch him in the face again and then the stomach. And even though hitting him won't bring my wife back, it feels good to let out some aggression.

I hit him again and again. He tries to fight back, but adrenaline and anger are on my side, and eventually, he hits the ground, begging me to stop.

"Enough," Dominick says, walking up next to me.

"Fuck that. I told you he was a dead man."

I kick him in the stomach, and he groans.

"He disappears, and you'll be suspect number one. While I don't give a shit if you end up in prison, my sister will."

I whip my head around to look at him. "She's back?"

"No, but she will be once you get your shit together and find her."

"I've looked everywhere. Unless you want to tell me where she's hiding …"

"You know I can't do that." He shakes his head and then nods toward Theo, who's out cold but still alive. "Drop this asshole off at a hospital," he says to his men. "And warn him what will happen if he speaks."

Dominick looks at me. "There's only one place my sister would go where she feels safe. Figure it out, and you'll find her."

"Title for her Porsche, college degree, bank account, bank account …" I've been going through Brielle's paperwork for over an hour, and one thing I've learned about my wife is that organization is not her strong suit.

As soon as I figure out where the hell she's hiding, I'm going to tell Jack to set up an office for her so we can get her organized.

I flip through several more papers, proving that Brielle is financially worth more than me, when my eyes land on a deed to a house … in Russia.

"My entire world had exploded, and I couldn't handle it, so I went to Russia to live with my grandparents and didn't return until Dominick showed up and forced me to come home after they both passed away."

I grab the paperwork and take a picture of the address. It's the only lead I have, so it looks like I'm going to Russia.

THIRTY-THREE

Brielle

"HE'S NOT GOING TO STOP LOOKING UNTIL HE FINDS YOU," Nicole says over the phone. "The man has practically torn this town apart in search of you."

"That doesn't prove that he loves me. I just made him look bad by leaving. If he loved me, he wouldn't have filed for divorce."

"Did he actually file?" Nicole asks, and I groan in annoyance. We've been through this a dozen times.

"Look," I start, but before I can finish my thought, the front door opens, and in walks my husband. "I've gotta go. I'll call you back."

I hang up and stand, torn between wanting to kiss Kane—because it's been a month since I've seen him and I've missed him more than I'll ever admit—and wanting to tell him to get out because I left for Russia to get away from him, needing time to think.

"You found me," I whisper, drinking him in.

He's dressed in a white button-down shirt with his sleeves rolled to his forearms and a pair of charcoal slacks. He's sporting a full beard and messy hair, like he hasn't shaved or gotten a haircut in weeks. His usually bright brown eyes are dull, and he has faint black circles under his eyes. My brothers told me that he wasn't taking my leaving well, which I didn't understand since he was literally the one who'd had the divorce papers drawn up, but seeing him like this has me wondering if they weren't wrong.

"I've been looking for you since you left," he admits, cutting across the room.

I take a step back, and he stops short and frowns.

"You should've let me explain."

"Explain why you not only messed with my birth control, but also pretended to care about me, only for you to have divorce papers drawn up?" I scoff. "I think it's all pretty obvious. You—"

"Love you," he interjects, stepping toward me. "I love you, Princess." He raises his hand like he wants to touch me, but then he shakes his head and puts the hand in his pocket. "That's why I had the divorce papers drawn up."

"That doesn't make any sense," I choke out, in shock that he just told me the very words I'd longed to hear, only to follow it up with it being his reason for wanting a divorce.

"It does," he says. "I love you enough to let you go. The truth is, when I came to town, I never planned to force you to marry me." He chuckles humorlessly. "My only goal was to fuck up the water-front expansion. But then I saw how profitable it was, and instead of fucking it up, I wanted in on it."

He takes another step toward me. Instead of refraining this time, he gently cups the side of my face, and instinctually, I lean into it, craving his warmth.

"And then I met you," he murmurs, using his thumb to stroke my jawline.

I should push him away. Insist that he not touch me. But I'm weak when it comes to Kane. He's the only man I've let in and let my guard down for. And even though his betrayal hurts like hell, I can't help the way my body and heart react to his touch. My entire life, I've craved control, but with Kane, I willingly want to relinquish it to him.

"We spent the night together, and I knew that one night wouldn't be enough."

"Why didn't you tell me?" I ask, confused as to why he let me leave without saying something. "I felt the same way," I admit. "The only reason why I left without saying anything was because you'd dismissed me."

"Because you were the enemy." He brings his other hand up and holds my face between his hands. "And I knew, once you learned who I was, there was no way you would willingly marry me. So, I told my-self, by forcing you to marry me, I was getting what was owed to my family. But there was never a moment that I didn't want you. Hell, I'm almost positive I was in love with you before I even said my vows."

"And to prove how much you loved me, you had divorce pa-pers drawn up?"

Kane shakes his head and steps back, and I immediately miss his touch.

"I had the divorce papers drawn up the day after you told me you had been raped and then forced to have an abortion."

My heart sinks.

I was right.

"Because I'm damaged goods."

"What?" he hisses, closing the space between us again. "No." He pulls me into his arms and moves us to the couch, settling me in his lap. "You are not damaged," he bites out. "You are the strongest fucking person I've ever known."

"Then why don't you want to be with me?" I choke out, hating how vulnerable I sound.

"I do," he argues. "I want more than anything to be with you, baby. But you've been forced into doing shit your entire life, and I knew that if I forced you to stay in this marriage, you would never truly love me the way I love you."

He drops his head against my chest, and without thinking, I delve my fingers into the soft strands of his hair.

When he glances back up at me, his whiskey-colored eyes are glassy. "You deserve to have a choice, Bri. So, I drew up the divorce papers so you could finally have a choice." His hands go to my hips, and his fingers dig into my flesh. "I never should've taken your choices away from you. So, the decision is yours. If you stay married to me,

I promise I'll love you for the rest of our lives. But …" He swallows thickly, his features turning pained. "If you sign the divorce papers, I'll let you go, no matter how hard it'll be."

He's giving me a choice.

He doesn't want a divorce.

And then I remember a crucial detail that he isn't aware of.

"I'm pregnant."

"What?" he breathes out.

"I'm pregnant. Looks like your placebo worked. I took a home test … well, several actually … and they all say the same thing—I'm pregnant. Still okay with giving me a choice?"

"Holy shit." His eyes descend to my still-flat stomach.

Though I can already feel my body changing. Since I don't know how long he's been messing with my birth control, I can only go by my missed period, putting me at roughly eight weeks along.

"You're pregnant?" His hand goes to my belly, and butterflies erupt in my chest.

"Because you switched out my birth control!"

Needing space, I push his hand away and climb off his lap.

"No, I didn't," he says, standing as well. "I put them under the sink and then moved them to my desk. I didn't know you'd found and taken them."

He smirks and then quickly reins it in. "I'd like to say I'm sorry, but I will never regret you being pregnant with my baby."

He steps toward me, and I shake my head, silently halting him, knowing if I let him touch me, I'll give in.

"This doesn't change anything," he says. "I won't force you to be with me. If you want to be with me, then I would love nothing more than to raise this baby together. I never imagined having a wife, let alone a baby. But I want it with you."

"And if I decide I want a divorce?" I quirk a brow, trying to remain strong.

"Then we'll figure it out," Kane says. "I will never force you to do anything again."

The thought of raising this baby without Kane by my side makes me sick to my stomach. And not because I'm incapable of doing it on my own, but because I've always wanted to have a family, and if we divorce, I'll be a single mom, and every dream I've had of having a family will be shot to hell.

"I love you, Brielle. And I have no doubt that the life we could have together would be fucking beautiful. But you have to want it too."

It would be so easy to go to him, to let him back in, and agree to stay married to him so that we could be a family. But a part of me would always wonder if I did it because I loved him or if I loved the idea of having a family with him.

"I need time," I blurt out. "This isn't how I envisioned my life," I say honestly. "I know I care about you, but I need to make sure that if I stay married to you, it's for the right reasons."

"Okay," he agrees. "I'll give you as much time as you need. But, please, consider coming home with me. If you want to live somewhere else, I'll understand—even though I'll fucking hate it. But I don't want to miss your pregnancy. If you don't come home, I'll have to move here, which will make running my company hard, but I'll do it because—"

"Breathe." I laugh softly. "I'll come home."

He releases a harsh breath and closes the space between us. "I know I'm not the husband you dreamed of, but I hope, one day, I'll be the man you can fall in love with because I've fallen so fucking in love with you, Princess, and I'll spend every day proving it to you."

I nod in understanding, unable to speak due to the lump of emotion caught in my throat. Because the truth is, I've already fallen in love with Kane.

Now, I just need to find out if I can forgive him.

THIRTY-FOUR

Kane

THE FLIGHT HOME WAS SPENT WITH BRIELLE hiding away in the bedroom while I got some work done. One of the hotel expansions in northern Florida is dealing with some red tape that's halting the renovation. I should've gone up there myself to deal with it, but I wasn't about to leave Harbor Point until I found Brielle, and now that I have, I'm not letting her out of my sight.

Since Giani and Kiril went to Russia with her, they insist on driving us home, and since I'm just thankful she's agreed to come home, I'm not about to argue.

When we step inside the house, Brielle lets Molly out of her travel crate, and she prances straight to the guest bathroom that Brielle has turned into what she calls her "princess pad."

"I'm tired," Brielle says with a sigh.

I heard her throwing up several times during the flight, but she locked the door, so I couldn't do anything to comfort her.

"You should take a nap. Do you need anything? I can run out and get you whatever you need …"

"As good as a nap sounds, I need to deal with my studio."

I debate on telling her it's already been dealt with, but now that she's made it clear she isn't sure she wants a future with me, I'm worried I overstepped.

"I'll go with you."

Her gaze lands on me. "You don't have to. I'm sure you have other things to do."

"The only thing I need to do is go with you."

After she showers and changes into a gorgeous dress that shows off her perky tits and toned thighs, we head out.

"I have a doctor's appointment scheduled for next week," she says once we're in the back of the town car with Giani driving and Kiril riding passenger.

"For the baby?"

"Yeah. I scheduled it on the flight back. I'm using the same OB-GYN practice Peyton and Dani used since my gynecologist isn't accepting new obstetrical patients." She stares out the window for a few moments and then says, "I'm nervous. I don't know if the abortion did any damage, and I've been too embarrassed to ask my doctors over the years."

I reach across the seat and thread my fingers through hers, forgetting that I don't have the right to do that anymore. But before I can pull my hand back and apologize, she tightens her grip on my hand.

"Whatever happens, we'll deal with it together," I tell her.

She nods and then goes back to looking out the window.

"Do you want to stop to get a coffee and a muffin?" I ask, imagining she's missed her friend Nicole.

"Sure."

Giani turns onto the street where the coffee shop is located—which is only one street over from Brielle's Pilates studio—and parks.

"We can walk from here," I tell them, hoping they'll give us a bit of space.

They nod in understanding and disappear, giving the illusion that they're gone.

"Oh my God!" Nicole screeches. "My main bitch is back!"

Nicole flies around the counter and bear-hugs Brielle, who laughs boisterously.

When they almost topple over, I jump in, worried about Brielle hitting the hard ground, and steady her.

"Protective much?" Nicole smirks, telling me she knows about the pregnancy.

We order two coffees—Brielle opts for one espresso shot instead of her usual three—and two muffins and have a seat at the table.

Of course, Nicole joins us, shooting questions at Brielle in rapid-fire succession.

But since Brielle has barely spoken a handful of words to me since we left Russia, I'm not going to complain. I not only get to hear Brielle talk, but Nicole is also asking a lot of the questions I want to ask.

"Have you seen the studio yet?" Nicole asks.

"No." Brielle pops a piece of her muffin into her mouth and frowns. "Kane and I are going over there after we leave here. I can't even imagine how bad it looks. Dominick refused to send me pictures, not wanting to stress me out since he overheard me tell Peyton I think I'm pregnant."

"Theo is a dick," Nicole says, making Brielle's back go straight.

"What does Theo have to do with anything?" Brielle asks.

Nicole glances at me, which has Brielle doing the same.

"Theo is the one who vandalized your studio," I tell her.

"Ugh, seriously?" Brielle groans. "He's such a man-child."

"Yep," Nicole agrees. "But he got his. From what I heard, someone"—Nicole side-eyes me—"beat the shit out of him and then dropped him off at the hospital. Normally, I don't condone violence, but in this case, he totally deserved it."

"Yeah, but it doesn't change the fact that he destroyed my studio, and now I'm going to have to spend weeks, possibly months, cleaning up the destruction." She takes her last bite of her muffin and stands. "Guess it's time to face the music."

Nicole frowns. "If you need anything, I'm here." She pulls Brielle into a hug. "I'm so glad you're home."

After we throw away our trash, we head to Brielle's studio.

When she unlocks the door and walks in, I wait with bated breath for her response. I ended up paying triple for the contractor to get it done in time, and since I was in Russia while they were finishing, I haven't had a chance to do a walk-through.

"Holy shit," she gasps, her hands covering her mouth as she takes the place in.

"What do you think?"

She whips around to look at me. "Did you do this?"

"That depends. Is it how you envisioned it?"

"It's exactly how I envisioned it." She walks through the main area and into the side rooms, a look of shock and awe in her features. "I can't believe you did this in a month's time."

She runs her hands over the state-of-the-art equipment I had shipped on rush order and smiles. "Thank you."

She throws herself at me, and for the first time since my wife walked out on me, I breathe a bit easier. With her face against my chest, I take a moment to inhale her sweet scent. She hasn't let me anywhere near her since I showed up in Russia, and before that, I spent two weeks avoiding her. It's been too long since I've felt her body against mine, and like an addict, I'm craving my next hit.

"I would do anything for you," I tell her honestly as I wrap my arms around her. "Whatever it is you want or need, Princess."

"I just need time, Kane," she whispers against my chest. "Just a little bit of time."

"Is it okay if we go by Dominick's house?" Brielle asks, glancing up from her phone. "Matteo and Dani are there, and they know I'm back and want to see for themselves that I'm okay."

"Of course, but if you want to go alone, I can drop you off, or Giani can take you."

I glance over at Giani and Kiril, who are standing guard on either side of the front door to Brielle's studio.

"I'd rather you go," she says. "You can be my buffer. I haven't seen them since they found out I'm pregnant."

"And what do you think they're going to say?" I quirk a brow.

"I don't know." She shrugs. "Sometimes, they forget that I'm a grown woman."

"They care deeply about you." I slide my arm across her shoulders. "Let's go. I'm sure they'll be so busy threatening to kill me that they won't even remember you're pregnant."

Brielle chuckles. "That works for me."

We slide into the back of the town car, and Giani heads to Dominick's house. When we arrive, Peyton and Daniella swarm Brielle, and Dominick extends his hand to shake mine.

"Brielle told us why you had the divorce papers drawn up," he says. "You're a better man than me. When I found out Peyton had my baby, I forced her and our son to come live with me."

"Yeah, well, I'm done forcing Brielle to do shit she doesn't want to do." I sigh, glancing at my beautiful wife.

She's holding Dani and Matteo's baby girl, and she looks so natural with a baby in her arms. It's crazy to think that before this year ends, she'll be holding our baby.

"Now, I just have to hope she chooses to stay married to me."

"Thank you for bringing our sister back," Matteo adds. "I still don't like you, but … I don't hate you as much."

"Matteo." Brielle glares at her brother.

"What?" Matteo shrugs. "It's progress. Besides, we don't even know if you're going to stay married to him. I'm not about to welcome him into the family, only for you to divorce him. Let me know once you decide."

Brielle rolls her eyes and then goes back to rocking the baby while I think about all the ways I can convince her not to sign those damn papers.

"If you want, I can just move the mattress into the hall, and then you don't have to decide where to sleep." I chuckle, leaning against the wall.

I was in my office, working, and clicked on the camera to check on Brielle. I didn't know what she was doing, until I checked on her again and found her in the same spot, her gaze bouncing between the master bedroom and guest room.

"I like sleeping with you," she admits softly. "But I don't know if it's because I don't want to be alone or if it's because I like you."

"Can't it be a bit of both?" I ask, pushing off the wall so I'm standing in front of her. "Isn't that why people go in search of someone to spend their life with? Join dating sites and go to bars in hope of meeting someone? Because at the end of the day, nobody wants to be alone."

Brielle looks at the guest room, and my stomach drops. If she chooses to sleep in a separate room, I'll have to accept it. I did this. I put us in this situation, and now I have to give her space while she sifts through her feelings.

"I … I think I'm going to sleep in the guest room tonight." Her voice is so low that I almost don't hear her. And when I look at her, her eyes are on the floor, as if she's ashamed of the decision.

"Hey." I tip her chin up. "It's okay. You're doing what you have to do … putting yourself first. I'll be right down the hall if you change your mind." I lean in and give her a soft kiss on her forehead. "I'll see you in the morning, Princess."

Since I can't sleep for shit—and haven't been able to since Brielle left—after I change into a pair of lounge pants and a T-shirt, I head back to my office to get some work done.

I'm neck deep in numbers when Brielle appears in my office doorway.

"Everything okay?" I ask, trying to keep the frustration out of my tone.

"I had a nightmare," she admits sheepishly. "And I went to find you, but you weren't in bed."

I turn my chair to the side, and Brielle pads across the room and straight into my arms.

I slide her across my lap, and she burrows her head into my chest.

"After what we did at Elite, I was hoping the nightmares would go away, but when I went to Russia, they seemed to get worse."

"You know," I tell her, trying to keep my tone light, "when you were sleeping with me, you barely had any."

She groans and buries her head deeper, and I chuckle at her lack of response.

After a few minutes, she glances up. "Are you working this late?"

"Unfortunately. I've been running these numbers for hours." I glance at the clock and see it's almost three in the morning.

"Don't you have an entire team to do that?" she asks curiously.

"Yeah, but something is off. David, my accountant, flagged the quarterly reports and asked me to take a look because he's not understanding why the numbers aren't adding up. There's a discrepancy internally. But when I asked Jim, my CFO, he swore that the numbers were correct."

"I can take a look if you want. Sometimes, a fresh pair of eyes helps."

I glance down at her. "Why did you major in accounting if you didn't plan to get a job in that field?"

She laughs softly. "I wanted to prove I could do it. Andrey had always harped about how it was a man's world and a woman's only purpose was to marry and be on a man's arm. I was nothing more than a bargaining chip. So, I majored in accounting, thinking once I graduated, I could show him that I could be useful to the family business. But then he ordered Owen to be killed and ..."

"Forced you to have an abortion," I finish, wishing I could

resurrect Andrey Antonov from the grave so I could kill him all over again, only slower, making it hurt. My father shooting him was too easy of a death for him. He deserved to be tortured for what he did to Brielle.

"Yeah," she breathes. "And then I left for Russia. I thought maybe once I was home and settled in, I could go to work for my brother, but then I fell in love with Pilates and decided to follow my own dreams instead of trying to prove something to someone else."

"So fucking strong," I murmur, cupping her face in my hands. "I wish I were half as strong as you are."

The blush that creeps up her delicate neck and cheeks has me wanting to lay her out on the desk and see where else I can make her blush. But instead, I lay a soft kiss to her jawline, inhaling her scent.

She shudders beneath my touch, so I kiss her again before I pull back, not wanting to push her too hard.

"If you're willing to look at the books, I would appreciate it. But not now. It's late, and you need to get some sleep."

I lift her into my arms and stand. She shocks me when she wraps her legs around my waist and her arms around my neck, enveloping me in her delicious heat.

I carry her toward the guest room, but before I step inside, she shakes her head.

"I think I'd rather sleep in our room," she whispers, "if that's okay. I sleep better in there with you."

"You're always welcome in our room."

I lay her on her side of the bed, and after using the bathroom and brushing my teeth, I join her. When I get under the covers, she glances at me like she wants to move into her usual position with her head on my chest and her leg slung over mine.

"C'mere, Princess."

"I feel like I'm leading you on." She bites the corner of her bottom lip nervously.

"You're not," I assure her, even if her ending up in our bed gives me hope. "I know the score. You need time. But how am I supposed to convince you to stay married to me if you keep your distance?"

I lift the blanket as a silent invitation, and she edges over to me. She nestles her face into the crook of my shoulder and swings her creamy bare leg over mine.

I run my fingers up and down her back, and within minutes, she's softly snoring in my arms, right where she belongs. Now, I just need to make her see that …

Her left hand is resting on my chest, and I can't help but notice her bare ring finger.

"… *the ring would symbolize that love.*"

Careful not to jostle Brielle, I reach into my nightstand and pull out the box that I placed in there a couple of weeks ago.

I told her it would be her choice, and it is, but that doesn't mean I'm not going to do everything in my power to convince her that the right choice is me.

THIRTY-FIVE

Brielle

TOLD MYSELF I WOULD REMAIN STRONG, THAT I WOULDN'T let Kane back in until I knew I was making the right choice. I even accepted that there was a chance we might not end up together. But not even a few hours and one nightmare later, and I was back in the comfort of his arms.

Not that it should surprise me. The man forced me to marry him to avenge his father's death. And I still fell for him.

But I can't help thinking about what he told me when he found me in Russia—he had drawn up the divorce papers because he wanted to give me a choice. That shouldn't be romantic, but it is.

Jesus, I'm fucked up.

And he didn't give me the placebo pills. I found the bag and took them myself.

That has to count for something, right?

Yep, I'm fucked up.

Oh, and when I returned home, thinking I was going to spend the next couple of months cleaning up and renovating my Pilates studio, I found out that Kane had already handled everything. And he followed my plans to a T.

It's probably the sweetest thing anyone has ever done for me.

Yeah, I know. I'm fucked up. We've already established that.

"I know you're awake," Kane murmurs, and even though my eyes are still closed, I can hear the humor in his tone.

"Don't overthink it," he says, his hand running down my back. "You had a nightmare, and we slept in the same bed together. It doesn't have to mean anything."

Except that it does. It means everything.

But I can't tell him that. Because I'm trying to be strong and think with my head and not my heart or libido.

I open my eyes, and I'm met with sunlight peeking through the windows. I'm not sure what time it is, but we most likely slept in. My gaze ascends to look at Kane, only before I make it there, I'm distracted by the black box resting on his torso, right next to my face.

"What's this?" I ask in confusion.

"Open it."

Since I can't do that while lying with my face smashed against his abs, I take the box in my hand and sit up. It's the size of a ring box, but that doesn't make sense because I already have a ring …

I pop the lid open and gasp when I take in the gorgeous engagement ring. It's a simple platinum band with a princess cut diamond in the center. It's flawless and beautiful and …

"When I saw it at the store, it looked like something you'd like," Kane says. "And then I asked the jeweler about it, and he said it's a princess cut diamond."

A boyish grin spreads across his face, and butterflies swarm my chest.

"Maybe it's cheesy as fuck, but I didn't even know princess cut diamonds existed, and I figured it had to be a sign."

"You bought me a new ring?" I whisper. "I left you, ran to Russia, and you bought me a second engagement ring?"

"Well, when you put it like that …" He chuckles. "I returned the other rings. You were right. I'd picked out the biggest ring to prove a point. But with this one, I hope the point I'm proving is that I love you."

I suck in a harsh breath. This isn't the first time he's told me he loves me, but every time I hear it, my heart pounds in my chest.

"You don't have to put it on," he says. "I meant what I said—it's your choice." He reaches into the nightstand and pulls out a manila folder. "I've already signed the divorce papers, so if you want a divorce, there's nothing to stop you."

He hands me the folder, but instead of taking it, I stare at it like it might attack me.

"My hope is that you'll rip them up and put on the engagement ring so I can marry you for real this time."

Just as he finishes his sentence, a horrible wave of morning sickness hits me. I hightail it to the bathroom and barely make it to the toilet before I throw up.

"Jesus," he says from behind me. "I know you're upset with me, but I didn't think the idea of marrying me would cause you to get sick."

My head pops up from the toilet bowl. "You want to get married again?"

"How else will I give you the wedding of your dreams … at the beach, with only family and friends?"

Oh fuck. This man.

"You're not playing fair," I whisper, my eyes stinging with emotion.

I stand and flush the toilet, and Kane steps toward me, cupping the side of my face.

"That's where you're wrong," he says. "I'm not playing at all. I love you, and I want to spend my life with you, and until you tell me otherwise, I'm going to spend every day showing you as much."

He lets go of me, and I instantly miss his touch.

"I need to get ready. I have to go into the office and deal with this accounting shit. Oh!" His eyes meet mine. "Can you send me the date and time of your doctor's appointment? I need to put it in the calendar so Jack can make sure I don't have anything scheduled that day."

"You're going with me?" I ask. "It's just to confirm the pregnancy. I don't even know if we'll get to see the baby."

"Bri," he drawls, "there's nowhere I'd rather be than with you at your appointment. And even if you decide that I'm not the man for you, I'm going to be the best father I can be. I was close with my father, but because of the circumstances, he hid us away from the world so that we weren't seen as his dirty little secret. He couldn't attend any of our sporting events or school functions. That's not going to be our child. I'm going to be active in their life, even if it means co-parenting with you."

He pulls off his shirt over his head, and I drink in his defined chest and abs like I'm severely dehydrated.

"I'd ask if you wanted to shower with me"—he smirks like the cocky bastard he is—"but I know that would be pushing it. So, I'll shower, and then you can get ready for your day."

He leans in and kisses my cheek, and it takes everything in me not to beg him to take me right here and now in the bathroom.

Because this man … he's the husband I've always dreamed of.

"Going into the office today?" Kane asks with a smirk as he hands me a cup of coffee and eyes the maroon pantsuit I'm wearing, which is a far cry from the workout clothes I usually sport.

"Actually, I saw on the calendar it was Take Your Wife to Work day, so I figured I'd tag along with you."

He quirks a brow.

"You asked for my help with the books, remember?"

"Oh shit." He shakes his head. "I didn't mean you had to do it today. If you have other stuff going on, it can wait. I know you have your studio and—"

I cover his mouth with my hand and smile. "And my studio will be there tomorrow. Today, I'm going to check your numbers. Besides, I've been married to you for months, and I've never seen your office."

Thirty minutes later, we arrive at his office downtown, and after we go through security, Kane escorts me to the floor where his office is. I know Jack, but he introduces me to a few other people who work alongside him, and then he directs me to his office.

It's your typical corner office with a beautiful view of downtown. A huge desk is in the middle of the room. And he has a couple of stuffy-looking couches in the corner as well as a bookshelf, filled with books that would put me to sleep.

I head straight for his desk, dropping into his comfy chair, while Kane stands by the door, smirking at me.

"What?" I ask, shifting to get comfortable.

"Nothing." He closes the door behind him and stalks over to the desk. "Every time I imagined you in my office, it was so I could fuck you on my desk. Didn't think when you finally came here, it would be to actually work."

My eyes go to his large mahogany desk, and my lady parts tingle at the thought of Kane bending me over the side of his desk, pulling my pants and underwear down to my ankles, and taking me from behind. I run my fingers across the cool surface, imagining the way it would feel against my sensitive nipples.

"You're thinking about it, aren't you?" He grins.

"No," I rasp, even though we both know I was. "Now, where are these numbers you need me to look at before I change my mind?"

Kane chuckles and steps around the desk and behind the chair, leaning over me so I'm forced to inhale his masculine scent.

"Right here," he says, waking the computer up. "My hope is that there's been an error in calculations …"

"There's no error. I've gone over the numbers a dozen times, and I've traced it back to right here." I point at the computer. "Your CFO has been siphoning from your accounts for the past month. That's why it only popped up for this quarterly report. He was sneaky, but your numbers are so perfect that your team was able to catch it quickly."

"Fuck," Kane hisses. "Tell me everything. I need to know exactly what this fucker did so I can fire him."

I glance at him, shocked that he's accepting what I said so easily. "You're not going to ask for a second opinion?"

Kane's eyes meet mine. "I trust you, Bri. And after you ran the numbers for the better part of the day, if you say my CFO has been stealing from me, I believe you. But I need to have the receipts so I can back myself up when I meet with him."

We spend the next hour going over what I found. The discrepancies in the books and the trail that led me to an offshore account, which I had Eddy locate and he confirmed it belonged to Jim Wallen, Kane's CFO.

"I don't get why he would do this." Kane exhales a frustrated breath. "He's paid a damn good salary, plus bonuses. And if he got himself into trouble, he could've come to me."

"I don't know, but maybe if you talk to him …"

"It's too late for that. Once you've lost my trust, there's no getting it back."

"Really?" I quirk a brow. "Seems kind of hypocritical. You fucked up, and you're asking me for a second chance. Should I never trust you again?"

Kane stares at me for several seconds before he sighs. "Honestly, I wouldn't blame you if you never trusted me again. I fucked up. But I love you, and I hope, one day, you can let me back in. But you and me … it's personal. This"—he nods toward the computer—"is business."

I don't necessarily agree with his logic, but on a certain level, I can understand where he's coming from. My brothers would give their wives a million chances if need be and then not think twice about killing a man who betrayed them.

"When are you going to speak to him?"

"Soon." My stomach growls, and Kane chuckles. "But right now, my concern is getting you and our baby fed."

"We don't even know for sure that there's a baby in there."

Sure, the pregnancy tests were all positive, and my period hasn't come two months in a row. And then there's the fact that my body is already changing, and morning sickness has also been in full swing. But until I see the baby myself, I don't think it'll sink in.

"Well, if there's not, we could always work on putting one in there."

Kane playfully waggles his brows, and even though he's only joking, the idea of having sex with him isn't funny.

Another symptom of being pregnant is being horny. And unfortunately, my vibrator and fingers don't compare to the way Kane expertly works my body.

My gaze bounces from Kane's face to his cock, and I briefly wonder if I could offer to suck him off. It wouldn't fill me up, but it would satiate a different hunger.

"You're thinking about me fucking you again, aren't you?" Kane laughs.

"No," I rasp. "I was thinking about sucking you off." I stand and round the desk. "But since you were a bad boy and fucked with my head and heart, it's not happening. Not only did you fuck up your sex life, but you fucked up mine too."

"Oh, Princess." Kane grabs me by my hips and pulls me into his lap. "Give me five minutes with that pretty pussy, and I'll show you just how *good* I can be."

The hardness rubbing against my center has me wanting to say yes, but then I remember everything he did, and I force myself to shake my head.

"Not yet," I choke out. "I need time."

Kane immediately sobers. "I know. I'm sorry. I got caught up in the moment." He kisses my temple and helps me stand. "You have time. I promise."

THIRTY-SIX

Brielle

MORNING SICKNESS SUCKS.

I used to start my morning with a latte and a muffin. Now, I start it with my head in a toilet bowl. I dread opening my eyes, knowing what's to come. If I could, I'd sleep until noon and then wake up, but my body is so used to getting up early that by seven in the morning, I'm awake, whether I like it or not.

"Hopefully, this will end soon," Kane says, handing me a warm washcloth. "But until it does, I got you a few things."

He leaves the room, and while he's gone, I brush my teeth and rinse out my mouth. I'm just turning off the sink when he returns, carrying a large wicker basket.

"What's this?" I ask curiously.

I follow him out to the bedroom, and he sets it on the bed.

Inside, there are several items such as a pregnancy journal, filled with blank pages I can write in. Fluffy socks, a water bottle, herbal tea, ginger gum, lotion for stretch marks …

I pick up the *What to Expect When You're Expecting* book, and Kane says, "I got one too. I was thinking we could read it together."

He glances at me sheepishly, and my heart squeezes in my chest.

"These are pregnancy pops," he explains, lifting a pack of lollipops that were hidden behind the journal. "They help with nausea. At least the woman at the store said they do."

"You bought all this for me?" I choke out, overcome with emotion. "When?"

"Yesterday, but I had to put it all together, so I did it after you fell asleep last night."

I glance at the basket, tears pricking my eyes, and then I throw my arms around Kane's neck. "You're not playing fair," I cry, repeating what I said to him a few days ago.

"I'm playing to win, Princess," he murmurs. "Especially since the prize is a life with you." He pulls back. "Go get ready. In case you forgot, your appointment is this morning."

"How could I forget?" I grin. "We finally get to find out if I'm pregnant or if I've contracted a deathly illness that causes me to lose my breakfast every morning."

Kane chuckles. "I think it's safe to say you're pregnant, but we'll let the doctor confirm."

"I can't believe there's this much paperwork to fill out just to have a baby," Kane mutters as I hand him the last form I had to fill out since he's been holding them for me as I go.

"I mean, I am going to be giving birth to an actual human being. So, the paperwork is probably necessary."

Kane grins, and I glance at him in confusion.

"What?"

"Nothing." His hand goes to my belly. "I just can't believe you're having my baby."

"*Our* baby," I choke out, trying and failing not to let his words and touch affect me.

"Our baby." His grin widens.

"Miss Antonov," the nurse calls out.

Kane's face falls, and even though I shouldn't care, my stomach knots. I hate to see the disappointment in his features.

"It's, um, it's Antonov-Morgan," I correct her.

"Oh, sorry," she says, glancing at the file in her hand. "Antonov-*Morgan*. Right this way."

She has me give a urine sample, and then she checks my weight and blood pressure. Once that's done, she takes a bit of blood, letting us know it's standard procedure.

"You're going to be seeing Dr. Drescher today," she says, "in room four."

We step into the hall, and we're about to make a left into the room when something—or I should say, someone—catches my attention.

I stop in my tracks, frozen in my spot, and Kane runs into the back of me. I nearly topple over, but he quickly encircles his arms around me, catching me. He murmurs something into my ear, but I can't hear him.

Short dirty-blond hair.

A belly that hangs over the belt of his pants.

No, it can't be him …

As if he senses me staring, he lifts his head from whatever he was reading, and his green eyes meet mine.

It's been six years, but I would never forget that monster's face.

He squints, trying to place me. The moment he recognizes me, his eyes go wide, his mouth opens and closes like a fish out of water, and then he dodges into the room closest to him.

"Brielle," Kane says, stepping around me so I'm forced to look at him. "What's wrong? Are you dizzy? Nauseous?"

"That was him," I whisper, flashbacks of that day nearly knocking me back.

"Don't worry. You won't feel a thing."

"Who?" Kane looks around. "That was who?"

"Dr. Moore?" the nurse asks. "He's one of the OB-GYNs at the practice."

Dr. Moore. I finally have a name to go with the face of the man who stole my baby.

"Can you give us a minute?" Kane asks curtly.

"Sure. If you want to step into room four, you'll need to change into the gown on the table. You can leave your bra on, but make sure to remove your underwear. Dr. Drescher is running a few minutes behind, so she should be in shortly. Please let me know if you need anything."

Once we're inside, Kane lifts me onto the medical table and looks into my eyes. "Talk to me, Princess. Who was that man?"

"He's ..." I choke on a sob.

It doesn't matter that it's been years. Every time I think about what he did at Andrey's insistence, my heart feels like it's being put through the grinder.

"He's the doctor who performed my abortion." I throw my arms around Kane's neck and cry. "He's a doctor. He's supposed to heal people, not hurt them."

THIRTY-SEVEN

Kane

H E'S A DEAD MAN.

Dr. Moore won't survive the day.

I hate that Brielle was forced to see the piece of shit who had ripped her baby out of her womb without her permission, but I'm glad that I now know who he is so I can take care of him.

"Kane, no," Brielle says, shaking her head.

"No what?" I lean back, hoping she isn't saying what I think she's saying.

"I don't want to kill him," she admits. "There's been so much bloodshed in my life. All I wanted was to move forward, find a man to spend my life with, and have a family. Killing him won't right the wrong."

"It will end his fucking life," I hiss.

"And the blood will be on my hands. How does that make me any better of a person than him?"

Fuck, this woman. She's too good for this damn life.

I could kill him behind her back, but if she ever found out, she would know I went against her wishes.

"Fine. But we can't just let him get away with this. Who knows who else he's done that shit to?"

"I agree," she says. "I don't want to kill him, but … I do want to make sure he can never do to anyone else what he did to me."

"Say the word, and I'll make sure he never practices medicine again," I promise her.

She swallows thickly and then nods. "Not by killing him though."

"He'll still be alive," I assure her.

"Thank you." She presses a soft kiss to my lips. "I'd better get into this ugly gown."

She jumps off the medical table and proceeds to take her clothes off right in front of me. When I glance at her, her eyes widen, as if realizing what she's doing.

"Sorry," she mumbles. "It's habit."

"A habit I'm one hundred percent okay with."

She laughs, finishes getting into the gown, and hops back onto the medical bed just as there's a knock on the door.

"Come in," Brielle calls out.

An older woman with a kind smile walks in. "Hello. I'm Dr. Drescher, and you must be Brielle."

"I am," she says, "and this is my husband, Kane."

Husband.

I know it's just a formality, but the thought that the title could be revoked doesn't sit well with me at all.

"I'm going to do a quick exam. Based on your last period, you're estimated to be around eight weeks, so we should be good to do an abdominal ultrasound. And once we're finished, your lab work should be done, so we can look at everything. But before we get started, do you have any questions or concerns?"

"Just one," Brielle says softly. "When I was younger, I had an abortion. I looked it up, and it said that, generally, it shouldn't affect future pregnancies, but it was, um …"

She takes a deep breath, and I step next to her, threading my fingers through hers for moral support.

Another exhale.

"It was forced and possibly not done in sterile conditions. So, um …"

Dr. Drescher reaches out and gently pats Brielle's knee. "We will double- and triple-check everything, I promise."

"Thank you," Brielle chokes out. "I've just wanted to be a mom for so long, and I don't want anything to go wrong."

The doctor does a quick exam, confirming everything looks normal, and then she grabs the machine and wheels it over.

"Go ahead and drape this over your legs so we can lift your gown," the doctor says, handing her what looks like a plastic towel.

When Brielle lifts her gown, exposing her belly, it's no longer flat.

"What?" she asks.

"Your belly's grown." I grin.

She glances down and smiles. "Yeah, I didn't think I would show so soon, but I read everyone's different. Dani didn't show until she was in her third trimester!"

Dr. Drescher chuckles. "I forgot you're related to Daniella. How is she, Matteo, and the baby doing?"

"Good," Brielle tells her. "Alba is growing so fast. I was gone for a month, and I swear she gained five pounds and grew four inches."

The doctor laughs. "They grow too quickly. Now, let's see what we're working with."

She squirts some blue shit on Brielle's belly and clicks the mouse a few times. The screen is grainy, and since I've never been in this situation, I have no clue what we're looking at.

After a few moments, the doctor reaches for the screen and turns a knob, and a loud whooshing sound fills the otherwise quiet room.

"This is your baby's heartbeat."

Brielle sniffles. "There's really a baby in there?" she whispers.

"Oh, yes." The doctor smiles. "You see this little flutter?" She points at the screen. "That's your baby. And based on my calculations, you're nine weeks along and due on November 8."

"And … does everything look okay?" Brielle asks, squeezing my hand tighter.

"You're still in the first trimester, so anything is possible. But your baby has a strong heartbeat, and everything looks good. I'm going to look at the blood work, and then we'll know more."

She clicks a few keys and then reaches down, pulling something out. "Here you go." She hands Brielle one set of images and me the other. "Your baby's first photo shoot."

THIRTY-EIGHT

Brielle

WHEN I ARRIVED AT MY APPOINTMENT, I KNEW I WAS pregnant—but knowing it and seeing it with my own eyes is a completely different story.

The blood work all came back good, and the doctor included an envelope with the baby's gender in case we wanted to do some sort of reveal.

She also gave me a pregnancy gift bag, filled with a bunch of goodies and information, and told me to make sure I take a daily prenatal pill—something I started as soon as the test read PREGNANT.

"Did you know that eighty percent of miscarriages happen in the first trimester?"

I'm reading one of the informational packets while Kane drives us home from the doctor's appointment with Giani and Kiril following behind. They weren't thrilled when I asked to take a separate vehicle, but I felt like this moment needed to be between just the two of us.

Thankfully, we never ran into Dr. Moore the rest of the time we were at the doctor's office, but I'm not sure if I can risk going back, which sucks because I really like Dr. Drescher.

"Let's focus on the positive," Kane says, plucking the pamphlet out of my hand. "You're healthy, the baby is growing inside of you, and everything else is out of our control."

Even though I agree, not having control is the bane of my existence, and the thought of having zero control causes panic to creep into my veins.

"I have a meeting I need to go to," Kane says. "Do you want me to drop you off at home or the studio?"

I glance down at the pictures, wanting to share them with the people I love—and not wanting to be alone right now. "Can you drop me off at Peyton's, please?"

I pull out my phone and text Peyton to let her know I'm coming over. She texted me earlier to wish me a good appointment and to let me know she'd be at home if I needed anything.

> Peyton: Yes! Please come over. Dani is already here. We can do a girls' day.
>
> Me: Is it okay if I invite my mom and Nicole?
>
> Peyton: Of course!

When we pull into the driveway, Kane looks at me. "Have dinner with me tonight?"

"Okay. I should be home by then. It's only—"

"Not like that." He shakes his head. "I want to take you out." He slides his finger across the sonogram image in my lap. "We have something huge to celebrate." He frames the side of my face. "I know you're freaking out right now. I can't empathize since I've never been pregnant, but I know how much you crave control, and being pregnant is making you feel like you have none."

I swallow thickly as tears prick my eyes. It's insane how in sync we are. Kane might've forced his way into my life, but I can't deny the way he's burrowed himself deep inside my marrow. I don't think there's anyone who knows me like he does.

"Focus on what you can control." He rubs his thumb down my

cheek, and I lean into his touch, craving the comfort he gives me. "You're taking vitamins. You eat healthy. The doctor said you can continue working out and doing Pilates, and exercise is good for you and the baby. You don't drink or smoke. You've got this, Princess."

His gaze descends to my mouth, his eyes filled with heat, and for a moment, I think he's going to kiss me, and I realize that I want him to.

I want his kisses and hugs and affection.

I want the love he gives so freely. Maybe we didn't start off the way most relationships should, but it doesn't change the fact that he loves me and I love him.

I love my husband. I've fought so hard to have the life that I want. And I can have it with Kane, if I just let him in.

I glance up at him, wanting to tell him, but decide to wait. Sitting in the car in my brother's driveway isn't the time or place.

Besides, I need to make sure this is what I want. That I can forgive and let go of everything that's happened.

THIRTY-NINE

Kane

"I NEED TO USE YOUR WAREHOUSE. I HAVE A SPECIAL DELIVERY I need to temporarily store."

While my father was deep in organized crime, he kept me out of it, and after he died, his connections to the underground world died with him. I could've kept them going, but that would've meant businesses, such as the Antonovs and Russos, knowing who I was, and the only way for me to revive his company was to start fresh.

Normally, I wouldn't ask Matteo for a favor, but since this has to do with his sister and his warehouse is the only place I know of where we have guaranteed control of the cameras, it's a necessity.

Matteo's quiet over the line for several seconds before he says, "I'll meet you there."

We hang up, and I glance back at Simon Moore, who's shifting around in the back seat like he has a prayer of loosening the zip ties binding his hands and legs together.

He mumbles something under his breath, but I can't make it out since he has a piece of duct tape covering his mouth. And thanks to the pillowcase I put over his face, he can't see anything either.

When I pull up to the port, the guard presses the button to let me in, and I drive straight toward the warehouse, making sure to pull in all the way so any cameras that the Antonovs don't have access to won't catch me yanking the good doctor out of my SUV.

"What do we have here?" Matteo asks when I drop the asshole onto the ground.

"You'll see."

I pull Simon onto his feet and cut the zip ties with the knife I brought with me.

"Bring him in here," Matteo says. "Are you killing him or—"

"No, Brielle won't let me kill him. I'm just going to make him wish he were dead."

At the mention of his sister, Matteo's eyes turn into thin slits.

I shove the guy into the metal chair in the middle of the room that Matteo must've placed there.

I pull a few more zip ties out of my pocket and bind his ankles to the legs of the chair. Then I pull the pillowcase over his face and rip the tape off his mouth.

"Please!" the piece of shit immediately starts pleading. "I didn't want to do it. But I was in debt from medical school and—"

I punch him square in his jaw, and his head flies to the side.

"Do you hear yourself?" I hiss. "You were in debt from medical school. Where you had taken an oath to heal people."

"What did he do to my sister?" Matteo asks lowly.

"You wanna tell him, or should I?" I ask Simon.

"You don't understand," he cries. "Andrey threatened my family."

I punch him again, this time in the nose, and crimson runs out of his nostrils and into his mouth.

"This is the asshole who performed the abortion on Brielle."

Matteo growls and then cuts across the room, punching the doctor with so much force that he flies backward in the chair. The back of his head hits the concrete so hard that I wouldn't be surprised if it caused permanent brain damage.

"We ran into him when we went to see Dr. Drescher."

"Are you telling me that fucker was working there when Peyton and Dani were pregnant?" Matteo seethes. "He's dead." He lifts the doctor and sets the chair right. "You're dead."

"No, he's not," I remind him. "Brielle doesn't want blood on her hands. All she wants is for him to never practice medicine again."

I smirk, and Matteo quirks a brow.

"Can't perform forced abortions without hands." I shrug.

Matteo chuckles darkly, and the asshole cries.

"You know," Matteo says, patting me on the shoulder, "I wasn't a fan of yours. But you're actually starting to grow on me."

He grabs a blowtorch and turns it on.

The doctor screams, "Please, no!"

I grab the torch from Matteo and walk over to the doctor. "Let me ask you this …" I lift his bound hands and extend his pointer finger. "When you forced my wife to have an abortion and she begged you not to do it, did you listen to her?"

He whimpers.

"Exactly."

I lift his finger to the fire, letting it slowly burn the flesh. He screams in agony, and I hope he feels an ounce of the pain and devastation and lack of control that Brielle felt when he sold his soul to Andrey over a threat and money.

The scent of burning flesh wafts through the air, and eventually, when the flesh is gone, the bone starts to burn.

At some point, the doctor pisses himself, and I have to force myself not to gag at the mix of piss and flesh.

I keep going, and he whimpers and then briefly passes out. Good.

But the torch is too hot, making it hard to hold on to his hand, so I turn it off and walk over to the toolbox, grabbing a Sawzall.

"Bring him over here."

Matteo cuts his zip ties off and drags him over to the workbench, forcing his hand onto the block of wood.

"I'll do anything," the doctor cries.

"Too late," I tell him. "My wife is more compassionate than I am, and I promised I'd keep you alive, but you will never practice medicine again." I switch the Sawzall on and start to cut off his fingers, one by one. "And if I find out that you told a single person about what happened today, I will end your life. Understand?"

Before he can answer, he passes out from the pain being too much.

"I think he understood," I say to Matteo. "But just to be sure, I should probably cut off a couple more fingers."

FORTY

Brielle

"YOU SCARED THE HELL OUT OF ME."

I blink several times and then glance at my husband, who's changed out of his suit and into a pair of gray linen pants and a white button-downed shirt, the sleeves rolled to his elbows, showcasing his toned forearms. His brown hair is still damp from the shower, and his whiskey eyes are shining bright today.

"You turned off your tracker on your phone when you left for Russia, so I have no way of knowing where you are. I called several times, and when you didn't answer, I assumed the worst. Giani assured me you were safe at home, but we already know he works for you and not me."

"What time is it?"

"Quarter after six."

"I'm sorry," I tell him. "I got home from Peyton's, laid down, thinking I'd take a little cat nap, and passed out."

"You obviously needed it."

Kane gives Molly, who's sleeping against my side, a quick pet, and then he leans in, giving me a chaste kiss. "The doctor has been taken care of."

My eyes widen.

"And he's still alive, as promised."

"Thank you," I rasp, sitting up and grabbing my phone that was on the nightstand.

Next to it sits the black box housing the engagement ring. I consider putting it on, but I second-guess myself. I've only been home for a week. Shouldn't I take longer to make sure this is what I want?

You already know you love Kane and want to be with him, my subconscious reminds me. *Just admit it out loud already.*

"Is it too late to go to dinner?" I ask, shoving my internal thoughts to the side.

I was looking forward to tonight. It would've been our first real date. And of course, I slept through it.

"We can eat anytime you want. How about you get dressed, and once you're ready, we'll go?"

"Are we going somewhere fancy?" I ask, trying to figure out what I should wear.

"Nope. Wear whatever you want. It's a bit warm out, so maybe something light."

Hmm … outside. Okay, I can work with that.

I find a lightweight, sleeveless green smocked minidress and pair it with my favorite wedges. I fluff my hair, brush my teeth, and touch up my makeup, and once I'm ready, I head downstairs, stopping at the bottom step when Kane rounds the corner with a bouquet of red roses.

"You look beautiful," he says, walking toward me as I take the final step into the foyer. "I can't wait to see your belly swollen with my baby."

He hands me the roses and gives me a kiss on my cheek.

I inhale the floral scent and set them on the foyer table. "Thank you."

Kane extends his hand, and I take it, hooking my arm into the crook of his elbow.

Rather than head to the garage, he confuses me when he walks us out the back door and onto the patio. The warm, salty breeze immediately assaults my senses, and I smile out at the ocean. There's just something so therapeutic about the beach.

I've come out here several times since moving in with Kane, and every time it's as though all the stress temporarily leaves my body.

We cross over the bridge that leads us out to Kane's private beach, and that's when I notice the picnic that's been set up.

Dozens of red roses surround the area, illuminated by soft tiki torches. A blanket is spread across the ground, and a wicker basket is sitting atop it.

Since sand and wedges don't mix, I tug them off and chuck them to the side and then head down to the picnic.

"I can't believe you did all this," I say to Kane, plopping onto the blanket. "When I give in and agree to marry you again, you'd better not stop this romantic stuff."

The second the words are out of my mouth, I widen my eyes, realizing what I just said, and Kane smirks.

"I'm totally wearing you down, aren't I, Princess?"

He lowers onto the blanket and pulls two glasses and a bottle of apple cider out of the basket. He fills our glasses and hands me one.

"To you falling in love with me," he says, clinking my glass.

"To me not drowning you in the ocean."

He chuckles. "I'll drink to that."

Kane pulled out all the stops for our date. Not only did he include all my favorite foods, but he also included several of my current cravings. We spend dinner and dessert talking about everything and nothing. The conversation flows easily, reminding me why I fell in love with Kane. He makes it too easy.

"Dark chocolate is my favorite," I tell him as he slides a chocolate-covered strawberry between my lips.

"I know." He chuckles when I moan around the berry. "Because it's the perfect amount of sweet and bitter and technically good for you," he says, repeating the words I once told him back to me.

"You know what else I like that's the perfect mix of sweet and bitter?" I flirt, my gaze descending to his crotch.

He grins, but shakes his head, making me pout.

"What do you mean, *no?*"

"That's not what tonight is about," he says, giving me another bite of the juicy fruit. "If I have it my way, we'll have the rest of our lives together. There's no reason to rush. I want you to be sure I'm who you want. Because, Princess"—he tips my chin until I'm looking at him—"if you agree to spend your life with me, there's no way I'm ever letting you go again."

I open my eyes and glance at the ring box.

Last night was one of the best nights I'd had in a long time.

After we finished dessert, we went for a walk along the beach, and then after we showered—together, at my insistence—Kane slid into bed behind me and held me all night long.

Maybe I'm being irrational or jumping the gun, but I love Kane, and I want to be with him. Not because I want to be in love or because I'm pregnant with his baby, but because I want to love him and spend my life with him. He's who I want, and I'm not going to waste another moment without telling him so.

When I turn over to talk to him, I'm met with the empty side of his bed and a note with his chicken scratch scribbled across it.

Princess,

I have an early meeting with Jim. I'll call you afterward.
I hope your morning sickness isn't too bad. I'll see you tonight.
XO,
Kane

Glancing from the note to the ring box, I make a decision.

I want to be with Kane, and I'm done wasting time.

I find his name in my text thread and send him a message.

> Me: Good morning. I hope everything goes okay with Jim. I'd like to talk to you tonight. Since you took me out on a date last night, I'd like to take you out on one tonight. <heart-eyes emoji>

And then I lift the lid and pluck the beautiful ring out of the box and slide it onto my finger. I stare at it for several seconds, waiting for my gut to indicate I'm making the wrong decision, but when it doesn't come, I breathe a sigh of relief, ready to start the next chapter of my life as Kane's wife.

Since I have a lot to do to get the studio reopened, I climb out of bed and jump in the shower. I'm blow-drying my hair when my phone rings with a call from Matteo.

Since he isn't one for idle chitchat, I answer it right away, hoping nothing has happened to Dani or the baby.

"Hey, is everything okay?"

"No," he says gravely. "But before I tell you, I need you to remember you're pregnant, so you need to stay calm."

"Telling a pregnant woman something is wrong but to stay calm is counterintuitive. Tell me what happened."

Matteo sighs. "You need to get to North Harbor Point Medical. Kane's been shot."

Kane's been shot.

My mind goes back to several years ago, watching Owen get shot and killed.

"He's been shot?" I whisper.

My heart is racing. My breathing labored.

Memories of seeing Owen on the ground, bleeding out. Begging him to live. Knowing he was dead and I'd never see him again.

My gaze goes to my ring.

My husband has been shot.

But isn't that how the world works?

The moment I say I want a life with Kane, he's taken away from me.

The same way Owen was taken from me.

The way my baby was taken from me.

My hand goes to my belly, and I take a calming breath.

Stress isn't good for the baby, and he or she is all I have left.

"Bri, you there?"

"Yeah," I rasp. "I'm on my way."

FORTY-ONE

Kane

One Hour Ago

"Mr. Morgan, Jim isn't here."

"What do you mean, he isn't there?" I bark at my assistant as I pull into the private garage of Morgan Enterprises.

I requested a meeting with my CFO, and he accepted it. The meeting is in three minutes, so he damn well should be there.

"He's not here, and all his stuff is gone, including the company laptop. According to Peggy in accounting, he was boxing up a bunch of stuff yesterday, and when she asked him what was going on, he told her he was cleaning out old files."

"Shit." I pull into the spot. "I'll call you right back."

I hang up and dial Matteo since he's the only person I know with access to Eddy. God knows what Jim took with him. I didn't lead on that I knew what he had done, but of course his guilt caused him to put it all together.

"Yeah?"

"I need a favor. Jim Wallen, my CFO, stole from me, and knowing I was going to confront him, he bolted, taking company files and equipment with him. I need Eddy to see where he's heading so I can get to him before he disappears."

"You owe me, Morgan."

Matteo hangs up, and since I can't do shit, I sit and wait for him to hopefully call me back. I consider calling Brielle, but if she hasn't texted me, it means she's still asleep. Since finding out she's pregnant, she's been sleeping a lot more, obviously needing it.

A few minutes later, Matteo calls me back.

"He has a private flight booked at North Harbor Point Airport. It's leaving in thirty minutes."

"Thanks."

Since my company jet is currently housed there, I make it through security easily. When I pull onto the tarmac, I see Jim standing at the bottom of the stairs, talking to someone with their back to me.

When I get out, Jim glances at me, and he must say something to whoever he's talking to because the guy turns around.

"Theodore fucking DeSantis." I laugh humorlessly. "Why doesn't this surprise me?"

"Mr. Morgan," Jim rasps. "I'm sorry, but Theo blackmailed me into—"

Before he can finish his sentence, Theo pulls out a gun and shoots the man in the chest. He falls to the ground, and I take a step back since I'm not armed.

"Fuck you!" Theo yells, pointing his gun at me. "You think you can come in here and steal my girl and my investment? I was trying to get in on the waterfront expansion, but Dominick wouldn't give me the time of day—even with me fucking his sister. Then the bitch told me she wouldn't date anyone associated with her brothers' business. Yet you walked in and took everything I'd wanted!"

I raise my hands, mentally trying to figure out if I can run fast enough to get behind my SUV when Theo pulls the trigger.

The bullet hits me somewhere in my chest, knocking me to the ground. It's hard to breathe, and before I can even consider calling for help, everything around me goes black. And my last thought as

I accept that I'm going to die is that I hope Brielle finds happiness for her and our baby.

Matteo

What Kane does isn't my fucking business.

But as I drive to the warehouse, a bad feeling comes over me. I've learned over the years to trust my gut, and it's telling me something is about to go down at the airport.

And I might not give a shit if Kane lives or dies, but my sister loves him, and she's been through too much.

"Fuck it." I make a right instead of a left toward the airport, and I accelerate to a speed that would have me arrested if I got pulled over by the wrong cop.

I get through security quickly, and when I pull up, I take in the situation in front of me and find that my gut wasn't wrong.

One guy is bleeding out on the tarmac while Theodore DeSantis is standing several feet from Kane, pointing a gun at him.

I grab my Glock from my glove box and slowly open the door, needing to get into place to shoot him. But before I can do that, Theo presses the trigger, and Kane goes down.

He hasn't lowered the gun, telling me he might shoot again, so without waiting, I step out of my car, aim for Theo's heart, and pull the trigger.

Game over.

I run over to Kane, who's bleeding pretty fucking badly.

"We need a medic," I yell to the worker who's watching from a distance, obviously not wanting to get in the middle of a fucking shoot-out.

I bend in front of Kane and shake my head. "You seriously fucking owe me, Morgan."

FORTY-TWO

Brielle

KANE'S BEEN SHOT IN THE CHEST, AND HE'S IN SURGERY.

I might lose my husband and the father of my unborn child—again.

He won't be here to watch our baby grow in my belly. He'll never know if they're a boy or a girl. He'll never get to hold them in his arms.

A sob bubbles out of me, and Matteo wraps his arms around me.

He arrived at the hospital at the same time as Kane.

I don't know what happened, but Matteo said it wasn't good. Kane was bleeding badly, and apparently, his heart stopped on the way here.

Since we're in a public setting, Matteo isn't going to give me the details, but it doesn't even matter. Kane is hanging on by a thread, and all we can do is wait to hear what the doctor says.

Peyton, Dani, and Nicole offered to come to the hospital, but with everything going on, I don't want to risk their safety, so I asked them to stay home and told them I'd let them know how he was doing.

"Excuse me," a woman says to the nurse at the front desk. "I'm here for my son, Kane Morgan."

"Ms. Morgan," I cry, rushing over to Kane's mom.

I haven't had a chance to get to know her since I was pushing

Kane away and then I left for Russia. Kane said she's excited about the baby, but she's been trying to give us space. She knows the marriage was forced, and he told me she didn't agree with it.

"Oh, Brielle, please call me Silvia. We're family."

She envelops me in a warm, comforting embrace, reminding me so much of her son. Kane gives the best hugs. He must get it from his mom.

"Thank you for calling me," she murmurs.

"Of course. He's in surgery, so we don't know anything."

"Do you know who did this to him?" she asks, pulling back and looking at me with tears in her eyes.

"No," I tell her honestly. "My brother was there but …"

"We'll discuss it later," Matteo tells us both. "But I can assure you, it's been handled."

Silvia sighs in relief. "Thank you."

She turns her attention back to me. "How are you doing?" She shakes her head. "That's a stupid question. Of course you're not doing okay. But you need to stay calm … for the baby. Do you need anything? Water? Juice? Are you hungry?"

I choke out a watery laugh. "You remind me of Kane … well, I guess he reminds me of you."

Silvia smiles. "Enrique was ruthless, like his father." She frowns. "Lacked compassion and all sense of right and wrong. But Kane … he's always been a nurturer, like me. He wears his heart on his sleeve."

I nod in agreement, and when I reach up to my face to wipe my tears from my eyes, Silvia's gaze lands on my hand.

"You're wearing the new ring," she breathes. "Does this mean …"

"I want to be with Kane." I sniffle back another sob. "But I didn't have a chance to tell him, and now—"

"You will get to tell him," she says. "He's so in love with you. There's no way he'll give up without a fight."

"I hope you're right," I whisper. "Because I'm so in love with him too."

Hours go by before the doctor finally walks out and tells us that Kane made it through surgery. They had to put him into a medically induced coma, but now that he's stable, they'll start waking him up. The next forty-eight hours are crucial. Since he's no longer in ICU, he can have visitors.

"You guys go," Matteo says. "I have some shit to handle." He kisses my temple. "I love you, sis."

"I love you too. Thank you for saving my husband."

Silvia and I arrive at Kane's room, and it's dark and quiet. The nurse tells us they keep the lights low so that it's not too blinding when a patient wakes up.

I pull a seat up to the side of his bed, and it's where I stay for the next two days while he sleeps and I pray he gets through this.

"So, is that all it took to get my ring on your finger?" Kane rasps, startling me awake. "Getting shot? If I had known, I'd have gotten shot sooner."

I blink several times and then glare at Kane. "Don't say stupid shit like that, or I'll remove the damn ring from my finger."

Silvia chuckles from in the corner. "I'm so happy you're awake," she says, walking over and giving Kane a kiss on his forehead. "I'm going to give you both a few minutes." She kisses the crown of my head. "Go easy on him."

Once she's gone, I release a relieved sob. "You're alive."

"I'm alive." He takes my hand in his and kisses the top of my ring. "And you're wearing my ring."

"I put it on before you got shot. I texted that I wanted to take you out so I could tell you that I'd made my decision, but you never read it."

I hand him his phone that Matteo gave me to hold on to and open it up to the text thread between us.

"Damn, it's been two days?"

"Yeah, you were shot in the chest, but you're going to be okay."

"And Theo?"

"What about Theo?" I hiss.

"He's the person who shot me," he says, confused. "Wait, how did I get here?"

"Matteo found you and called for help, and you were brought in by ambulance. He didn't tell me what happened, but he said that everything was taken care of."

Kane exhales heavily. "I owe your brother big time. Jim was working with Theo to steal from me. Apparently, Theo had wanted in on the waterfront expansion, but your brothers said no, and then you told him you wouldn't date anyone working with your brothers. So, when I showed up and claimed you and got in on the waterfront expansion, he was pissed. Blackmailed Jim into stealing from me. Theo shot Jim and then me."

"Ugh, and to think I thought Theo was a green flag." I shake my head. "I guess looks can be deceiving. What a freaking psycho."

"Enough about him," Kane says. "I want to hear about this decision you made."

"I made it days ago, but I was afraid to say anything. I kind of felt stupid since I'd told you I needed time, and then not even a week later, I knew I wanted to be with you."

"Come here." He nods toward the bed and shifts slightly so I can climb in and snuggle next to him. "So," he prompts, "you're giving us another chance?"

"I love you," I tell him for the first time. "I love you with everything in me, and if we're being honest, I've probably loved you since before we got married. I knew from the first night we spent together that you were the one for me, and I'm done wasting time. I want this life … the marriage and babies and happiness … and I don't want it with anyone but you."

"Good." Kane brings his lips to mine. "Because I don't want it with anyone but you."

FORTY-THREE

Brielle

Two Months Later

"So, what do you think?" Kane asks with a boyish grin. "Last chance to make your guess."

We're standing on the beach, under a pavilion Kane had brought in for today, with our closest friends and family surrounding us. There's a table in the center, and on it are elegant-looking cake pops.

When he asked how I wanted to find out the gender, I told him that even though it's super cheesy, I wanted to do something sweet, like having cupcakes or cake pops made for everyone in attendance—with pink cake for a girl or blue for a boy inside. But that I wanted to wait until after the first trimester.

He didn't laugh at me. He simply said he'd handle it, and for the next few weeks, I didn't give it another thought. Between Kane recovering from his bullet wound and having to hire a new CFO and me getting the studio up and running and preparing for the grand reopening, we were busy.

So, when he told me not to make any plans for today, I didn't think about it and was beyond shocked to walk out onto the beach and find our friends and family here to celebrate our pregnancy.

"I just want them to be healthy." My hand goes to my belly.

I'm four months along, and just being pregnant by the man I love is enough for me. It doesn't matter whether they're a boy or a girl.

"Well, I, for one, hope you're having a girl." Peyton laughs. "We need as many girls as we can get."

She side-eyes her three rambunctious boys, who are currently playing in the sand, and everyone cracks up.

Peyton might act like they drive her nuts—and I'm sure they do—but she wouldn't have it any other way.

"Peaches," Dominick coos, "if you want a girl so badly, I'll give you one."

He waggles his brows, and Peyton scoffs.

"Yeah, okay. You might think you're God, but even you can't determine the gender of a baby, and your track record isn't exactly good in that department."

"Well, if they're not a girl, we have three more tries since I want at least four kids," I say.

"Four!" Peyton hisses. "You're insane. Talk to me after you give birth."

"Yeah, I thought I wanted to have a few, but with Alba being colicky, we haven't gotten a good night's sleep since she was born," Dani says, giving her baby girl an affectionate kiss on her forehead. "I'm thinking one more, and we'll be done."

"Just make sure you're on strong birth control then," Peyton notes. "Because if Dominick is anything to go by, these Antonov men have strong sperm."

"And on that note"—Kane coughs through his laugh—"let's find out what we're having."

He hands out the cake pops to everyone and then hands me one.

"Ready?" he asks.

We bite into our cake pops at the same time and then expose them.

"It's a girl!" we say in unison.

Kane pulls me into his arms and kisses me while everyone claps and cheers.

"You know what this means, right?" he murmurs.

"What?" I rasp.

"We have a princess on the way … which means you're being upgraded to queen."

His lips capture mine again, this time more passionately, and butterflies attack my belly. But before I can deepen the kiss, never having enough of him, he pulls back and then gets down on one knee.

"Brielle Antonova-Morgan," he says with a grin spread across his face, "today wasn't only for the gender reveal. I invited our friends and family here because I have a question for you …"

"Yes!" I squeal. "Yes, I'll marry you!"

Everyone laughs, and Kane's grin grows wider. And I realize I didn't let him finish.

"Sorry," I mutter. "Blame it on the pregnancy brain."

"I love you," Kane says, standing. "And I want to give you the wedding of your dreams, on the beach with our friends and family. And I'd like to do it before this baby comes. So, my queen, what do you say? Will you go to the Bahamas with me next month and *willingly* marry me?"

"Yes!" I repeat, throwing my arms around his neck. "I will marry you as many times as you want."

Kane lifts me into his arms and kisses me, and it takes everything in me not to beg him to carry me back to our house so he can make love to me.

On second thought …

"It's not happening," he murmurs, laughter in his voice. "Right now, we're going to celebrate. And later, I'll show you how thankful I am for you over and over again."

Kane

Today has been a damn good day.

We found out we were having a little girl and Brielle agreed to marry me again.

I hadn't been thinking when I asked her to willingly marry me, so we had to come clean to her mom about the truth of our marriage. She wasn't thrilled, but when Brielle told her she wouldn't change anything because it was what had led us to where we were now, she understood and congratulated us.

After saying goodbye to our friends and family and making sure the cleanup crew has everything under control, I walk my wife back to our house.

The second we're through the door, she jumps into my arms.

"Thank you for today," she murmurs, peppering sweet kisses all over my face.

"You never have to thank me for giving you what you deserve," I tell her. "Every day, you give me everything I've ever wanted."

"Oh, yeah?" She smirks. "And what is it you want right now?"

She slides down my body and then removes her sundress, exposing her perfect tits, covered in sexy white lace, and her swollen belly.

"Do you want me?" she asks, reaching behind and undoing her bra.

She lets the material fall to the floor, and her breasts, which have grown since her pregnancy, drop slightly.

"I always want you." I palm her breasts and gently pinch her nipples, making her moan.

"Hmm." She steps back and shimmies out of her lace panties, giving me the perfect view of her neatly trimmed pussy. "How about this?" She backs up and drops onto the ottoman and spreads her legs. "Do you want this?"

I step toward her and cup her cunt. "I always want this."

I lean over and capture her mouth with mine. My tongue parts her plump lips and delves in, stroking hers for several seconds before she pulls back.

"What about this?" she murmurs, sitting up and reaching for my dress pants. She unbuttons and unzips them and then pulls my cock out. "Do you want this?"

Before I can ask her to clarify, she does so by leaning over and taking my hard length into her mouth.

"Fuck," I hiss, running my fingers through her blonde locks. "I always want this."

I watch her suck my dick for a few minutes, enjoying the way her warm, wet mouth slides up and down my shaft, and then I pull her off me.

"But what I want the most is to pleasure you," I tell her as I lift her gently onto the ottoman since we're clearly not making it to the bedroom.

I spread her legs and lean over her, kissing her chastely before I move my lips down the slim column of her neck and over to her breasts. I lick and suck each sensitive nipple, making her mewl in pleasure. And then I continue my descent to her belly. It's not big, but because she's so toned, there's an obvious bump there, and every time I see it, knowing she's carrying our baby, it turns me on.

I trail kisses down her bump, and when I get to her cunt, I spread her lips and lean in so I can taste her.

"Kane," she moans, "I'm too turned on. Don't tease me, please."

I chuckle. "I'm not teasing you," I argue. "The gift of your pussy is the *second*-best thing you've ever given me."

"What's the first?" she rasps, not missing a beat.

I glance up at her. "Your heart."

I work Brielle's body over, making her climax twice before I get up and sit on the couch, pulling her on top of me.

"Ride me, Queen," I tell her, guiding her onto my cock. "You're in charge, baby. Take us both over the edge."

With her arms around my neck and her soft lips slowly caressing mine, she sinks onto me. She fucks me slow and steady, grinding her hips. My wife knows exactly what to do to get us to climax, and within minutes, she's screaming my name as she comes around my cock, and I drain every drop of my orgasm into her.

"This is what I want," I tell her, pushing strands of hair away from her eyes. "I want you every day for the rest of my life. I fucked up, Bri, but I promise, I'll cherish you and love you every day. And I'll remind you that even though I betrayed you, what we have is worth having."

"Our love isn't simple," she murmurs, leaning in and brushing her lips against mine. "But it's so fucking beautiful. And I know we'll spend the rest of our lives never taking it for granted again."

EPILOGUE

Brielle

Two Months Later

BLOOD-RED ROSES ARE SPREAD ELEGANTLY AROUND THE pavilion that's on the beach overlooking the Atlantic. Our family and friends are here, sitting in chairs behind us.

I'm in a white midi maternity dress, and Kane is wearing a pair of khaki dress shorts with a button-down white linen shirt. His hair is messy from the ocean breeze, and his face is scruffy since I told him I loved his facial hair. While I'm wearing a cute pair of Valentino sandals, he's sporting Christian Louboutin leather boat shoes.

It's nothing like our first wedding and everything like what I dreamed of when I was a little girl.

The officiant says a few words and then turns it over to us.

Like last time, Kane goes first.

"I never thought I'd be married," he says. "My only goal was to be successful, and I measured that success with dollar signs. But what I didn't understand at the time was that there's a different type of success, one that can't be measured with money …"

"It's in the way you smile at me when I do something that makes you happy. The way your body calms at my touch. When you're having a bad day and I pull you into my arms and you tell me that I made it better. Success is when you and Molly snuggle against my side while we watch our shows. Or when you light up because I remembered your favorite coffee or muffin."

I choke out a sob, and Kane palms the side of my face.

"I thought I had found success until I met you. But now, with you by my side, every time you look at me with happiness and love in your eyes, I feel like the most successful man in the world. And I vow to spend every day of the rest of our lives working to ensure that you look at me like I'm all you need in life, even though we both know you don't *need* anyone."

"Kane"—I sniffle back a sob—"it's not me that makes you successful. It's *us*." I reach up and cup the sides of his face. "It's having each other's back, no matter what. Sharing our goals and hopes and dreams and supporting each other through them.

"And I vow to spend every day of the rest of our lives sharing my hopes and dreams with you. And when things get hard, I'll be here because this life we're creating is beautiful, and all I want is to spend it with you."

I glance at Matteo, who stands and brings me over the box I asked him to hold.

"Thank you," I tell him, plucking the ring out of the box and handing it back to him.

"You remembered," Kane rasps.

"Not only did I remember, but I had it engraved—*I give myself to you*."

I look into Kane's eyes, and he swallows thickly, understanding what I'm saying.

I've always craved control. But with Kane, I no longer need it because I trust him with every part of me.

I take his fourth finger and slide the ring onto it. "I, Brielle Antonova-Morgan, give myself to you in every way, till death do us part."

Kane nods, his eyes teary. "Thank you, Princess," he chokes out, taking my hand in his. He reaches into his pocket and pulls out a new wedding ring that matches the engagement ring he bought me.

"I, Kane Morgan, give myself to you in every way, till death do us part."

Kane

Waking up next to my pregnant wife is something I could do every day for the rest of my life. Given, she wouldn't be thrilled if I kept her knocked up, but thankfully, she wants a few babies, which means in a couple of months, when she gives birth, it won't be the end of getting to see her pregnant.

"What are you thinking about?" Bri croaks out, rolling over so her bump is pressed against my torso.

"How long I have to wait to get you pregnant again."

Brielle laughs. "Let's have this one first, and then we can discuss it." She glides her creamy thigh between my legs and presses her lips to mine. "But we can definitely have fun practicing."

I reach between us and find her clit. But with her belly, it's hard to do what I want. So, I gently roll her over and then proceed to remove her underwear so I can make her come.

It only takes a few strokes to her needy clit before she's screaming my name, and then I'm pushing my boxers down and guiding myself into her.

"I love this," I murmur, my hand going to her belly. "I love you."

Her face splits into a beautiful smile, and I vow to make sure she smiles as much as possible.

"I love you," she says, pulling my face down to hers for a kiss.

Careful not to put pressure on her stomach, I make love to my wife, thanking whatever god there is for bringing her into my life.

When we both find our release, I drop onto the bed and pull

her into my arms, not ready to let her go yet. My hand goes to her belly, and when the baby kicks, I hold her even tighter.

"I can't wait for our little girl to get here," I murmur into the crook of her neck.

"You say that now, until you realize you're stuck with not only me for life, but a mini version of me as well."

I chuckle at the thought of a mini Bri. "It's going to be—"

My words are cut off at the sound of someone shouting.

Immediately on alert, I fly out of the bed, grabbing my sweats and throwing them on.

"Stay here," I tell Bri, who, of course, doesn't listen.

When we step into the hallway, we find Lorenzo standing in the doorway with Nicole's stepsister, Vanessa.

"Is everything okay?" Brielle asks.

"No!" Lorenzo barks. "This crazy bitch is trying to tell me that we got married last night."

His hand cuts through the air, and the gleam of a wedding band catches my eye.

Lorenzo must see it, too, because his eyes widen in shock as he takes in the ring on his fourth finger. "Fuck," he hisses. "I got married last night."

Want to see how Kane's private Pilates class goes?
Go to my website to read the bonus chapter.

Want to see more of Kane and Brielle, as well as the others?
There's one final book in the Tempting Love series.
Check out Lorenzo's story: *Secret Seduction.*

ABOUT THE AUTHOR

Nikki Ash is a *USA Today* Bestselling author of contemporary romance, focusing on single parent, secret baby, and surprise pregnancy romances. She spends her days and nights getting lost in words. When she's not writing, she's reading. From the Boxcar Children, to Wuthering Heights, to the latest single parent romance, she has lived and breathed every type of book.

Nikki resides in South Florida with her husband, two children, and dog that she considers to be one of her kids. When she's not reading or writing, she's traveling the world with her family—in search of inspiration.